VOICES
IN THE
DARK

A CHARITY ANTHOLOGY

FOR DISABILITY AND MENTAL HEALTH AWARENESS

EDITED BY
ALAIN DAVIS, STEVE DILLON,
AND EUGENE JOHNSON

Copyright Notices

"Donald, Duck" by Peter Straub © Copyright 2008
"There's No Light Between Floors" by Paul Tremblay © Copyright 2007
"Ocular" Copyright 2007 Mick Garris

All other stories not reprints are copyright 2022 their respective authors.

Cover Art: © Copyright Paul Moore, 2022
Interior layout and typography: Steve Dillon, 2022

Proofread by: Alain Davis & Anna Ray-Stokes

© Copyright Eugene Johnson, 2022.
First Published 2022 by Eugene Johnson.
A *Saturday Mornings Incorporated Press LLC* publication in association with Gestalt Media.

ISBN: 978-1-7356644-2-2 (Paperback)
        978-1-7356644-3-9 (eBook)

Dedications

For all the Essential Workers who were on the front line during the COVID-19 pandemic; for all those who struggle each day with mental illness; for those lost during this horrible time: You are not alone. And you are not forgotten.

To my loving family: Angela, Hannah, Bradley, Oliver, and my grandparents. You make my life blessed and so much brighter.
- Eugene Johnson

To my husband, James, who is my North star, always helps me stay grounded and guides me home when I am feeling lost.
- Alain Davis

Contents

The Stacks by Chris Mason…7
The Girl Who Bled in The Tree by Tim Waggonner…25
SHH by David Wellington…35
There's No Light Between Floors by Paul Tremblay…52
A World of Ghosts by Christina Sng…60
Vigil at Singer's Cross by Matthew R. Davis…62
The Library of Half-Read Books by Norman Prentiss…84
It Only Hurts When I Dream by Lucy A. Snyder…94
Donald, Duck by Peter Straub…95
Disremembering Me by Christopher Sartin…120
Drink, Drink from the Fountain of Death by Eric J. Guignard…121
Lost by Jason Stokes…134
Lost in the Forest of My Mind by Hannah Elizabeth…145
Step Right Up to Marcy Lynne's Amazing Wunderkammer!
by Gwendolyn Kiste…147
Ocular by Mick Garris…158
Wide-Shining Light by Rio Youers…183
Biographies…211

Introduction

by Cindy O'Quinn

April 20, 2021, was a day like most, until my husband died... I was suddenly a widow after being a wife for nearly thirty years. Our sons no longer had their dad. A good man was gone.

As usual, the sun shone, the temperatures rose, as well as the humidity, but those things certainly didn't put an end to the virus. The world continued on, but it wasn't the same. And hasn't been the same since early 2020. If one wanted my opinion, it would be that the virus known as Covid19 & its variants started months prior, back in the Fall of 2019. I saw the signs in the posts on social media. Whispers of illness.

I wish this anthology wasn't necessary, but here we are. My hope is it will benefit those who need it most. The young children who have suffered unspeakable loss. This season of darkness for the world has lasted far more than just one season. Death and long-term illness from Covid19 have not ended.

The common thread of this anthology is loss. Each writer brought some of their best writing into this book. There's not a single story or poem that won't move you in some way.

Christopher Sartin's poem, "Disremembering Me", is heart wrenching. "There's No Light Between Floors", Paul Tremblay's short story left me holding my breath on more than occasion. Christina Sng's poem, "A World of Ghosts" is one of her finest. Tim Waggoner's story, "The Girl Who Bled in The Tree", will really get you thinking. As I mentioned earlier, every piece in this anthology is excellent. And it is for a needed charity.

THE STACKS

CHRIS MASON

Tissue thin, the page had been torn from a bible, the numbers 20022020 hastily scrawled in pencil across the small black print. Claire stared at the row of twos and zeroes, then redirected her attention to the sprawling university campus before her. "Remind me why I agreed to do this," she asked.

"We couldn't let today pass and not be here. I've been waiting forty years to prove my theory," Jacquie replied.

"It feels weird."

"To be back here...? Why?"

"I don't know. It's the unknown I guess."

"Don't tell me you're worried."

"A little bit," Claire admitted. "I just wish I knew why I'm supposed to be here, that's all. Assuming the numbers actually *are* today's date."

"Well, I can't wait to find out."

Claire pocketed the page. "Where is the library anyway, I can't even see it?"

"Over there," Jacquie pointed.

The building was definitely not as Claire remembered. The original architecture–mid 1800's sandstone with a classical façade–had been covered along the western side by a series of large contemporary red brick and glass boxes.

"Good God, they've ruined the place," said Claire.

"I think it's called progress," said Jacquie. "I wonder if the library will remember us?"

"How could it possibly forget?"

"If those walls could talk, eh?" Jacquie smiled.

"Perhaps it's good they can't. I seem to recall you vomiting into a wastepaper basket behind the loans desk after the Christmas party one year."

"You held my hair back."

"What else is a best friend for?"

Jacquie's smile broadened to a grin. "C'mon, let's go in and see if we can find the scene of the crime."

Entering the building to a hive of student activity, Claire felt out of place. The last time she'd been inside the library was 1979. Jacquie had worked in cataloguing, Claire in undergraduate loans. The library had been austere and gloomy back then; books spread over three floors, four counting the little extension that housed *Special Collections*. Now it was a vast sprawling labyrinth.

Their first stop was the Reading Room; a great hall of dark wood with rows of ancient desks, each adorned with a green glass lamp. Below the vaulted ceiling, shelves of leather-bound journals shared the walls with portraits of proud men, eyes casting judgement over all who dared utter more than a whisper in the hallowed space.

"At least this still looks the same," said Claire.

"I always felt like I was doing something wrong in here," said Jacquie.

"Probably because you usually were. You never could keep your voice down. Do I need to remind you of the pigeon fiasco?"

"It shouldn't have flown in here. I hate pigeons."

"We heard you screaming up on the second floor. Students thought it was a fire alarm."

"Can I help it if I'm naturally loud?"

A girl in denim shorts and a mouth full of silver looked up from her book. She raised a sculpted eyebrow at Jacquie.

"Calm down, luv, we won't be joining your tutorial anytime soon," said Jacquie.

Claire cringed and moved out of earshot. "When did they get so young?"

"I know, right? She's probably doing a PhD. Ever wish we'd come here as students instead of library assistants?"

"Sometimes," said Claire. "But we did okay, didn't we? Considering we never read Marx or Sartre or Nietzsche."

"We read *The Joy of Sex*, that had to count for something."

Claire wasn't sure if giggling together over the drawings could be classed as reading, but she had learned a thing or two for which a number of partners had been extremely appreciative.

"Looks like nothing much is happening in here. Where to next?" asked Claire.

"How about we try and find Record Services, see if Miss Rickles is still there."

"The old tyrant would have to be dead, surely."

"Don't bet on it, I always suspected she was a vampire."

After discovering the entire Records Services department had been replaced by an iMac (Miss Rickles, long gone, and quite possibly turning in her grave, stake and all), they explored the acres of shelving on the ground floor. Transformed for a new era, this part of the library was now a confusion of specially created bright spaces, and existing ones, resized, refitted, and repurposed. They were about to head up to the next level to see if the mezzanine floor still existed when Jacquie spied the service lift that went down to the basement.

Claire stared at the grey doors. She wiped a slick of sweat from beneath her chin. "Do we have to?"

"It's part of the tour."

"I hate that bloody thing."

The elevator to the basement was similar to those used in hospitals, with doors opening on both sides. Instead of transporting patients on gurneys, it was used for book trolleys.

"Do you think Ghoulman is down there?" asked Jacquie.

Claire had been waiting for Jacquie to bring up the subject. "Oh, don't start with the ghost nonsense."

"From what I hear, the ghost has been making a few appearances of late. Check out the University's Wikipedia page, he gets a whole paragraph."

"So, this is a ghost hunt now?"

"Not at all, but I wouldn't be surprised if we do see him. Ghoulman wanted you to come back to the library today for a reason. Why else would he have given you the note with the date?" said Jacquie.

Claire had asked herself the same question a thousand times.

Ghoulman, aka Clive Collins, had been a professor of physics at the university until a sudden and marked decline in his mental health ended his tenure. When the brilliant, but confused, professor discovered he'd been locked out of his old faculty, he took refuge in the last place left on campus that would have him—the library.

By day he'd wandered the stacks, and at night, regularly moved on by Security who found him sleeping in the service entry. His impromptu lectures on the fall of civilization, and his habit of carrying a bible and a rolled-up newspaper, the latter used to swat undergraduates canoodling between the shelves, became infamous. At six-foot-tall, and with more than a passing resemblance to Charles Manson, it was little wonder students and library staff had started referring to Collins as 'Ghoulman'.

A short time before his death, Claire had her own strange encounter with him. Late one afternoon, on her way back from the basement, she'd entered the service lift alone, pushing her trolley and humming *I Will Survive,* when Ghoulman rushed out of the shadows, shaking his bible at her. Pressing buttons frantically in an attempt to get the doors closed before he could get in, Claire watched him tear a page from the Good Book, screw it up and toss it into the lift. He'd then vanished between the shelves. Knowing she was vulnerable, Claire had spun around to the door behind, to find him already standing there on the other side of the lift. How he'd managed to get there so quickly, was something Claire had never quite figured out.

With the doors finally closing, she had stared in disbelief as Ghoulman pointed a finger at her and screamed, "It was *you*, Claire! You're next," as if they were playing some hideous game of tag. By the time Claire got back to the loans desk, she'd been a blubbering mess. Her name wrapped in spittle from Ghoulman's mouth had shocked her to the core. Ghoulman had clearly not chosen her at random. He'd known who she was. Security made a search of the basement and found Ghoulman in the women's toilets, smashing mirrors. The once esteemed member of staff had been terrorising students for years, but it seemed damaging university property was the last straw. The police were called and Ghoulman escorted off campus.

A week later his naked body was pulled from the river Torrens. It was a sad ending to a remarkable life and had left Claire even more confused about the page he'd thrown at her. In the days following his death, students began reporting mysterious sounds and movements among the shelves, and rumours of Ghoulman's return spread like a wildfire across the campus. Sightings of his ghost, although never substantiated, were well established by the time Claire and Jacquie had moved on.

***

Claire stepped out of the lift into the gloom of the lower floor. Standing against the southern wall was the compactus, a bank of grey metal shelving, once used to house archive boxes and science magazines.

"Can you believe this old thing is still here?" said Claire, deliberately directing the conversation away from the ghost of Ghoulman.

"Remember when I squished you in it?"

Claire nodded. How could she forget being trapped between the rolling shelves? It was the type of thing Jacquie did when she got bored. Writing out index cards and stamping book returns wasn't exactly riveting stuff. Pulling pranks on Claire had been half the fun of going down to the basement. The other half was springing students fucking one another in the narrow aisles where the periodicals were kept.

Claire ran her fingers along a shelf full of outdated textbooks, covers faded, and spines ruined. She identified completely. The passing of time was rarely kind.

"I made out with a post-grad called Sam Lambert down here once," said Jacquie.

"You did not!" Claire feigned shock. "How was it?"

"Quick and dirty. We nearly got caught. I wonder what happened to him."

"He's probably overweight and balding…with grandkids."

"I was thinking loaded and a lawyer, but okay." Jacquie glanced over her shoulder. "If he's down here, I'm going to scream."

"Sam?"

"No, Ghoulman."

"Oh, we're back on *him* again, are we?"

"You can't tell me you're not a little scared about the prospect of a reunion."

"Ghoulman was sick. I understand that now. But when I saw him, he was also very much alive. I don't believe his ghost is roaming the building. And despite what you think, I don't believe he set a date because he wanted to catch up with me again."

Claire wasn't in the mood to entertain her friend's vivid imagination. Over the years, Jacquie had come up with a number of theories as to why Ghoulman had written the twos and zeroes on a page torn from Leviticus: they were a code for a briefcase containing a stash of secret documents; they were related to Schrodinger's equation and a ground-breaking new discovery in quantum field theory; they were linked to highly classified Russian intel; they had something to do with the disappearance of Prime Minister Harold Holt. The arrival of Google had only intensified Jacquie's quest to seek an answer to the digits. It had taken Claire a long time to accept the idea that in the end, the numbers were perhaps simply a date. 20022020. The 20th of February 2020. Why, back in 1979, this date had been so important he'd needed to write it down and give it to her, she hadn't a clue.

"But it's the reason you came, isn't it?"

Claire gave Jacquie an exasperated look. "Really? I'm not here because of Ghoulman, Jacquie. I'm here to finally put this thing to rest so you'll stop badgering me about those bloody numbers. You know, as soon as I walked in here, it was bleeding obvious. The library has moved on without us. I can't see a thing that ties us to this place anymore. Maybe we should move on too." Claire inhaled, held her breath for a second or two then let it go. "Now, are we done?"

"Not yet. Follow me."

Claire didn't stay cross at Jacquie for long. Experience told her it was pointless, and she'd end up feeling like she'd picked a fight with a puppy. She checked herself and gave in to Jacquie's relentless reminiscing.

"That's new." Jacquie nodded at a freshly painted green and white emergency exit.

"Smart move. It always felt like a fire trap down here." Between rows of books, Claire spied pockets of students hunched over laptops. She looked at her watch. For half-past four on a Friday afternoon, this new breed was keen. "Is it me or does this space feel a lot smaller than it used to?"

"No, you're right. Where are the newspaper stacks?"

"They must have closed them off."

Jacquie studied the wall in front of them.

"I guess that's that then," said Claire.

"I guess." Jacquie sounded disappointed.

They exited through the emergency door, where a brand-new set of stairs encased in glass led up and out of the building. To the right was a dimly lit corridor. It ran the length of the wall then made a sharp turn.

"Bingo," said Jacquie. She took off before Claire could stop her.

Around the corner, Claire found herself in familiar territory. Jacquie gave her a triumphant grin. She stood before a metal gate: galvanised chain link mesh with a sliding bolt lock. It was the entrance to the old newspaper stacks, a vast collection housed directly below the historic Reading Room.

Claire peered through the gate into a black void.

"We used to bundle up the papers and bring them down here at the end of each week," said Jacquie.

"Not my favourite thing in the world, if I recall." When Claire had been on her own at work, it was a quick trip in to dump the load and then out again. The newspaper stacks were dark and dingy, and she wasn't one to linger long.

"Let's go in," Jacquie said, without a hint of trepidation.

Claire nodded at the 'Do Not Enter' sign on the gate.

"When did that ever stop us?"

"Do I have to remind you we don't work here anymore." Claire shuddered. "And sorry, no way. These stacks always gave me the creeps."

Jacquie tried the bolt and it slid open. "There you go. If they were serious, it'd be locked." She beamed. "C'mon Claire, humour me, it'll be like old times."

It was exactly what Claire was afraid of.

Inside, a sensor-switch automatically activated a fluorescent strip. It flickered on, brightly illuminating the immediate area as they stepped past the gate. Beyond the entrance, spaced at long intervals down the main aisles, bare bulbs lit up one by one throwing splashes of greasy light onto the concrete floor. The place smelled dry and dusty.

"Quick, before anyone sees us." Jacquie darted into the shadows of the first row of shelving, pulling Claire with her.

Sweat pooled in Claire's cleavage. As she followed Jacquie into the bowels of the library, her jaw tightened. Inches of dust covered the shelves, towers of old newspapers packed in from top to bottom. One sneeze and there'd be an avalanche. From the look of it, no one had been in the stacks in recent times.

They wandered up and down a dozen rows, Claire feeling increasingly claustrophobic. Sound did not travel well in the stacks. The noise their heels made was dull and flat; when they spoke, it was as if the print absorbed their conversation. The low ceiling; the thick wooden cross bearers and stone foundation pillars; the weight of the books in the reading room above; the endless rows of newspapers stretching into the darkness; the stale air; all added to Claire's growing unease. Among the sea of brittle pages, she felt like she was drowning.

"I hope they're still laying rat baits. Those damn things used to grow big as dogs down here," said Jacquie.

"Ugh. I think I've seen enough. Let's go. There's nothing here to connect us with a page from the bible. And what a surprise, no ghosts."

"Where's the fire? I want to have a good look. I was never brave enough to see how far back it went when we worked here."

"It's just more shelves and newspapers. We're going to be covered in webs and dust if we keep going."

"Did you ever walk all the way to the far wall?" asked Jacquie.

"On my own? What do you think I am, an idiot?"

There was a clicking sound followed by faint footsteps.

"Did you hear that?" asked Claire.

"Don't panic."

"We're not supposed to be in here, remember."

"No one knows we're *in* here."

"Shush. They will if you don't keep your voice down."

The footsteps came closer. A shot of static from a walkie talkie giving away it was a security guard.

"Hello, is anyone back there?"

Claire silently cursed and ducked her head. They waited, like two naughty schoolchildren, Jacquie with one hand clamped over her mouth as she suppressed laughter. Finally, the footsteps retreated, a click and rattle of the gate indicating they were alone again.

"Great, we're probably locked in now," said Claire.

"You always think the worse, don't you?"

Overhead the lights buzzed and went out.

"Shit," said Jacquie.

***

"This is working out well. What do you suggest we do now?" asked Claire, squinting in the dark.

"Hang on, we can use the torch on my phone. Here it is." Jacquie shone the light in Claire's face, almost blinding her.

"Which way is the gate?"

Jacquie turned and shone the torch down the row. "Back that way, I think?"

"You think?"

"Well, it can only be one way or the other, can't it?

They walked to the end, where the row met a cross aisle, and stopped. Jacquie aimed the torch left, then right. Claire stared at the shelves, stretching off in every direction.

"Not that way, then," said Jacquie.

There were too many shadows for Claire's liking. "No shit, Sherlock. Let's go back."

They retraced their steps. The view from the next aisle was more of the same.

"Well, that sucks," said Jacquie.

"How can we be this far from the exit?"

Jacquie shrugged.

"Which way do we go?" asked Claire.

"No idea."

"You are of no help whatsoever, you know that?"

"Then why don't you navigate, captain."

Claire ignored the accompanying giggle and directed them across the aisle to another row. They kept walking. After ten minutes, she put up her hand. "This is pointless. I feel like we're going around in circles."

"We're walking in a straight line," said Jacquie.

"Then why haven't we hit a wall yet?"

"How do I know? This place seems to be getting bigger, the longer we're down here."

"Don't be ridiculous."

"Well, you explain it."

Claire couldn't.

"I hate to say it, but I think we're lost," said Jacquie.

"Seriously? We're in an area the same size as the reading room above. It's big, but it's not *that* big."

"Unless the newspaper stacks are larger than the footprint of the library."

"If that's the case we should be across the river and in the parklands by now." Claire looked at her Fitbit and frowned. She tapped it, tapped it again. "Look at this. It says I've done 28,296 steps. I'd only done six thousand when I met you at the cafe."

"No wonder my feet are killing me. What's the time?"

"4.50pm."

"We've only been in here twenty minutes? That can't be right. It feels like we've been in here for hours."

Claire cleared her throat. "I could do with a drink."

"I could do with a wee."

"Maybe we should have skipped the wine at lunch."

"Why, you think we're drunk?"

"It might explain why we're so… disorientated."

"One hell of a bottle of chardonnay and a mighty long kick in, if that's the case."

There was a humming sound and the lights flickered on. The offer of hope was brief. Claire did a slow turn, trying to find a reference point. The light made little difference. There appeared to be no end to the shelves.

***

Claire pulled a newspaper from a pile and shook the dust from it. She searched the top of the front page for a date. "14 January 1862," she said. "When did the library open?"

"1850s I think."

"That means we have to be somewhere near the back of the stacks, yes?"

"I see where you're going with this."

"If we keep moving forwards in time, we have to find our way out of here."

"It's a rudimentary filing system, but it should work." Jacquie's face lit up "A breadcrumb trail of history, I like it."

"Have you got a lipstick on you? We should mark the shelf with the date, in case we have to backtrack."

"Good thinking." Jacquie produced a lipstick and drew a bright red '1862' on the middle shelf.

"At the end of each row we'll check to make sure we're heading in the right direction."

"Go Claire. When we get out of here, you'll be my first pick for an escape room team."

"When we get out of here, I'm going to have an extremely large gin."

"Might need to go top shelf."

"Oh, I'm planning on it."

They walked a short way and checked a front page. The date was July 1862.

"So far, so good."

"Do you think Ghoulman ever came in here?" asked Jacquie.

"Who knows. Stupid fucking numbers. Why did he have to pick on me?" Claire marched ahead to the end of the row and checked another paper.

"Date?" asked Jacquie.

"This one is March 1863."

"Excellent, the system appears to be working."

"Hallelujah, we might just get out of here after all."

"Claire?"

"Yes?"

"Lighten up will you. It's not the end of the world."

By the time they reached the newspapers of the '70s Claire had read headlines reporting the sinking of the Titanic, the Great Depression, two world wars, and the arrival of the Beatles in Adelaide.

"We're up to the years when we were working here," said Jacquie. "It feels odd."

"I know what you mean. Imagine if young Claire Hogan walked in right now."

"What would you do?"

"I'd whisper a few things in her ear."

"Like what?"

"Like stay away from that girl Jacquie, she's bound to get you into all sorts of trouble. Especially on February 20, 2020."

Jacquie elbowed Claire. "C'mon I'm serious. If you had the chance to tell your younger self something, something that would help her get through life, what would it be?"

"I don't know…maybe lighten up and not worry so damn much." Claire gave Jacquie half a smile.

"Do you think she'd listen?"

"Probably not."

"I'd tell myself not to shave my eyebrows," said Jacquie.

Claire laughed. "Sage advice."

The lights brightened momentarily then went out again.

"What the hell is going on with these lights?" Claire rummaged through her handbag for her phone, couldn't find it. "Jacquie, give me some light will you, I'm damned if I can find my phone."

"Claire?" Jacquie's voice was small and distant. "Where are you?"

"I'm right here."

"No. No, you're not."

Claire reached out in the dark and felt nothing but air. "Seriously, if you're messing around, I will kill you."

A pin prick of light appeared through the shelves, two rows over.

"What the hell are you doing?" asked Claire.

Silence.

"Jacquie?"

"I'm not sure how I got here."

Claire went cold. She tapped her Fitbit…59,320 steps, doubled since the last check. Impossible. "Okay, stay put and hold up your light, I'm coming to you."

"Make it quick, because I'm starting to freak out."

When Claire reached Jacquie, she was shaking. "What the fuck just happened?"

"I don't know, I didn't move, not a single step," said Jacquie.

Claire stiffened. There was no way Jacquie could have moved fast enough to get as far as she had in such a short amount of time. And Jacquie was frightened, not a good sign. "I believe you," said Claire.

"It's like the stacks are trying to separate us." Jacquie whispered.

The suggestion sent a tingle down Claire's spine. "Let's think about this for a minute."

"Maybe we should scream for help."

"I have an awful feeling no one is going to hear us."

Jacquie's mouth opened and closed. It was the first time in their long friendship, Claire had seen Jacquie speechless.

"How much juice have you got in your phone?" asked Claire.

Jacquie peered at the screen for what seemed like an eternity then said, "53 per cent."

"Okay let me try and find mine again." Claire fumbled about in her bag, felt her purse and keys, a forest of tissues. "It's not here. I must have left it in the car."

"Should we call someone?"

"Who?"

"I don't know, the police?"

"And what, end up in tomorrow's papers. I can see the headline now: SENIORS FOUND AFTER MISSING IN LIBRARY. My family already think I'm showing early signs of dementia. Do you want them to put me away?"

"What? You're sharp as a tack."

"Tell that to my house keys. I lock myself out more often than not these days."

A rustling noise came from somewhere behind them. It sounded like fingers turning pages.

"Rats?" asked Jacquie, a tremble in her voice.

"Let's keep moving," said Claire.

Jacquie led this time, taking slow deliberate steps. She found the end of the row, stopped and turned towards Claire. "Continue on across the aisle or try going left? Or right?" She swung the light around at Claire and gasped.

"Now what?"

"There's somebody standing behind you."

Every hair on Claire's body stood to attention. She felt a trickle of breath on the back of her neck. For a second, she couldn't move, then Jacquie reached out, grabbed her arm, and screamed, "RUN!"

The light from the torch bounced around, illuminating the shelves in snatches as they fled. When they came to the intersection between rows and the wider aisles, Jacquie didn't stop, pulling Claire randomly left and right. Even when they started to slow, they kept going, switching directions in a frantic attempt to confuse whoever was in the stacks with them. Finally, out of breath, Jacquie came to a halt. She let go of Claire, crouched low, and turned off the flashlight.

"This is insane," said Claire, sliding down beside her.

There was a beat of silence before Jacquie said, "It was him."

"Ghoulman?"

"It sure as hell looked like him. You don't forget a face like that, it had crazy written all over it."

"You saw his ghost?"

Jacquie shook her head. "He looked pretty solid to me."

"How could it possibly be him?"

"I don't know. Maybe because we were back in the '70s…."

"Not literally, Jacquie. It's just newspapers."

"It was Ghoulman, I tell you. It *was* Ghoulman!"

Claire's mind raced. Had Jacquie been right? The mad professor had somehow been waiting down here all this time for Claire to return. She tucked the silly thought firmly away and set her mind on what to do next.

"Are you good to keep going?"

"I think so, but I think I might have peed my pants a little."

"Give me your phone. I'll check a paper to see where the hell we've ended up this time."

***

In silence, the two women walked into the new millennium, tracking their progress through the Global Financial crisis, the Fukushima power plant disaster, Trump's inauguration, and the much-debated Brexit. They were still no closer to the gate. The shelves continued. To Claire, it felt like the year 2020 had abandoned them. For a time, frustrated, they stopped looking at the papers altogether, instead turning off the phone to save the battery, and stumbling through the blackness in search of a sliver of light that would indicate the exit and a way out of the mess they had gotten themselves into.

After what felt like days, Claire asked Jacquie to turn the torch on again. She grabbed a paper from a pile on her left and froze. The date was the 13th August 2038. The front page had a black and white photo of Sydney. The city was in ruins; the bridge gone, the Opera House a tangle of steel floating in the harbour.

"This is a joke, right?" said Jacquie.

Claire leaned across to the opposite shelf and pulled down another paper.

The headline: CANADA CALLS FOR PEACE TALKS WITH THE US, dated 25 September 2038.

Claire ripped the newspaper open and scanned the next page. She found an article about a Mars landing accident, another about wildfires burning out of control in Indonesia, and an advertisement for a seawater filtration unit.

"I'm calling bullshit," said Jacquie. "Why are newspapers still in print in 2038? If we're landing on Mars, what's happened to digital media?"

"What if the general population can't access technology for information anymore?" Claire paused. "Or aren't allowed."

"That's dark."

Frowning, Claire studied the page. "This typeset isn't right."

"So?"

"Feel the paper, look at the ink. I've looked at enough print in my life to know this has been done on an old press."

Jacquie stared at the front page with her. "You've lost me."

"What do you do when the power goes out?"

"Sorry?"

"When the power goes out at home, what do you do?"

"I light a candle."

"You go back to the old way of doing things. Tried and trusted."

"Yes, but—"

"If Sydney has no bridge, I think the world in 2038 might be in all kinds of pain." She held up the paper. "They've gone back to good old-fashioned print to get the news out."

Jacquie shook her head. "You tell me you don't believe in ghosts, but you're entertaining this shite?"

"Ghosts are the past." Claire walked a few paces, and pulled down another paper, this time from the top shelf. "This is the future… our future." She unfolded the broadsheet and started to read from the lead article. New Zealand had put a cap on their refugee intake and were no longer taking Australian citizens over the age of thirty.

"Put it back," snapped Jacquie.

"Why?"

"Don't look."

"Why on earth not?"

"Because, if it's true, this is what sent Professor Collins mad."

***

Jacquie switched off her torch and together they huddled in the dark. Claire could hear her friend quietly sobbing. She let her have a few moments. The suggestion that Ghoulman had been here before them was not stupid. And it did provide answers to some questions. *I saw you, Claire!* Had Ghoulman followed her out of the newspaper stacks forty years ago? Had he given her the date because he'd already seen another version of her between the shelves? But if so, how could he have possibly known who she was back in '79? Claire sucked in a breath as the penny dropped. If he'd overheard her conversation with Jacquie about passing information across time, he'd heard her say her name… Claire Hogan. All he had to do was go back again and find her.

"I wonder how long he spent down here, reading," said Claire after a while.

"Too long is my guess," said Jacquie. "The only good news is, if Ghoulman warned you, it means he found a way out. That means we can too."

Claire barely heard her. How far into the future did the newspaper stacks go?

"Claire?"

"What?"

"We need to turn around, *now*."

This irritated Claire more than it should. "Why?"

"Because I'm worried about what you're thinking. What you might want to do next."

"You weren't too worried when you dragged me in here."

"That was different. We were supposed to be having fun."

"You're scared," said Claire. It came out more accusatory than she intended.

"Damn tootin' I am. We've jumped the bloody shark, Claire, and I've had enough." Her voice had a shrill edge to it.

"Calm down."

"I don't want to be calm."

Claire waited a beat. "Don't you find this fascinating?"

"No, not at all."

"You're not one bit curious about what the newspapers could tell us?"

"*No*. And I don't see why you should be either. No good will come of it."

"But it's like enjoying a book and being told you can't read the final chapter. Jacquie, I want to read all the way to the end."

"Spoiler alert: it's a shit ending."

"You don't know that. Give me your phone."

"No, and I'm not turning the torch back on until you promise me you're not going to look at the papers on these shelves."

"Really? You're going to tell me what I can and can't do now?"

Jacquie sniffed.

"I came back to the library because you wanted to. You've harped on about this day for all these years. Now, when I finally have the chance to find out what Ghoulman was trying to tell me, you want to pick up your bat and ball and go home."

"We seem to be taking the long route."

Claire softened her tone. "I tell you what. Let me go to the end of this row, and I'll stop, I promise. It's not far, it'll only take me two minutes. You don't even have to come with me."

"You're not leaving me here in the dark by myself! Not after what happened before. We have to stick together, Claire."

"Hang on to me then, and keep your eyes shut if you want. I won't tell you what I see."

"Why do I feel like I'm about to let you jump off a cliff?"

"I'm not. I'm just going to read a few pages." A moment passed before Claire felt the phone push into her hand. She swiped the torch on. The battery bar showed 23 per cent. "Thank you, I'll be quick."

Jacquie looped her arms around Claire's waist. Together they inched forward.

Claire read a dozen front pages, skimming through articles that begged her eye. While her brain absorbed the information, she chewed into her bottom lip.

As promised, she didn't venture past the end of the row. Claire returned the phone to Jacquie and let her again take the lead. It made no difference to Claire which direction they took now. Her world was spinning.

They'd barely crossed into the next row when the bulbs overhead buzzed loudly. The aisle ahead flooded with warm light.

Jacquie let out a nervous excited laugh. "I don't believe it. Look down there. I can see the gate."

Claire blinked.

"Claire?"

Claire blinked again. *You're next.*

"We made it." Jacquie clapped her hands. "Do you see? There," she pointed, "and it's been left open. Thank God for small mercies."

A smile formed on Claire's lips as Jacquie dragged her towards the exit.

Outside, in the late afternoon sun, Claire raised her face to the sky, felt the warmth on her face, and took in a long, deep breath. She let Jacquie's chatter wash over her as they walked the main avenue through the university campus towards the city.

"You're quiet," said Jacquie, when they'd sat down in the front bar of the Richmond hotel. She slid a gin and tonic across the table. "Not still mad at me, are you?"

Claire picked up the glass and took a sip. You're next. You're next. You're next. You're next. You're next. You're next…

"Is everything okay? I don't want to know anything, it's not what I'm asking. Blissful ignorance is fine with me, but you haven't said a word since we left the library."

Claire took another sip, her gaze directed at the wall.

"Earth to mothership, are you in there? C'mon Claire, you're starting to scare me."

But Claire wasn't listening.

She was hardly there at all, her mind elsewhere.

Deep in thought, Claire returned over and over again to the stacks, where beyond that last row the shelves stood empty, and a page from the bible was pinned to a strange blue door.

The Girl Who Bled in the Tree

Tim Waggoner

Terri Marshall swings her Altima onto the street where she grew up, heart pounding, hands gripping the steering wheel tight. She looks up at the rearview mirror every few seconds, afraid she'll see a pair of headlights reflected in the glass, relieved when she sees only dark road behind her. She knows she hasn't lost Duane, knows he's still following, but she's managed to put some distance between them, and that's enough for now. When her car's headlights wash across the front lawn of her parents' house—illuminating the For Sale sign in the yard—she hits the brakes too hard, and her car fishtails, tires squealing in protest. It's late, after two in the morning according to the dashboard clock, and she fears the noise might wake some of the neighbors, prompt them to peer between cracked curtains to see what's going on, maybe place a worried call to 911. She isn't concerned the sound of her car skidding will wake her parents. They're both dead and buried.

She whips the Altima into the empty driveway, parks with the passenger side wheels on the grass, and cuts the engine. She gets out, the garage door a smear of garish white in the headlights' glare, and slams the door shut. *Too loud*, she tells herself, but really, what does it matter? If Duane catches her, it's going to get a hell of a lot louder.

She hasn't been here for six months, not since she and Duane got the place ready to sell. It's been on the market for a while, long enough for Duane to start losing patience. *I don't know what the hell's wrong. I've sold houses in that neighborhood before. Maybe it's got some kind of bad karma or something.*

Two stories, white siding, black shutters, new roof, new windows. The front yard is well-maintained—Duane pays a service to take care of it—and while the lawn isn't huge, it's big enough for a good-sized oak tree. The tree is close to the house, and Duane considered cutting it down. *An old tree like that makes people nervous, makes them think about it falling down on their house during a bad storm.* The idea appalled her, but rather than make a big issue of it, she told him the tree was charming, and that it would look good on the photos for the brochure and the house's online listing. He agreed, one of the few times he actually listened to her, and the tree still stands where it has all her life.

She needs it now.

She hurries across the lawn, the night air cold on her exposed arms and legs, the grass cool beneath her bare feet. It's mid-August, temperature in the high seventies, but it feels more like early fall to her, and she shivers. She wishes she had on something more than a Queens of the Stone Age T-shirt and shorts, but she had no time to change, not if she wanted to get out of the house before Duane grabbed hold of her. She almost didn't escape as it was.

When she reaches the tree, she takes hold of its lowest limb and hauls herself up. When she was a child, she needed to jump to grab the limb, and while she's by no means tall, she grew enough during adolescence that she can reach it easily now. Once on the limb, she crouches, bare feet on corrugated bark, one hand pressed against the trunk to steady herself. She reaches up, wraps her fingers around the next highest limb, and begins climbing. How far can she get? She has no idea. She was twelve the last time she climbed the tree, and she was able to get two thirds of the way up then. She's bigger now, of course, and she doesn't know if she can get that high, fears the thinner limbs won't support her weight. She decides to go as far as she can and hopes it will be high enough to conceal her.

She hears the engine of Duane's SUV before she sees the headlights. She feels a deep chill that has nothing to do with the temperature, and with it comes a mental flash of him standing in the open doorway of their master bathroom, a home-pregnancy test gripped in his hand, held up as if it were evidence at a trial and he the prosecuting attorney. *When were you going to tell me, Terri? When?*

The Altima's automatic headlights have switched off, but the vehicle is clearly visible from the street, and her less-than-stellar parking job makes it even more noticeable. She hopes the oak's leaves will provide cover, but they're sparse this low. She's tempted to climb higher to where the leaves are thicker, but she fears the movement will attract Duane's attention. There are no streetlights in this neighborhood—the residents think they spoil the area's aesthetics—and the SUV's headlights won't reach this far. Her clothes are dark, and if she remains still, the shadows might conceal her, and he'll drive past without noticing her. She presses herself close to the trunk. If there was a limb on the side opposite the road, she would move onto it to better hide herself, but there isn't. She watches the SUV approach. If Duane drives on, she'll wait several minutes to make sure he isn't coming back, then she'll climb down, hop in her car, and get the hell out of here. She won't need the tree then.

But as the SUV draws near the house, the vehicle slows, and Terri imagines Duane peering through the driver's side window to get a good look at her car. This is her parents' house, and he's been here many times over the years—and he's the goddamn realtor selling it. He *knows* there shouldn't be a car parked here this time of night, and of course he'd recognize her Altima. A second later, he guns the engine and turns into the driveway.

The limb she's crouched on has smaller branches coming off it. She takes hold of one of these, snaps it off, and drops it to the ground. She then raises her hand and brings it down fast and hard onto the jagged stub she's created. Pain flares bright and hot in her palm, and she can't stop herself from crying out.

The SUV door slams, and she hears Duane shout, "Where the *fuck* are you, Terri?"

She looks down, sees him standing in the driveway, sees that he's holding a gun.

She pulls her hand off the broken branch-end, biting her lip hard to keep from crying out again. She turns the palm upward, sees the blood welling forth, watches it begin to spill over the edges of her hand, run between her fingers.

Help me, she thinks. Please . . .

***

"I bring all the money into this house, and that means I get to spend it anyway I want!"

Terri sits at the top of the stairs, listening to her father yell. She's twelve years old and wearing her favorite pajamas, the ones with little Eeyores on them, feet bare, legs drawn up to her chest, arms wrapped around them, chin resting on her knees. Her mother says something, but she speaks so softly that Terri can't make out the words. She's always quiet, and the louder Dad gets, the quieter she becomes. *Yell back!* Terri thinks. She knows it won't happen, though.

From where she sits, she can't see her parents. She hears water running in the kitchen sink, knows Mom is rinsing dishes so she doesn't have look at Dad. When he yells, his face turns a deep red. When this happens, Terri always hopes he'll have a heart attack, collapse to the floor, and die. So far, he hasn't, though. Maybe tonight she and Mom will get lucky.

Dad bought a new car today—a Lexus—without consulting Terri's mother. Dad may make money, but he's terrible at managing it, so he leaves that job to his wife. But he's an impulsive spender, which puts her in the impossible position of trying to budget around his splurges.

"Carl, we can't afford a new car now, especially one so expensive." Mom's voice is whisper-soft, her tone apologetic.

A harsh smack of flesh on flesh, followed by a gasp then a sob tells Terri Dad has slapped Mom. She's seen him hit her—and worse—many times before. Her insides go cold and tears well, though they do not fall. She won't let them.

A moment of silence, and Terri expects Mom to say she's sorry, that of course he's right, what was she thinking? But when she speaks there's a thread of steel her voice. Just a thread, but it's there.

"If we keep the Lexus, we won't be able to afford Terri's dance class. You know how much it means to her."

Terri's gut knots with tension. Dance class is *everything* to her right now. It's her whole world, and she's good at it—her teacher says so—maybe good enough to become a professional one day. She'd like that. She wants to rush down the stairs, go into the living room, and beg her father to allow her to continue with her class. She could help pay for it. She's only twelve, but that's old enough to start babysitting, isn't it? Or maybe she could rake leaves and mow yards. She's willing to do whatever it takes. She doesn't move, though, just sits and listens and tries not to cry. Tries *hard*.

"What did you say?" Dad practically roars these words, and another slap follows them. "That girl is so goddamn uncoordinated, I'm surprised she can take more than three steps without tripping over her own damn feet. Sending her to dance class is like sending a three-legged hippo—a waste of time and money!"

Terri feels as if she's been slapped now, and the tears finally come. Before she realizes it, she's halfway down the stairs, then she's at the front door, then she's outside, the world a shimmering blur seen through her tears. It's a late Saturday afternoon in October, the air crisp and cool, but even though Terri isn't wearing a jacket, she doesn't feel the cold, doesn't feel anything except hurt and shame and anger—so much anger. Without thinking, she runs toward the oak tree in their front yard, her stocking feet crunching dead leaves beneath them. She reaches the tree and starts climbing it as easily as if it were a ladder, her young, strong body moving with speed and grace. This is where she goes when her father's cruelty becomes too much to bear, high above the world, surrounded by branches and leaves, alone, secluded, safe. She's spent countless hours up here, hiding and crying and wishing things were different than they are. In a way, the tree's her friend, her guardian, her protector, and she desperately needs it now. The tree's leaves have turned brown and orange with the season, and only two thirds of them remain on the branches to provide cover for her. She climbs as high as she can, does her best to conceal herself, and hopes it's enough.

She waits.

She hopes that Dad's too angry at her mother to have noticed her running out of the house, and she's ashamed to hope this, for it means that her mother is still bearing the brunt of Dad's anger, drawing it to herself and away from Terri. She shouldn't wish more pain on her mother, should take her fair share of it, give her mother some relief, but she's too scared. The front door flies open then and Dad storms outside.

"Terri! Where the hell are you?"

She doesn't answer, holds her breath. She can see him through gaps in the leaves, face red, eyes burning, hands clenched into fists . . . And then the tension drains from his body, and he smiles.

"Sweetie? Honey? Everything's okay. Your mother and I just had a little misunderstanding, that's all."

He glances toward the Lexus parked in their driveway, and his brow furrows, as if his anger is returning. But then he smiles wider and his brow smooths. She knows the smile isn't real, that he's putting on an act for her, trying to lure her out. He's done it before. But she wants the act to be real, wants him not to be mad at her, wants her kind, lovable Daddy back, even if he's an illusion. She shifts her position so she has a clearer view of him, but in doing so snags the left pajama sleeve on a broken branch. The sharp end pierces the fabric, bites into her skin, and the pain makes her wince. She draws in a hissing breath but doesn't cry out. She feels blood running down her forearm, fears she's seriously injured herself, but she won't call out to her father. Better to bleed to death in the tree than to let him get his hands on her. She wishes she understood where his anger comes from, why he is the way he is. Maybe if she understood it, she could do something about it, help him overcome it, or at least better know how to keep it at bay. She tried asking her mother once, but all her mother said was, *We are who we are*. She smiled grimly, then added, *'Til death do us part*. Terri didn't understand her mother's response, but she felt the woman's despairing bitterness, and she's never asked her about Dad's temper again.

She will never know what prompted her father to look upward, some sixth sense, maybe. But look up he does, and when he sees her his Nice Daddy mask falls away, and Angry Daddy returns.

"Come down," he says, tone cold. "Now."

She doesn't move. Her pajama sleeve remains caught on the branch, the end embedded in her flesh, and she thinks she can feel a pulling, a draining, as if the tree is absorbing her blood. Dad's features darken, and he stabs an index finger toward the ground, as if he thinks she's lost the ability to comprehend English.

"*Now*," he repeats, like he's summoning a stubborn dog.

She stays where she is, lets the tree continue drinking her blood. Why not? It's been more a friend to her than her father ever was. It stands just outside her bedroom on the second floor, so close she can almost reach it when the window's open. How many times has she stood at the window looking out at the tree while her father yelled and hit her mother? Watched it change with the seasons, listened to the wind stirring its leaves and rustling its branches? How many times has she imagined jumping out the window in the middle of the night, catching hold of one of the limbs, shimmying down monkey-swift, until she reaches the lawn and starts running, never stopping, never looking back? There's no escape now, though. She knows that, but she can't bring herself to climb down and face her father. Instead, she wraps her free arm tight around the tree's trunk, and—gaze fixed on her father's face—almost imperceptibly shakes her head no.

Her father smiles, cold and cruel.

"If you're not going to come down on your own, I'll just have to come get you, won't I?"

He walks toward the tree, grabs a low-hanging branch, pulls himself up with a soft *oomph* of effort. He climbs slowly, testing hand and footholds as he goes, angry but still in control. She wishes he climbed swiftly, recklessly, because then he might slip and fall, might hurt himself when he lands, giving her a chance to get down and run off before he can recover and grab hold of her. She wishes, wishes *hard* . . .

A dry brown leaf near her left shoulder detaches and falls, spiraling downward. It passes near her father's face, brushes his cheek, and he winces. A thin line of blood appears on his skin, and Terri realizes the leaf has cut him. He touches a hand to his small wound, frowns as he regards the blood on his fingers.

Another leaf breaks free, this one close to her right hip. Like the first, it spirals downward, and it slices the back of her father's left hand, which currently grips a branch not much wider than

Terri's thin arms. This time the cut is deeper, and her father lets out a sharp cry of pain. There's more blood, too. A lot more.

Terri smiles. "Get him," she whispers.

All around her leaves quiver, and then they burst away from the tree in an explosion of red, brown, and yellow. They descend rapidly toward her father, so many that he's temporarily lost to Terri's sight. They cut and cut and cut, and his screams are like sweet music to her. He tries to hold onto the tree, but he's in too much pain, and his hands are too slick with blood to maintain a solid grip. He slips, falls, hits the ground head-first. There's a loud *crack*, like a branch breaking, and her father—a tattered, bloody thing—lies on the grass, not moving, eyes open and staring. Terri looks at him for a moment, and then she slowly pulls her left arm free of the broken branch that pierced her flesh. Blood trickles down her forearm, onto her wrist, then onto her hand and fingers. She presses those fingers gently against the tree's bark.

"Thank you," she says.

***

As Terri grew into adulthood, she promised herself that whatever else happened in her life, she wouldn't end up with a man like her father. But of course, she did. She was cautious in her dating life, kept close watch for red flags –a quick temper, a lack of patience, simmering resentment, nurturing grudges . . . But she hadn't realized that people like her father didn't reveal their true selves right away. They were like carnivorous plants that create a sticky sweet substance to lure and trap their prey, and by the time you realize what's happening, it's too late. They've got you. Duane was like that, kind and attentive at first, but once he had his hooks into her, he dropped the act and reverted to the sadistic, controlling bastard he'd always been. Terri found herself living in the very hell she'd sworn to avoid, and she literally has the scars to show for it. Now here she is, clinging to an old oak tree in the middle of the night, her abusive spouse standing on the ground below, gun in hand. The gun—a 9mm Glock—surprises her. She knew he had one, but he's never threatened her with it. But then, she's never tried to escape him before, has she?

He walks up to the front door to check that it's still locked and finds it so. She wishes she had the presence of mind to unlock the door before climbing the tree. Duane might've gone inside then, giving her a chance to run off before he found her. A missed opportunity, hopefully not a fatal one. He thumps his fist on the door, as if to punish it for not granting him access to her, then he turns around and sweeps his gaze around the yard. This could go one of two ways, she thinks. He could decide to check the backyard, see if she's there, or if she's unlocked the rear door and entered the house that way. This *was* her parents' place, after all, and she has her own keys to it. Or it will occur to him—whether consciously or subconsciously—that she's up in the tree, just as it had to her father over two decades ago? One thing Duane won't do is give up and leave, not with her car parked in the driveway. He knows she's here somewhere.

She only has one option left.

She presses her bleeding hand to the trunk of the tree, hard, ignoring the pain, willing the tree to drink deep.

"Please," she whispers.

For a moment nothing happens, and she fears that the memory of how her father died has become cloaked in childish fantasy over the years. The tree didn't do anything to save her that day. Her father slipped all on his own, fell, and broke his neck. An accident, nothing more. She's an idiot for coming here hoping to find safety in the arms of her old friend. Years of enduring Duane's physical and psychological abuse has damaged her mind more than she realized. There's no other explanation for why she's come to believe that this tree is a sentient thing, and more, that it actually cares for her.

Does she move without knowing it? Is it the wind? Whatever the reason, the leaves around her rustle, drawing Duane's attention. He looks up, and despite the darkness and the foliage, he sees her. His eyes widen in surprise, and then his mouth stretches into a slow grin. He's been holding the gun down at his side, but now he raises it and aims it directly at her.

"Come down," he says. "*Now.*"

He speaks the words, but she hears them in her father's voice.

Can she shift position, put the tree trunk between her and the gun, shield herself from his bullets? That's assuming he'll even shoot. She *is* pregnant with his child, after all. But even if he empties the clip without hitting her, he'll simply climb up and get her, just as her father tried to do. The outcome is inevitable, and from Duane's darkly amused expression, he knows it too.

She lifts a foot from the branch she stands on, begins to lower it . . .

Then the tree starts to move. Gently at first, as if swaying in a light breeze, then faster, more violently, as if buffeted by gale-force winds. Sudden panic grips her, and she wraps her arms around the trunk to steady herself, presses her still-bleeding hand tight against the bark, and as she does this, she remembers Duane's words.

An old tree like that makes people nervous, makes them think about it falling down on their house during a bad storm.

Branches and leaves flail around her, blocking her view of Duane, but she imagines him standing frozen, gun raised, eyes wide, mouth open, as he watches her friend's increasingly wild gyrations. Branches curl around her then, enclose her in a sphere of leaves, as if to protect her. And then she feels the tree begin to fall. For a moment she's flying weightless, but then her flight comes to a jarring halt as the tree crashes into the house. She's bounced around some, but the leaf-sphere cushions the impact, and she's uninjured. She lies there a moment, heart racing, breathing heavily, and then the branches curl away from her, and she's able to crawl out and step onto the ground.

The top of the tree has smashed what was once her bedroom window and caved in a good portion of the house's façade. It snapped in the middle, and its lower half slammed into the ground, broken limbs burying themselves in the earth—and in Duane. He lies beneath the tree, thick branches impaling his chest and abdomen, pinning him like a dead, dried insect mounted for display. Blood courses from his wounds, runs from his mouth, and his unblinking eyes are glazed and sightless. His outstretched hand is empty, the gun lying some distance away.

She looks at him for a time, dimly aware of lights coming on in houses up and down the street. *I should hide the gun,* she thinks. *Before anyone gets here.* She walks toward it, but halfway there, her bare foot comes down on something hard. She bends down and picks up an acorn in her wounded hand. She holds it in front of her face, turns it this way and that, then she smiles, closes her bleeding palm around it, and continues toward the gun.

SHH

David Wellington

Six suns up, five suns down. She splayed her fingers, all the fingers of one hand, one finger of another. Shoved that many fingernails into the flesh of her thigh, thinking the pain would make the words come. It didn't work.

It was dawn and the broken-down semi-trailer was already hot and stank of dead food. Dead. Not just dead but. Decaying diseased corrupted. Rotten food. The high acid-y bouquet of rotten citrus, the floral undernotes. Like the words people used to use to talk about – about – rotten fruit, something made of rotten fruit. Something liquid, something rotten liquid something something. She forced herself to let it go because the rotten fruit liquid didn't matter. Not right now. Last night she'd eaten oranges, rotting oranges, choking them down, gnawing on the rinds. Dead oranges were better than—

Rotten. Not dead. Rotten. Rotten oranges.

It wasn't just the words, it was the… conceptuals? The metastasis. No, no, *metaphors*. You'd think the nuances and the shades of meaning would stay, but they were all contingent. You couldn't think *rotten* without *dead*, without *old*, without *toxic*, and those were all words, too.

They were all slipping away.

She pushed open the doors at the back of the, the trailer and sunlight spilled across her, made her body warm. That and the fresh air made her smile, a little. Then she opened her eyes and looked around for Daughter. One of two words she'd been able to hold onto the best. *Daughter.* Daughter, where? Where is Daughter?

There were people walking past the back of the trailer, a line of people headed…somewhere. People carrying all they could of. Of things. *Belongings*. People who looked tired, who look down. Down at the ground. Daughter was going up to each one. Holding up a piece of paper. The thing. The thingy Daughter made, because Daughter is so good at. At thingy.

Daughter makes noises with her mouth as she pushes the paper toward passers-by. Passersfly cannot understand, of course. How could they? No **IMMUNE** among them. **IMMUNE** had already gotten out. Gone. Somewhere.

None of the passengers (*passersby?* that couldn't be right) looked at the paper. The paper that had a portrait… painting… television *drawing* of Husband

(the other word she's held onto)

drawing of Husband.

Husband. A word she could hold almost as well as Daughter. But not quite. She hadn't seen Husband in nearly a week, and he was fading, except when she looked at the drawing.

Is good drawing. Is…is good, it is an excellent drawing, because Daughter is so good. At drawing. It's how they're going to find Husband. Somebody will have seen him.

Six fingers, still splayed out. So, she can remember. Another thing you need words for: remembering. You can't hold everything in your head. If you can't say them, if you can't repeat them out loud, things just slip away.

Daughter makes noises. As if someone will understand. A big man is there, looking at Daughter, listening to the noises. Big man does not look at paper, at – at drawing. Looks at Daughter.

Smiles.

This is a thing that she understands. She knows what that smile says.

She feels her heart explode in her chest, it feels just like that, is not metaphor, is real, is explosion. Of fear. Rushes to jump down from the back of trailer, runs toward Daughter and the man. Get away! Get away!

She makes noises with mouth. No good, noises. Worth nothing. Daughter does not look up.

***

The first letter is tall, and thin. Like Husband. Arms at sides, feet together.

***

It started six days ago, in the kitchen. She'd called out, called Daughter's name, called her to dinner. Mindy. No. That was wrong, and she knew it. They laughed. Mandy. Except that was wrong, too. Daughter thought she was making a joke. Maybe I am, she thought. Maybe I am. That night she kissed Husband good night. She was turning in early, because she had a yoga class in the morning, first thing, while Husband wasn't expected into the office until eleven for a meeting, so he was going to stay up and play some – some—

Oh, God, that stupid game. That game he always played with his headphones on, so he couldn't hear her. Couldn't hear her when she called his name.

She'd finished a glass of wine, kissed him good night, and gone to bed. She had an audiobook she was working on, but she was tired enough she didn't need it. There was supposedly a bad flu going around, and she wondered if maybe she'd caught it. She'd been tired and a little achy all day, and she had a bad headache, which wasn't so much. She got headaches sometimes. The best thing for them was sleep. So, she went to bed.

When she woke up, she couldn't remember what breakfast was called. Or the car. Or the address of the yoga studio, or what it was called, or how to look that up on the, on the thing she couldn't remember what it was called.

Her headache felt like someone was digging into her head with a trombone. No, no, no. Not a trombone. An armchair. A– a claymore? What the hell was a claymore?

The words were still there. They were a big cloud, swirling inside her head, there and she knew them but if she tried to reach for them, they fled from her, like mischievous birds, like trying to catch a, a, thingy, a thingy that is…hard to…catch.

If she focused hard enough, she could almost get one word at a time. This time, the word she was looking for, the word that described the headache, was:

power drill

Shh

It took her half an hour to come up with it. By that point she was lying on the floor of the front hall, down on her yoga mat, crying. The foam mat wasn't designed to absorb tears. She thought she was going to die. She was certain, absolutely certain that there was a brain tumor in her head, a big fat ball of fat of fatty fat of fat and it had the fat had the thing, the tumor had popped, and the fat thing had burst, and she was going to die.

Daughter found her there, on the floor.

Daughter had been sent home early, from school. The school principal had gotten on the intercom and said something about artichokes, something about gold. Something about fishbones, and that was enough.

The teachers sent the children home.

Broca's Area of the Brain. Daughter's science teacher said those words and they were sing-songy, head rhyme-y enough that she could hold onto them, for a while. She had Daughter help her look it up online. Broca's Area of the Broca. It was exactly where her headache was, her left temple. Her left area of brain. Of Broca. Of the... it was where your language lived. Where lovely letters and lexicons and linguistics and logomachia lived loved and laughed, in the Brain's Area of the—

"Mom? Mom, you're not making—"

Famous last words. After that, there were fragments. Sounds that sounded right and sounds that sounded wrong. The television was turned on and there were pictures, which felt easier to work with, pictures made more sense. Pictures of people out in the street, looking confused and scared and then running and screaming. Daughter looked scared. Daughter looked terrified.

Shh, she told Daughter. *Shh*. It was what she could manage. *Shh*.

Husband didn't come home from his meeting. He didn't come home that night.

She was scared, but she had to be strong, for Daughter. *Shh*.

***

The second letter is two mountains, next to one another. Touching at their bases, at their foothills. This is my favorite letter. It hurts that I can't remember why.

***

They kept the door locked. They kept the windows closed and curtained until it was dark inside as a stormy day. They could hear people outside, shouting. There was a lot of shouting. Daughter spent much of the first day with her phone, making noises into it, looking more and more confused. More and more angry. She would stare at the phone like it was the stretched open mouth of a snake, and it had bit her ear.

They switched on the television, which was just more noises, and pictures she couldn't understand. Daughter started crying, looking at those pictures.

On the television there was a very serious looking man holding a piece of cardboard. There were shapes on the cardboard, and the man kept pointing at the shapes. It reminded her of an eye test, at the doctor. *How much of this can you read?*

None, doctor. I can't read it at all.

The piece of cardboard had six shapes on it, shapes in a row, a line. Together they formed one shape that looked like this:
IMMUNE

The man on the television clutched the cardboard like it was an amulet, a magical talisman. Like it would make everyone safe. She saw that in his eyes, that he wanted everyone to feel safe, but that just made her feel worse that she couldn't understand. This kind man wanted to help, and she couldn't…

Can you read any of this?

No, doctor. No. I'm so sorry.

That night the television switched off. So did their lights.

The shouting outside continued.

She led Daughter by the hand, in the dark. Took her into the kitchen. Took out candles and matches. Took ice cream out of the freezer, which had gone very, very quiet. Together they sat on the kitchen floor and ate ice cream and laughed and cried and then they just held each other, waiting.

"Huh," she said. "Huh." It wasn't a word. Part of one, maybe. "Huzz. Husband."

Daughter made noises and shook her head. Daughter didn't understand. Daughter was crying again. She didn't understand what Daughter was trying to say. For a long time, they were like that, scared together, unable to say what they were scared of. Unable to tell each other it was going to be okay. Unable to say what they thought was going on.

In the morning she woke, and Daughter was standing in her bedroom, looking worried. Looking scared. Daughter had something in her hands. The sketchbook. The big sketchbook she took to school every day. The sketchbook nobody was supposed to look at.

She took it from Daughter. Daughter was always so good at drawing. She opened the cover, and touched the paper inside, shiny, slightly greasy paper. There were so many drawings in there and she was shocked to realize – Daughter wasn't just good. She was amazing. She had real talent. Half-naked girls riding on rockets and looking cute in sunglasses. Animals with sly expressions. A smiling sun winking at a smiling moon. A better world than this, a more fun world, a cuter world. Some of the drawings were colored in, in soft pastels that didn't exist anywhere real. That couldn't. She started crying, for this little glimpse, this view through a long, long telescope into Daughter's private little planet.

Daughter sighed in frustration and yanked the sketchbook back out of her hands. Daughter had a pen, a marker, even though the other drawings were mostly in pencil or fine line pen. Daughter flipped toward the back of the sketchbook, then slashed a few quick scribbles across a page.

She looked over Daughter's shoulder, trying to understand what was happening. On the page she saw a weird freeform shape, round and curvy. There were bubbles inside it, and it had a fringe of hair like eyelashes.

She had no clue whatsoever as to what Daughter was drawing. A thing that was gooey, and slimy, but alive, somehow. More a puddle than an animal, but it looked like it was about to move, to creep across the page.

A…a germ? A microbe? She could only shrug.

Daughter roared in frustration and tore the sheet out of the sketchbook. Balled it up and threw it away. Then she started another drawing. A brain, sketched out in just a couple quick lines. Daughter was so good at this. She tried to hug Daughter, to pull her close, but Daughter pushed her away and kept drawing. There was a hole in the brain now, on the left side, and something was spilling out of the hole. Squiggles, just random shapes, or maybe—

Words. Yes! She recognized they were supposed to be words, though she couldn't make any of them out.

One by one Daughter drew a line through each word.

She shrugged, again. Not understanding.

Daughter was weeping now, with the effort, the desperation of trying to be understood. She drew pictures in rapid succession, just the barest sketches but they were all recognizable, understandable. A cityscape, with tall buildings. The shape of America, the country. Then a planet Earth. Under each one she drew the same symbol, which made no sense. A curve, like a crescent moon. Hanging from its lower tip was a short straight line and then a dot that looked like it had dripped from the short straight line.

She shook her head. She didn't understand.

For once Daughter didn't get angry or upset. She just nodded with determination, resolution. Then she turned to a new page and started drawing again. Taking her time now, taking care with each tiny line, each curve. Really putting her heart into it this time. Not just using her talent but her skill, her craft. She was so proud to see Daughter working like that, head down, tongue pressed up against the inside of her pursed lips, so deep in concentration. Eventually, Daughter finished. For a while she sat there with her hands over what she'd drawn, as if afraid to let it out into the world. Afraid it wouldn't make sense.

She rubbed Daughter's back in small circles, the way she did when Daughter was little and would come home from ballet practice, and her feet would hurt so much she would whimper. Daughter hadn't danced in so long, maybe she should—

Daughter took her hands away. She was trembling. Why was Daughter so afraid?

She looked down at the drawing. Saw a man there, a thin man in a nice shirt. Drawn so carefully, so precisely, that she thought she could lean down and smell that shirt, smell the skin underneath it. The man in the drawing had Husband's face. The soft beard. Those tired, sweet eyes.

She touched the drawing. Rubbed at it with her fingers, as if she could make it real. As if she could make him step out of the paper and into the house. Oh, it hurt. Oh, it felt so good.

Daughter grabbed her by the shoulders. Shook her. Then Daughter jabbed at the paper with the blunt end of the marker, again and again. Then she lifted one hand to her eyes and turned her head back and forth, as if she was searching for something.

Where. Where is Husband?

Wouldn't she like to know. Oh God how she wanted to know. Eventually she realized Daughter was asking a question. She answered it as best she could. She pointed at the window, at the outside.

For the first time she was glad she had no words.

Daughter took a deep breath. Then she reached up both hands to her throat and fake-squeezed. Made horrible sounds, stuck her tongue out the side of her mouth. Then she shrugged.

Her eyes were so terrified. Her face was pale.

Is Husband dead?

Why didn't he come home?

Words, no words. No answers. No answers.

***

The third letter is the same as the second letter. Make it just the same, exact. Has to be just the same, or they'll know.

***

Opening the front door was hard. The shouting outside had changed, grown periodic, but there was no way to know what they would find out there. Daughter kept grabbing the hem of her coat, as if afraid a wind would come and blow them away from each other.

"*Shh*," she said, and smoothed down Daughter's hair. And then she opened the door and stepped out into the garden. And nothing happened. For a long while it was like any other sunny, cold day. There were birds chirping in the trees, and tiny buds growing on the ends of twigs. The blue sky turned ever so slowly over their heads.

The two of them went to the detached garage like they had a million times before and climbed into the car, which chimed and thrummed around them like it always had. There was something so very deeply comforting about the car. About its sounds and its vibrations and the smell of the thin, dusty fake leather of the dashboard, of the steering wheel, of the gearstick. Shifting stick. *Shifter.*

Daughter reached over to switch on the radio. She reached out at first, to stop Daughter's hand. Then pulled her own hand back. It didn't matter. There was nothing on the radio but white noise. Static.

Or did it just seem that way? Were there words on the air, a river of words, and they just sounded like the rush of waves on the beach, to her?

It didn't matter. She pulled out of the garage and started driving. And that was when she realized she was going to have to remember the whole route. She couldn't make out anything but white squiggles on the green street signs. If they lost their way…

It was only fifteen miles or so to Husband's office, the place they thought they would look for him first. She had driven there before. How many times? She tried to count, then gave up. Not often. Not very many.

She glanced over at Daughter and smiled. Daughter smiled back. She would let muscle memory guide her, her body remember the right way.

Three hours later they ran out of gas. They left the car by the side of a road, and she knew that they would never see it again, never find their way back here once it was out of sight. There was nothing else to do but keep moving.

Daughter kept making noises. Trying to talk, to make herself understood. Daughter was just clinging to the memory of words. The comfort of them. By that point she understood it wasn't just her and Daughter, it was the whole world that had forgotten the alphabet. They had met other people, in the streets, in the winding little roads that passed house after house after house. Other people who came up to them babbling, came at them shouting or wailing or just miming, making gestures she couldn't understand. So many more who didn't even try to talk, who just implored with eyes and faces creased with grief, with hands

Shh

grabbing for her, reaching for her clothes, to grab her sweater, her coat, as if she had something to give them. The silent people were the hardest. Because they understood, they knew what was happening, and that meant she had to admit it, too. Had to recognize the facts of this.

So many people. So scattered and alone, all of them, without their words.

It was Daughter who hit on the new plan. Daughter who tore her beautiful drawing out of her sketchbook, held it up high so people could see it. Husband's drawing. *Have you seen this man? Have you seen him?*

People shook their heads. Some barely glanced at the picture, some stopped and looked for a long time, like it gave them comfort, though she knew they would eventually shrug and walk away. Daughter's energy seemed boundless, for a while, as she turned circles in the street. Gabbling and warbling away, like the birds in the budding trees.

She followed along after Daughter, kept her in sight. Always. She knew — and it hurt, knowing this — knew, if they were separated, she wouldn't know what name to call out, wouldn't know how to find Daughter again.

Daughter's name was...it was Muh. It was Mmm. It was not Mary, or Millicent, or Meg. It was — it started with — muh. Muh. Muh.

She wiped a tear away and forced a smile, when Daughter turned to look back over her shoulder, still holding up the picture, the picture of Husband.

***

My Daughter, I show you, like the moon lying on its back is four four four fourth. One two three four. Again. One, two, three, four: the moon, on its back.

***

They walked until their feet were sore. They walked until their feet blistered and bled. It was something to do. In the middle of town, in the commercial district, they saw people gathered. They heard a great commotion, a roaring like the sea.

Daughter hurried forward but she ran and grabbed Daughter's shoulders and held her back. Careful. Slow. See what you can see, first. There was no way to explain.

There was a big military truck parked in the center of town. People sat in the back of the truck, not soldiers, just normal people, their heads ducked low, their faces covered by hands or the hoods of coats. She thought maybe they were being taken away, taken somewhere to be imprisoned or, or shot, or…

Soldiers had made a cordon around the truck. A ring of bodies in green, and rifles, and shouting orders. Shouting, so much shouting. Someone wriggled through, got through the ring of bodies and – and then rifle butts came down, hard, again and again, and the interloper, bloodied and clothing torn, was shoved back out of the circle. It didn't stop others from trying the same thing.

Daughter looked back at her, questioning. She didn't have any answers. People wanted to get on that truck, then. They wanted to get inside the protective ring? But how? How did you make it through, how did you…?

Someone came running toward the ring, waving a sign. A sign covered in black squiggles. She couldn't make any sense of them, they were just shapes, shapes in a row that looked like **IMMUNE**. It meant nothing, except when they man holding the sign came forward, desperate-faced, shaggy, the soldiers stopped shouting. They pushed the crowd back. It was like a magic trick.

IMMUNE. She studied that shape. She'd seen it before, hadn't she? Shapes like that, shapes made of squiggles just squirmed when she tried to grab them, squirmed away from her. Tore at it with her brains, with her, her thingies, worked at the shape with her teeth. If she could make sense of it, if she could capture just this one word, maybe, maybe—

The soldiers barked words at the man with the sign. He muttered back, as if he understood them. It was some kind of trick. He couldn't possibly – no, he couldn't understand, his words had been taken like everybody else's.

Hadn't they?

It was a trick. It had to be. Yet the soldiers pulled him inside their ring. Put him in the back of the truck. He put his head down, like the others. Waiting. He was waiting for the truck to move.

They saw two more people come up with signs, signs with the **IMMUNE** shape. Like somehow these people had figured out a magic spell. Or someone had taught them a trick, one foolproof trick to…

She tried to understand. She tried to figure out how it worked. But…

It slipped through her fingers like water.

They walked away, because the sight of hope was somehow worse than not knowing, not having anything. They walked away and kept walking, kept looking, kept holding up the picture of Husband.

After the sun went down, they found themselves right back there, in the center of town. The army truck was gone. They found a place to sleep, in the park. There were lots of people there, families, so maybe it would be safe. It was cold sleeping in just their coats, but she didn't know what else to do.

After that the days flowed by, and it was hard to keep track. They ate when they could find food, in abandoned stores or houses with no people. Houses were dangerous. More than once they merely walked too close to a house and someone would come roaring out, gun or rifle in hand, and drive them away. Once someone actually fired, shot at them. They ran as fast as they possibly could.

Daughter was so scared. She shook so hard in her mother's arms.

The night they found the truck full of oranges was a good one. The truck was so warm inside, with the heat and smell of decay, and some of the oranges were still edible. She couldn't believe their luck, that they'd just stumbled on bounty like this.

So funny to think that a week earlier, rotten oranges would have disgusted her. Made her sick. Not anymore.

She woke up in the warm, bright smell, and light creeping in under the doors at the back of the trailer, and she smiled, for the first time in a long time.

Six suns up, five suns down. She splayed her fingers, all the fingers of one hand, one finger of another. Shoved them into her leg to wake herself, to get the blood moving. Where was her Daughter? Where did Daughter go?

She threw open the doors and saw Daughter talking to the man, the smiling man, and her heart died in her chest. Daughter was smiling back. No, no, you can't, you don't, you never!

She jumped down out of the back of the truck. Grabbed Daughter and pushed her around behind her coat. The man was in her face right away. Of course he was. She held her ground, frowned and scowled and tried to look crazy.

The man laughed. He laughed at her. He reached for Daughter. She wouldn't let him have Daughter. She clawed at his eyes. For a second it worked.

Then she looked up and saw the man had friends. Men.

Everything after that happened very fast. There was a rock she picked up from the side of the road. There was a man's skull cracking open, and then hands on her shoulders, her hips, fingers snatching into her hair. Then her feet were off the ground and—

***

I will always love you. Wherever you are. The fifth letter is close to the second and third, but there is danger in thinking they are too close. Two tall men, between them a woman slumps, so tired. She needs to lie down and knows she cannot, that she will never get up again.

***

A kind of silence. Her brain had stopped struggling, stopped trying to find the words. To hold onto them. Daughter wasn't a word anymore. It was a picture, a picture of a smiling girl in a little dress with a red raspberry juice stain on the cuff of one sleeve. A stain that had never come out. The girl had short hair, and a cute headband.

Husband was – thin. Always so thin, in college and even now, when it wasn't fair anymore. She could hold on to that thinness. The chewy fatless solid compactness of his body, of his muscles under the smell of him. The shirt smell, the – the—

A kind of silence, if you didn't fight. A kind of peace, deep down.

It didn't matter what the men did to her.

She could find that peace, deep down, where there were no words. Just flashes of light, and the impacts, the shoes and boots finding her the soft spots between her ribs. She would hurt later, but what was that? Time?

Time was a word.

Enough time passed. Maybe a day and a night and a day? A day or a day or—

Words. She smiled, because Daughter pushed her hair back from her forehead. Daughter brought her water, and even a piece of bread. How had Daughter found bread? Somewhere. She ate of it and was fulled. Filled up. Stop—

Daughter brought out the sketchpad, and the marker, and drew pictures. Pictures of people, just quick caricatures but Daughter was so very good at this. Man, first, the man who had smiled and then laughed, and in the picture his eyes were hard. More men, the man's friends. She frowned to see this but Daughter kept drawing. More people, people with different faces. Kind faces. People who grabbed Man and Men and pulled them away, just in time.

There were good people in the world, Daughter was telling her. Kind people. She tapped the picture of Man and Men, though, tapped and tapped until Daughter understood, maybe. The existence of good people wouldn't always save you.

There was so much she needed to teach Daughter, and without words, without—

That was when she realized something. Something she had been seeing for days, and not understanding.

As Daughter walked her through the story, showing her each drawing, Daughter's lips moved. Sounds came out of her mouth. Daughter was still trying to talk, still trying to form words, phrases, speech.

Just... just trying?

She reached over and touched Daughter's mouth. Very gently. Daughter pulled away, looking embarrassed.

But then... if... she struggled, as usual, to get the ideas to line up. The concerts and the metatarsals. No, no, the similars and figures of spinach.

She tore at her hair, shook herself even though she hurt everywhere. There was something, something she could do, something she could make happen. But it meant sacrifices. Such incredible sacrifices.

Not least, a word. There was one more word, one she needed to hold inside her, to master. It meant letting go one of the so very few words she still had. A word she was going to miss, she knew.

The word she was going to let go was Husband.

Because if he was still alive, if he was out there somewhere, he would have to find her. She had put so much energy into looking for him. She needed that energy for another purpose, now. She was going to focus on another word, or at least, the shape of it. The shape it made on paper. She forgot what that was called. The shape – the shapes. Six shapes. Yes. Squiggles, marks. Most of them just lines, straight up and down, that would help. The hardest thing she could imagine doing. The only thing worth doing.

Make a picture of a word. *Daughter, help!* You are good at this. You draw good. Make the shape. Make a – a sign.

Six symbols shapes forms characters *letters*. We can do this, together. Daughter made noises with her mouth, worried noises. Scared noises. Noises of negation, refusal, of insistence. Somehow she made herself understand, not the noises but the meaning behind them.

I can't do this, Daughter was saying.

I can't do it without you.

Shh, she said.

Shh. It was motherese. A word in a language before there were words or language. A word mothers whispered to their daughters since always. *Shh*. Not even a word. *Shh*. Just a sound, but the most famous sound. The number one smash hit sound of all time. Top of the charts. There had always been mothers and daughters and together they whispered the sound, the *Shh*, that made everything okay.

Daughter took out the pen. There were tears on her drawing pad, and the thick, slightly grease paper wasn't designed to absorb tears, so they just ran down the page, making little valleys, little furrows when they dried. Daughter used the pen and drew the drawing, the shape. The shape of one last word. **IMMUNE**.

***

Take this. It is all I have left. It is the letter called "E", which is one of the letters in Daughter, but not in Husband. It is the last. It is the last gift. It is at the end. *End* has an E... I think. I think I remember that. I hope I am right. Please you are so good at drawing. Draw this just so. You must.

***

Daughter looked back. She shook her head and Daughter looked down. Looking down was okay, it wasn't a challenge. It made you less dangerous.

The soldiers had brought their big truck back and they were in a ring around it, pushing people back. A lot of people were trying to just rush their way through, to push as if they could push back against bullets. The soldiers held their position. How did the soldiers work together so well? How did they communicate, make plans? Was it possible all of those soldiers were **IMMUNE**? It didn't seem possible unless – unless somehow there was a, a, what was it called? A thing in a needle. A thingy that went in your arm thingy and then you didn't get thingy.

Was it possible there was a thingy and they hadn't told anybody? Until it was too late?

The soldiers pushed back, pushed back. One of them lifted a gun and pointed it right at Daughter's face, and her heart shrieked no, but Daughter knew what to do.

Don't look them in the eye. Just lift the sign, the sign we made.

Daughter held her ground, held her sign. After so so so so long the soldier lowered his gun – and grabbed Daughter. He grabbed her and spun her around, looked at her from every angle.

She fought back the urge to run forward, to shove through the crowd, to get to Daughter. No. She had to let this happen. She had to let this play out, now. Her big scam. Sham. Scheme. Plan. She had to give it a chance.

Eventually they finished roughhauling Daughter. Eventually they shoved Daughter back, inside their ring.

Daughter climbed up into the truck, where she sat with her head down, to wait. To wait to go.

Daughter was through.

Gone.

She turned. Turned and walked until she couldn't see Daughter anymore, ever step a supreme effort. Had it worked? She could hope. She could do that. She could hope. She walked, for a long time after that. Back toward town, and the house, the house where she lived with her – with – with the thingy, that was called—

The house she knew she wouldn't be able to find again.

Something rattleplanned inside her pocket. There was nothing there before. She pulled it out and felt the stiff, slightly greasy paper of Daughter's sketchpad. Unfolded the carefully folded. Unfurled, un—

A picture, a drawing. Of her. Of herself, and it was good. Not an idealized version, the wrinkles were there, the tiredness. In the eyes, though – love. There was love in those eyes, and at the bottom there was a series of squiggles, and the first one looked like two mountains standing next to each other, touching at their foothills. That first squiggle was the first letter of the name of Daughter.

She let the sounds breathe through her. It didn't matter if they weren't right. They were sounds she had chosen, sounds she'd given to Daughter, a very long time ago. Or something like them.

Mindy. Mandy. Melusine.

She sat down on a rock, and cried, just cried. Maybe Hustler would find her. Hustle, Histogram, Hinderance? She'd had the word, just last night, she'd known what he was called, the thin one with the shirt smell, he was called—

Shh, she told herself. She wrapped her arms around her cold body. Wrapped it and said over and over again:

Shh.

There's No Light Between Floors

Paul Tremblay

My head is a box full of wet cotton and it won't hold anything else. Her voice is dust falling into my ear. She says, "There's no light between floors."

I blink. Minutes or hours pass. There is nothing to see. We're blind, but our bodies are close, and we form a Yin and Yang, although I don't know who is which. She says the between floors stuff again. She speaks to my feet. They don't listen. Her feet are next to my head. I touch the bare skin of her ankle, of what I imagine to be her ankle, and it is warm, and I want to leave my hand there.

She's telling me that we're trapped between floors. I add, "I think we're in the rubble of a giant building. It was thousands of miles tall. The building was big enough to go to the moon where it had a second foundation, but most people agreed the top was the moon and the bottom was us." Her feet don't move and don't listen. I don't blame them. Her toes might be under sheetrock or a steel girder. There's only enough room in here for us. Everything presses down from above, or up from below. I keep talking and my voice fills our precious space. "Wait, it can't be the moon our building was built to. Maybe another planet with revolutions and rotations and orbital paths in sync with ours so the giant building doesn't get twisted and torn apart. Or maybe that's what happened, it did get twisted apart and that's why we're here." I stop talking because, like the giant building, my words fall apart and trap me.

She flexes her calf muscle. Is she shaking me away? I move my hand off her leg and I immediately regret it. I feel nothing now. Maybe her movement was just a muscle spasm. I could ask her, but that would be an awkward question depending on her answer.

She says, "There are gods moving above us. I can hear them."

I listen and I don't hear any gods. It horrifies me that I can't hear them. Makes me think I am terribly broken. There's only the sound of my breathing, and it's so loud and close, like I'm inside my own lungs.

She says, "They're the old gods, and they've been forgotten. They've returned, but they're suffering. And despite everything, they'll be forgotten again."

Maybe I'm not supposed to hear the old gods. Or maybe I do hear them, and I've always heard them, and their sound is nothingness, and that means we're forgotten too.

I put my hand back on her ankle. Her skin is cool now. Maybe it's my fault. My chest expands and gets tight, lungs too greedy. My head and back press against the weight around me. I'm taking up too much space. I let air and words out into the crowded void, trying to make myself small again. I say, "Did the old gods make the building? Did they tear it down? Did they do this to us? Are they angry? Why are they always so angry?"

She says, "I have a story. It's only one sentence long. There's a small child wandering a city and can't find her mother. That's it. It's sentimental and melodramatic but that doesn't mean it doesn't happen every day."

She is starting to break under the stress of our conditions. I admire that she has lasted this long but we can't stay in this no-room-womb-tomb forever. I should keep her talking so she doesn't lose consciousness. I say, "Who are you? I'm sorry I don't remember."

She whispers. I don't hear every word, so I have to fill in the gaps. "Dad died when I was four years old. He was short, bent, had those glasses that darkened automatically, and he loved flannel. At least, that's what he looked like in pictures. We had pictures all over the house, but not pictures of him, actually. My only real memory of Dad is him picking up dog shit in the back yard. It's what he did every weekend. We lived on a hill and the yard had a noticeable slant, so he stood lopsided to keep from falling. He used a gardener's trowel as a scoop and made the deposits into a plastic grocery bag. He let me hold the bag. His joke was that he was transporting not cleaning as he dumped the poop out in the woods across the street, same spot every time. It was the only time he spent out in the yard with me, cleaning our dog's shit. I don't remember our dog's name. My father and the dog are just like the old gods."

The old gods again. They make me nervous. Everything seems closer and tighter after she speaks. My eyes strain against their lids and pray for light. They want to jump out and roll away. I say, "What about the old gods?"

She says, "I still hear them. They have their own language."

I wait for another story that doesn't come. Her head is next to my feet but so far away. Her ankle feels different but that's not enough to go on. Finally, I say, "Maybe I should go find the old gods and tell them you're here, since you seem to know them. Maybe I'll apologize for not hearing them."

My elbows are pinned against my chest and I can't extend my arms. I do what I can to feel around me and around her legs. I find some space behind her left hip. I shift my weight and focus on my limited movement. Minutes and hours pass. My body turns slowly, like the hands of a clock. If the old gods are watching, even they won't be able to see the movement. Maybe that's blasphemous. I'll worry about it later. In order to turn my shoulders, I have to push my chest into her legs and hips. I apologize but she doesn't say anything. I make sure I don't hit her head with my feet. I pull myself over her legs, scraping my back against the rubble above me, pressing harder against her, and I'm trying the best I can to make myself flat. It's hard to breathe, and small white stars spot the blackness. I climb over her and reach into a tunnel where I'll have to crawl like a worm or a snake, but I have arms and I wish I could leave them behind with her. I can't turn around, so I roll her back with my feet into the spot I occupied. Maybe it'll be more comfortable and after I'm through she can follow. I say, "Don't worry, I'll find your Dad." But then I remember that she told me he died. What a horrible thing for me to say.

In the tunnel opening I find a flat, square object. It's the size of my hand. The outer perimeter is metal with raised bumps that I try to read with my fingers, but they can't read. It's not their fault. I never trained them to do so. The center of the square is smooth and cool. Glass, I think. I know what it is. It's a picture frame. Hers or mine. I don't know. I slide it into my back pocket, and I shimmy, still blind always blind, into the tunnel. Everything gets tighter.

My arms are pinned to my side. My untrained hands under my pelvis. My legs and feet do the all the work. Those silly hands and useless digits fret and worry. The tunnel thins. I push with my feet and roll my stomach muscles.

The tunnel thins more. My shoulders are stuck. I can't move. Should I wait for her? She could push me through. Do I yell? Would the old gods help me then? But I'm afraid. If I yell, I might start an avalanche and close the tunnel. I'm afraid they won't help me. My heart pumps and swells. There isn't any room in here for it. The white stars return. Everything is tight and hard in my chest. I feel a breeze on my face. There must be more open space ahead. One more push.

My feet are loud behind me. They're frantic rescue workers. I hope they don't panic. I need them to get through this. My shoulders ache and throb. Under the pressure. Legs muscles on fire. But I squeeze. Through. And into a chamber big enough to crawl in.

I feel around looking for openings, looking for up. I still can't see. I'll use sinus pressure and spit to determine up and down. My legs shake and I need to rest. I take out the picture frame. My hands dance all over it. Maybe it's a picture of her father in the yard. He's wearing the flannel even in summer. I remember how determined he was to keep the yard clean. He didn't care if the grass grew or if my dog dug holes, he just wanted all the shit gone.

I need to keep moving. I pocket the picture frame and listen again for the old gods. I still don't hear them. There's a wider path in the rubble, it expands, and it goes up and I follow it. Dad had all kinds of picture frames that held black and white photos of obscure relatives or relatives who became obscure on the windowsills and hutches and almost anything with a flat, stable surface. He told me all their stories once, and I tried to listen and remember, but they're gone. After Dad died, Mom didn't take down or hide any of the pictures. She took to adding to the collection with random black and white photos she'd find at yard sales and antique shops. She filled the walls with them. Every couple of months, she moved and switched all the pictures around too, so we didn't know who our obscure relatives were and who were strangers. Nothing was labeled. Everyone had similar mustaches or wore the same hats and jackets and dresses, and everyone was forgotten even though they were all still there. I can't help but think hidden in the stash of pictures were the old gods, and they've always been watching me.

The path in the rubble continues to expand. My crawl has become a walking crouch. There are hard lefts and rights, and I can't go too fast as I almost fall into a deep drop. Maybe it's the drop I shouldn't be concerned about. What if I should be going down instead of up? The piled rubble implies a bottom. There's no guarantee there's a top. What if she did hear the old gods but her sense of direction was all messed up? What if they're below us? Maybe that's fine too.

I continue to climb, and I try to concentrate. Thinking of the picture frame helps. In our house there was a picture of a young man in an army uniform standing by himself on a beach, shirt-sleeves rolled over his biceps. Probably circa-WWII but we didn't know for sure. He had an odd smirk, and like the Mona Lisa's it always followed me. I also thought his face looked painted on, and at the same time not all there, like it would float away if you stopped looking, so I stared at it, a lot. If I had to guess, I'd say that's the picture in my back pocket.

My crouch isn't necessary anymore and now I'm standing and level and the darkness isn't so dark. There are outlines and shapes, and weak light. My feet shuffle on a thin carpet. I avoid the teeth of a ruined escalator. I'm dizzy and my mouth tastes like tinfoil. There's a distant rumble and the bones of everything rattle and shake loose dust. She was right. The old gods are here. I imagine they are beautiful and horrible, and immense, and alien because they are all eyes or mouths or arms and they move the planets and stars around. I take the picture frame out of my pocket and clutch it to my chest. It's a shield. It's a teddy bear. I found it between floors. There's a jagged opening in the ruined building around me and I walk through it.

I emerge into an alien world. I'm not where I used to be. This is the top of the ruined building, or its other bottom. The air here is thick and not well. Behind me there is a section of the building's second or other foundation that is still intact. My eyes sting and my vision is blurry, but the sky is red and there are mountains of glass and mountains of brick and mountains of metal and I stand in the valley. Nothing grows here. There are eternal fires burning without smoke. Everything is so large, and I am so small. There are pools of fire and a layer of gray ash on the ground and mountains. I'm alone and there's just so much space and it's beautiful, but horrible too because I can't make any sense of it and there's too much space, too much room for possibility, anything can happen here. I shouldn't be here. She was right not to follow me because I climbed through the rubble in the wrong direction and I think about going back, but then I see the old gods.

I don't know how she heard them. They're as alien or other as I imagined but not grand or powerful. They're small and fragile, like me. There is one old god between the mountains, and it walks slowly toward me. The old god is naked and sloughs its dead skin, strips hanging off its fingers and elbows. Its head is all red holes and scaly, patchy skin. The old god must be at the end, or maybe the beginning, of a metamorphosis. There is another kneeling at the base of the mountain of glass. The old god's back is all oozing boils and blisters. Its hands leave skin and bloody prints on the mountain. It speaks in a language of gurgles and hard consonants that I do not understand. The old god is blessing or damning everything it touches. I don't know if there is a difference. I find more old gods lying about, some are covered in ash, and they look like the others, but they are asleep and dreaming their terrible dreams. And she was right again; they are all suffering. I didn't think they were supposed to suffer like this.

I walk and it's so hard to breathe but I shouldn't be surprised given where I am. There's too much space, everything is stretched out, and I'm afraid of the red sky. Then I hear her voice. Her falling dust in my ears. She's behind me somewhere, maybe standing at the edge of our felled building and this other world. She asks me to tell the old gods that I'm sorry I forgot them. My voice isn't very loud and my throat hurts, but I tell

There's No Light Between Floors

them I am sorry. I ask her if I'm the small child in the city looking for my mother in her one-line story. She tells me the old gods have names: Dresden and Hiroshima and Nagasaki. She knows the language of the old gods and I know the words mean something but it's beyond my grasp, like the seconds previously passed, and they all will be forgotten like those pictures, and their stories, in my mother's house.

I'm still clutching the found picture frame to my chest. There's a ringing in my ears and my stomach burns. The old god walking toward me spews a gout of blood, then tremors wrack its body. Flaps of skin peel off and fall like autumn leaves. Change is always painful. I take the frame off my chest and look at it. Focusing is difficult. There's no picture. It's empty. There's only a white sticker on the glass that reads $9.99. I feel dizzy and I can't stay out here much longer. It's too much and minutes and hours pass with me staring at the empty picture frame, and how wrong I was, how wrong I am.

There's a great, all-encompassing, white light that momentarily bleaches the red sky and I shield my eyes with the empty frame. Then there's a rumble that shakes the planet, and well beyond the mountains that surround me a great grey building reaches into the red sky. They're building it so fast, too fast, and that's why it'll eventually fall down because they aren't taking their time, they're not showing care. It's still an awesome sight despite what I know will happen to it. The top of the building billows out, like the cap of a mushroom, and I try to yell, "Stop!" because they are constructing the building's second foundation in the sky. The building won't be anchored to anything; the sky certainly won't hold it. It'll fall. I don't want to watch it fall. I can't. So, I turn away.

She speaks to me again. She tells me to leave this place and come back. I do and I walk, trying to avoid the gaze of the old gods. They make me feel guilty. But they aren't looking at me. They cover their faces. They're afraid of the great light. Or maybe they're just tired because they've seen it all before. I walk back to our ruined building, but she's not at the opening. She's already climbing back down. I'll follow. I'll climb back down to our space between floors and bring her the picture frame. I'll tell her it's a picture of my Dad in the yard with flannel and his poop-scoop.

I ease back into the rubble, dowsing paths and gaps, climbing down, knowing eventually down will become up again. Or maybe I'll tell her it's a picture of that army guy I didn't know, him and his inscrutable Mona Lisa smirk. Did he have the confidence and bravado of immortality or was he afraid of everything? She won't be able to see the picture, so I won't really be lying to her. The picture will be whatever I tell her it'll be. I won't tell her about the new giant building, the one that was grey and has a foundation in the sky.

The gaps in the rubble narrow quickly and everything is dark again. I once asked Mom why we kept all those old, black and white pictures and why she still bought more, and why all the walls and shelves of our house were covered with old photos and old faces, everyone anonymous, everyone dead, and she told me that they were keepsakes, little bits of history, she liked having history around, then she changed her mind and said, no, they were simply reminders. And I asked reminders of what? And she didn't say anything but gave me that same Mona Lisa smile from the photograph, but I know hers was afraid of everything.

The picture is in my back pocket again. I am going to tell her that everyone who was ever forgotten is in the picture. We'll be in the picture too, so we won't forget again.

I'm crawling and the tunnel ahead will narrow. I can feel the difference in the air. There is another rumble above me and the bones of everything shake again, but I won't see that horrible light down here. I'll be safe. I wonder if I should've tried to help them. But what could I have done? I suppose, at the very least, I could've told the old gods that there is no light between floors.

A World of Ghosts

Christina Sng

My dearest Momma,
Your spell worked.
I am safe now, me and Teddy.
But something went wrong.
The rest of the world is dead,
Even you and Kitty.

I guess
When you cast the spell
Wishing for me to be safe,
You didn't expect
The solution would be that
Everyone else had to be dead.

Does it mean they were
All carriers of the deadly virus
That would infect me,
Causing me to die early?
Even you and Kitty?
Is it my fault you're gone?

How do I live in a world
Without you, Momma?
It is quiet and scary
And full of ghosts
Whispering all day
That they are lost

Like me,
Wandering down
Empty, dusty roads,
Carrying Teddy
Who is getting heavy.
He hugs me to sleep

Keeping us warm,
Reminding me of you
And our bedtime cuddles
When you read poems
And we sang a sleepy song.
The memory keeps me strong.

I need it to go on.
Because
There is nobody, Momma,
No one around.
I've checked everywhere,
Even the ghosts are gone.

I'm so cold and hungry,
I'm gonna sit here for a while.
Maybe I'll lie down,
Curl up into a ball.
I can't stop shivering,
Even when hugging Teddy.

And the sky,
The sky is so dark.
I can no longer see
The moon through the fog.
Snow has started to fall.
It's getting colder now.

I think I'll see you soon, Momma.

Vigil at Singer's Cross

Matthew R. Davis

An hour after sundown, Justine Cho sat at the edge of the world between a sea of darkness and a sea of light.

On her sinister side, sand gave way to water so black that it blended seamlessly into the horizon, with only glimmers of light from the waning moon dancing on the gentle waves to dispel the illusion that the night had swallowed everything beyond the beach. To her right, a hundred candles burned, their flames wavering but holding steady like hope, each casting its yellow eye upon a countenance either taut with grim compassion or shimmering with fearful tears. The only face that bore a smile was printed upon placards and held aloft in prayer for its safe return.

Justine carried no candle, was trying to keep her distance from the faithful as they gave their yearning speeches and passed around their tokens of support. She wondered why she'd bothered to come to this vigil if she felt so detached. It wasn't like she and Laura-Lee Walters had ever been friends.

Oh, they shared classes at school, and had exchanged casual conversation on occasion. But they lived separate lives outside of education hours, and Justine had always been a little grateful for that, for there'd been a few instances when the sainted Laura-Lee—*beloved daughter, dearest friend*—had proven herself equally capable of bitchery as any other girl at school. She'd never bullied Justine as such, but she'd made jokes at her classmate's expense—laughing at her heavy eye makeup or newly-applied dye jobs, mocking the music that lent her life meaning, generally calling her out as a weirdo worthy of no real respect. If that were all she'd ever known of her, Justine would've found it hard to imagine herself ever missing the girl.

And there it was again, the word that had tripped off many a tongue this past week, impossible to ignore: *missing*.

Singer's Cross was a small town, and such tragedies rare here. People milled about like sheep, baaing the platitudes they felt appropriate in a situation like this: *time, prayers, hope*. Fair enough, but Justine couldn't help feeling a little disgusted that people who barely spoke to Laura-Lee were weeping as if their own sister had disappeared, that the whole community was buzzing with goodwill for someone whose wellbeing would otherwise scarcely concern them. She didn't resent the show of compassion and support, just the hypocrisy of hollow bromides that showed their speakers didn't know the missing at all. How many times this week had she heard Laura-Lee referred to as an angel? Justine must have misremembered the meaning of the word, or else no-one had bothered to look up the definition, because *angel* was so wide of the mark as to be insulting.

But that was true for everyone, she told herself as she rose to her feet and dusted sand off the rump of her black jeans. Angels would be bland and boring according to the popular conception of such things, or, if one went back to brass tacks, they would be ruthless and terrifying. She pictured Laura-Lee looming above this hopeful gathering, burning with harsh heavenly light, her eyes dispassionate as she raised a flaming sword to judge all she found wanting, and managed a small smile. It wasn't the worst image that came to mind when she thought of her classmate these days.

A couple of stray schoolgirls passed her by as she stumbled up the beach toward the vigil, frowning as if they'd spotted her smile and found it inappropriate. They'd surely deem it well within character for her, the weird chick who always wore black and kept to herself and watched all those freaky movies, but when they stopped to address her, Justine realised they had another reason to be dubious.

"Where's your candle?" asked Mikayla Paulsen.

"Oh." Justine realised how strange it was that this hadn't even occurred to her. "I, er, don't have one."

"Go see the pastor," Sharni Beck said, her tone falling just short of an order. "The prayer group are handing them out."

And here I was thinking it was BYO, Justine managed not to say. She nodded and flexed her mouth in a way she hoped looked forlorn. Her classmates moved on, no doubt intending to mutter imprecations once they were out of earshot.

And that right there was the other side of things, the equal and opposite reaction to all this holy folderol. Justine had heard at least half a dozen theories as to why Laura-Lee had disappeared, and most of them were petty, small-minded shit-talk. Laura was in hiding while she got an abortion; she'd been raped, murdered, and dumped by one of her teachers; she'd fled to the city to become a porn star, stripper, or prostitute—a charming collection of prospects, considering the missing girl was sixteen years old. Justine found these rumours offensive to Laura-Lee and sickening to her own sensibilities. Why did they all have to be about sex in some way, assuming you'd be so asinine as to define rape as such? The gulf between the sweet-beloved-angel bullshit and the secret-dirty-slut slander was appalling, revealing both hypocrisy and a tragic lack of imagination. There were so many other possibilities to consider, some that no-one here tonight could ever open their minds enough to even conceive.

Nevertheless, Justine had to admit that even she might have gone along with the mundane explanations had she not known better.

She stumbled up the beach toward the esplanade, sick to the stomach of everything she'd seen and heard tonight. Someone wandered by waving one of the placards that had been furnished by the local print shop, an A2 reproduction of Laura-Lee's class photo. The missing girl smiled at all who looked her way, bright blue eyes a-sparkle with love of life, silky long locks gleaming fresh and pure as if to represent the state of her soul.

Justine tore her gaze away, taking care to hide her sneer from the sympathetic mob. Would anyone give a shit if the unfortunate girl hadn't been white, blonde, born of parents well-connected in the community? She well recalled that time last year when Agozie had run away from home due to an abusive stepfather, and barely anyone had noticed. Sure, he'd been back within a week and the abuser taken into custody, but there hadn't been any vigils for the poor guy, and citizens had been notably quiet on the subject. As if this kind of thing was to be expected from such people, and the best response was to pretend it wasn't happening in the hopes that it—or they—would go away.

As she neared the flight of cement steps that led up to the esplanade, she caught sight of Mr. and Mrs. Walters, left alone for a moment by the crowd of well-wishers. The woman's face was a taut mask that hardly concealed her grief, and her husband clung tight to her arm like he was terrified he'd lose another loved one if he let go. The brief glimpse left Justine choking on her cynicism, ashamed. No matter how white or well-connected the Walters family might be, they were suffering through a living hell right now. Loss was a universal experience, the great leveller. It tore down boundaries as well as hearts and made supplicants of rich and poor alike, reduced class and race to arbitrary distinctions. In a way, loss was the only true justice in this world.

Justine reached the foot of the stairway that wove upward through a wall of rocks, and here she reigned in a sudden impulse to dash up them at full pelt—for just a couple of metres away, sat upon a flat-topped stone, was Marjorie Bartholomaeus.

The woman's generous girth was draped in a shawl and skirt as black as Justine's own outfit, her close-cropped skull swaddled in a purple knitted cap that poked woollen horns into the air as if to mock her reputation. Instead of a candle, her hands cradled the severed head of a dead rose, and she watched the vigil with an indulgent smile that she periodically coupled with a tiny shake of her head. As Justine reached the stairway, Marjorie's eyes flicked toward her, and she pretended not to notice as her boots trod up the sand-gritted steps.

Despite Justine's nominal approval and support of an eccentric single woman clad always in black and widely rumoured to be a witch, she didn't feel comfortable in Marjorie's presence. The look that woman wore tonight only deepened her misgivings—Justine got the impression she wasn't here to lend her sympathy, but rather to amuse herself with the misguided antics of idiots. And if her condescension implied she knew better than the rest of Singer's Cross, did it also hint that she knew the truth about Laura-Lee's disappearance? Justine, who considered herself privy to more of those facts than anyone else in town, couldn't resist a shudder at the inference. It made a disquieting amount of sense. After all, where had the seeds of her suspicions about the nature of things been planted, if not in Marjorie Bartholomaeus' strange little shop?

Reaching the top of the stairway, Justine turned for a moment to look down upon the beach. One hundred candles braved the night, each flickering in the gentle breeze as if to remind its holder just how easily its life could be snuffed out. Shivering herself, she left the esplanade behind and began walking back toward the centre of town, where the roundabout that served as the heart of Singer's Cross waited to point her in one of three directions.

Justine would follow none of them.

As she had done every night this week, she would sit by the roundabout and think of all the things she had no choice but to keep to herself. She would remember the half-hour she'd spent with Laura-Lee Walters on the night she disappeared, the things they'd said, the terrible mistake that had been made.

And she would wait.

***

Justine was halfway through her usual late-night loop of the town when she realised she was no longer alone.

Harmony Park was the one part of the walk that gave her cause for concern—not enough to avoid it, but enough that her senses went on alert as soon as her boots began crunching the gravel path that wound its way through the tree-spotted sward. She knew the risk of traversing such a place after midnight, away from the streetlights and anyone who could lend help should it be needed, but she kept her headphones on and blaring regardless. It was her way of whistling past the graveyard, and these days, it was her own little secret.

She'd made the mistake of mentioning it to her father once, and he had told her that a girl walking through such a place, at night, *with headphones on*, was just asking to be assaulted. The implication pissed her off, but she had to admit he was coming from a place of concern. It didn't stop her, though. She just told him she'd be wiser in future and kept trudging that unlit track regardless. Never mind whistling past the graveyard—this was Justine Cho flipping her middle fingers at fate. She would not be told where to go, what to do, how to do it. She would not be meek. She would do as she damn well pleased.

That said, she wasn't *stupid*. Her hands curled into fists within her jacket pockets as soon as she stepped into Harmony Park, one of them clutched tight around her *Fortnite* Funko Pop! keychain, her house keys poking out through her fingers like stubby blades. And tonight, she squeezed Cuddle Team Leader twice as hard as she approached the footbridge that ran over the small pond in the centre of the park, for someone was sitting on the stone post closest to her.

Her free hand flew out of her jacket pocket and swept the headphones back down around her neck, opening her ears to the night, and a dry, dark voice in her head muttered: *If I prove Dad right, I'll never hear the end of it.*

"Yo, Cho," said the shadow as it slipped off the post, the voice feminine and familiar. "Got a smoke?"

"Fuck, man! You scared the shit out of me." Justine fumbled in her pocket to mute the track still spilling out of the phones. "What are you *doing*, hanging around here at this time of night?"

"I could ask you the same question," replied Laura-Lee Walters, "but I won't bother, because you're a weirdo, and walking around in the dark is totally the sort of thing you would do. Smoke?"

"Er, sure. Hang on." Justine fished around for her cigarettes, one of many small pleasures she took in these night walks—there was no risk of being rumbled and guilt-tripped by her parents.

"Thanks." Laura-Lee produced a silver Zippo, an oddly masculine touch for someone whose sneakers and nails were bedazzled with glitter. They stood and smoked by the pond, two girls with little in common and less to say to each other. Eventually, the blonde thought of something.

"What you listening to?"

"Depeche Mode."

Laura-Lee shrugged, evidently no wiser for being told. "This is so *you*, Cho. Creeping around in the dark, dressed in black, listening to music I've never heard of. You do this on the regular?"

Justine swallowed her first response and instead asked, "What about you? I never expected to find *you* lurking in public parks after midnight."

"Oh, I'm on my way home. I had business to attend to." The smirk on her lips implied a certain self-satisfaction at the fact but gave away nothing else. "I stopped off to have my last smoke and, you know. Think about shit."

"Deep," Justine said, noncommittal. "Well, if you're going my way, I'll walk with you. Less chance of being raped and murdered that way, right?"

"Who knows with you? Just kidding."

They crossed the footbridge and left the pond behind, a puddle of oil that lay flat and gleaming beneath the night sky. Justine wondered at the incongruity of her company; she and Laura-Lee had just exchanged more words in a minute than they had during the previous month.

"You're not going to ask?"

"Ask what?" Justine wanted to know as they walked out of Harmony Park and into the antiseptic glow of the streetlights.

"About the business I had to attend to. You're not itching for goss?"

"None of my business."

"Ah, I like that about you, Cho. You might be a shady goth who wears butch clothes, but you don't give a shit about high school politics or trying to be cool."

Justine looked down at her black t-shirt and jeans, her chunky Doc Martens, and winced. "Actually, I think I *am* kind of cool."

Laura-Lee just grinned and patted her arm: *you do you, honey*. Justine decided to let the condescension slide.

Now they were advancing along the footpath into the modest central business district of Singer's Cross. This late at night, the town's life-signs were few—the discreet hum of powerlines hung overhead between poles like slack guitar strings, the red eyes of alarm systems that winked through darkened shop windows, the LED sign that flashed 24/7 behind the glass frontage of Chrissie's Cuts—and they walked the street alone, accompanied only by shadows the harsh white streetlights threw at their feet. They passed Imminent Domain, the odd little store owned and run by Marjorie Bartholomaeus, and Justine couldn't help staring through its front window into the shadows beyond.

Laura-Lee noticed. "Hey, you think she's actually a witch? She's got to be, right? I mean, dreamcatchers and incense and crystals and all that hippie shit, that's one thing. But her shop is just *weird*."

Justine shrugged. She'd browsed the place a couple times out of curiosity, and it seemed more like a display centre for eccentric tchotchkes than a place where one could buy anything of practical use. Many unusual things were offered up for sale, from bags of mugwort and wormwood to ceremonial thuribles and even, oddly, singing lessons that Marjorie claimed would protect one from otherworldly harm. The item that had intrigued Justine most was kept in a glass cabinet alongside the counter where the proprietor sat all day sharing tea and chatter with spooky-spinster friends: a single sheet of yellowed paper, its face stamped with words in an archaic typeset. They spelled out lyrics that any local would have found familiar.

"Walking the Cross" was attributed to Mare Gilly, the woman who'd given birth to Singer's Cross when she established the roundabout in 1837 and built a pub on its corner to refresh weary travellers; other businesses had sprung up nearby to meet other needs, including the still-standing feed store and the building that now held a Lebanese restaurant but was once, if rumour was to be believed, a brothel. Mare Gilly was an accomplished singer and had come out from behind the bar to give impromptu performances whenever a decent crowd had gathered, or whenever the mood took her. She'd even established a town anthem, to which the lyric sheet in Imminent Domain was dedicated—it must have been an original publication from around the time of Singer's Cross's incorporation and worth a tidy sum, hence its display and cage of glass. The song itself could still be heard at town fêtes and the annual Christmas Carols celebration held in Harmony Park, and even now, Justine could call some of the words to mind. The part that really stuck was the ending refrain, and without thinking, she sang it quietly as they walked away from Marjorie Bartholomaeus' shop window.

Back around,

Around, around.
Around, around, around.

Laura-Lee threw her finished cigarette toward a bin and a curious glance at Justine. "What's that? Depeche Mode?"

"Philistine! It's our town song. You must have heard it."

"Needs a trap beat."

Something very much like that boomed out at them as a low-slung car cruised by, bright eyes peering along the empty streets. Laura-Lee bopped her head to the familiar rhythm until it faded into the night along with the car's taillights, leaving them alone again in what might as well have been a ghost town.

Justine took these walks because she enjoyed feeling like the only person in an abandoned world; it spoke to her sense of isolation from the mundane mainstream, from her fellow humans. Before tonight, she'd have thought that sharing this delicious emptiness with anyone else would ruin it, but Laura-Lee made for surprisingly amenable company. She didn't gab on about moronic YouTubers or rattle off slanderous school gossip, and much of the time, the only sound from her was the soft clap of her glitter sneakers on the footpath.

Soon the pair of them reached the very core of Singer's Cross: the large roundabout around which the settlement had grown, its three asphalt arms pointing off to the north, east, and south. In the centre stood a cenotaph listing the names of locals who'd lost their lives in conflict; this three-metre needle, shaped from marble the colour of Himalayan rock salt, was ringed by three concentric rows of red rosebushes. The town's first building and cornerstone, the Bard's Rest, loomed on one side of the southernmost road, its two-storey bulk watching over the Cross like a stern but benign grandparent, or perhaps old Mare Gilly herself. Past that, the west was walled off by a deep expanse of woods that had refused to be corralled into a reserve or park, and instead brought the wilderness right to the heart of town.

"You know what I always found strange?" Justine asked, as much to break the silence as anything else. "This roundabout was the first thing here, right? Mare Gilly put it here as a point where travellers could diverge—south to the city, north to the hills, east along the coast—and she chucked a pub on it to make herself some money. But why only *three* roads? Why not go the whole hog and make it four?"

Laura-Lee shrugged, disinterested. "Maybe they couldn't cut a western road through the bush. What do I care?"

"And here's the thing: the town's called Singer's *Cross*. Implying a crossroads. And yet, no."

"Mayor Mare probably decided that Singer's T-Junction didn't have the right ring to it. Whatevs! You're starting to bore me, Cho."

With that, Laura-Lee dashed across the circle of bitumen and came to a halt on the roundabout itself. Glancing about for oncoming traffic, Justine swore under her breath and followed, wondering why she should even as she did. By the time she joined her classmate on the paved ring that encircled the memorial, Laura-Lee had plucked a rose from the nearest row and was tucking it behind one ear, turning to throw a model pose that Justine had seen online a thousand times.

"What now, then? Instagram selfie?"

Her tone must have been more scathing than she'd thought, for Laura-Lee replied, "You really think I'm shallow, don't you? Lighten up, Cho. I'm just trying to make my own fun in this dead-end town."

Justine couldn't quite bring herself to apologise. "Okay, fine."

The other girl narrowed her eyes, skeptical. "All right. You want to see a proper Insta pose?"

Laura-Lee looked for an opening in the rings of rosebushes, found none, and quickly slipped between thorny fingers once, twice, three times, until she reached the cenotaph that stood twice her height. With a glance of challenge at Justine, she turned and leaned against the marble needle, arched her back and threw a peace sign, pooching her lips into a perfect teenage pout. Then she extended both arms above her head and slipped into a more seductive pose, her chest pushed forward, her hips canted suggestively. Justine couldn't help but think of a saucy sacrificial maiden chained happily to a rock, Andromeda welcoming the approach of her darling beast.

"Are you done?"

Laura-Lee slumped, deflated. "You're no fun at all. No wonder we don't hang out."

"So sorry I don't meet your high standards, Walters. Maybe if I accepted Cardi B as my lord and saviour you'd see me as a worthwhile person."

"Oh, come on." Laura-Lee picked her way back through the prickly bushes to stand alongside Justine on the ring of pavers. "You're okay, Cho, and I've totally not really minded hanging out with you tonight. Let's go so I can get some sleep before school tomorrow. Where do you live? You going my way?"

Justine pointed down the northern road, where the edge of the business district faded into the beginning of the Cross's higher-end residential streets.

"Yeah, me too. Well, that's a relief. At least we don't have to go back around." Laura-Lee twirled one finger before gesturing the way they'd come.

Back around.

Justine frowned as several pieces of information crashed together inside her head, threatening to make an odd sort of sense.

"Hang on, I think I'm having an epiphany here. You want to try something weird?"

She regretted that choice of words as Laura-Lee arched an eyebrow at her. "Don't get carried away just because I said you were okay. I'm not into girl-on-girl."

"That's not what I meant."

Laura-Lee leaned forward, a smile crooking the corners of her mouth. "Are *you*?"

"None of your business. Look, what I meant was, I think I've worked something out. I want to try a thing. It's probably dumb, but hey, like you said, we've got to make our own fun, right?"

"I don't know if I like the sound of this. You've probably got strange ideas about what constitutes *fun*."

"I'll give you another cigarette."

"Okay, I'm in. Explain."

Justine spun on the spot, taking in the roundabout on which they stood and the three roads that radiated out from it. "Have you ever heard of widdershins?"

"Is that a kids' TV show?"

"It means anti-clockwise, dingbat. Look, this will only take a minute. Just follow me."

Justine walked past Laura-Lee, around the rim of the roundabout, in the opposite direction that traffic would take—widdershins, as she'd said. The other girl trailed after her, saying nothing until they'd completed a full revolution.

"So, when does the fun start?"

"That's *back around*," Justine said. "Keep going."

She led her classmate in another lap of the roundabout, and then another. No cars came by at this late hour to disturb their impromptu ritual.

"What are we even doing?"

"*Back around, around, around.* Get it? Three more times, and then we'll see."

Justine was acting on impulse, trying to ignore the voice that told her nothing would happen, Laura-Lee would laugh at her, this story would do the rounds at school and dropkick her reputation straight to *total freak*. But she was committed to this lunacy now, so she determined to see it through.

Laura-Lee was sighing in exaggerated boredom as they rounded the cenotaph for the sixth time, but that sigh became a *whuff* of surprise as she walked into the back of Justine, who had come to a dead halt on the pavers.

"What's the deal, Cho?"

Justine found herself struck momentarily dumb, so she raised one hand and pointed across the road.

On the western side of the roundabout, the curb admitted no entry to the bush that crept up to its edge—but the eucalyptus trees that kept their vigil against Singer's Cross had now parted, leaving a gap wide enough for a truck. And within that gap, there was now a packed-earth trail that led dead on into the dark depths of the woods.

"No fucking way!" Laura-Lee breathed. "What the *hell.*"

"I was right," Justine sighed, not sure if she should be glad of that fact. A tingle of terror and awe shivered her spine. "There *is* a fourth road, if you know how to find it—and Mare Gilly put the instructions right there in the town song!"

"It looks like something out of a fairy tale," said Laura-Lee, articulating Justine's unspoken feeling about this new vista before them. The plain path promised wonders and terrors. Did wolves lurk within those sylvan depths? Would the trail lead to a village, a witch's hut, a castle? And at the end of it, would they discover true love, or find themselves made an abject lesson in bedtime tales for unruly children?

"We've got to go in," Justine whispered.

"Do we *fuck*," Laura-Lee retorted. "You know what happens in fairy tales, right? You want us to get eaten by wolves or witches or some shit? Make it go away, Cho. Now."

"I don't know how. Come on, Walters." Justine turned and threw her a daredevil look that masked her own anxiety. "I'll give you *two* cigarettes."

"Piss off. Seriously. I'm going home."

"Whatever happened to making your own fun in this dead-end town? This is *amazing*. Wouldn't you regret it forever if something magical happened and you just *ignored* it? Come on. Let's at least just go in a little bit, and if it gets too freaky, we'll bail."

"It's already too freaky!" Laura-Lee hadn't taken her eyes off the mysterious new path for even a moment. "But... ah, man... you're right, aren't you? I won't be able to stop thinking about this. We'd be nuts to take a peek, but we'd be nuts *not* to. I just don't want to end up as wolf droppings, okay? We see anything weird, like gingerbread houses or singing dwarves or whatever, and we do the bolt. Deal?"

"Deal."

"*And* two cigarettes."

The girls crossed the road to stand on the curb before this fresh wonder, casting glances back to be sure nothing else had changed. Singer's Cross looked on, unfazed by this sudden breach of reality's law—but then, why should it be surprised? It must have seen this happen countless times over the decades, as those in the know walked back around and followed the fourth path to... *where*, exactly?

"Well." Justine blew out a long, shaky breath. "Don't say I never take you anywhere."

With a shared nervous glance, they stepped together into the trees.

It didn't feel like slipping through a magic portal; they might as well have been walking onto the path through Harmony Park, only the air here seemed a little sharper, colder. The track lay solid and true as any other beneath their feet, so this was no illusion. Justine felt Laura-Lee's hand creep into hers and marvelled at the turn this night's events had taken.

"Do you think anyone else can see this?"

A good question. Justine turned to look behind and, at that moment, heard a familiar throaty hum as an engine approached the roundabout. Together, they watched as a delivery truck came from the south and traversed their side of the circle, passing straight through and onwards to the north without a moment's pause. They were close enough to see the driver's head turn their way and then back, apparently not seeing them nor anything else worth a second glance.

"Just us, then." Justine squeezed her companion's hand. "Come on. Let's check it out."

"What if it closes up and we're stuck here?"

Justine sucked her teeth at the thought. "Good point. We'll be quick. Just a couple of minutes, okay? We can always come back again later."

Laura-Lee scowled, but let Justine pull her along. Together, the two of them walked deeper into the trees and toward the heart of this impossible forest.

The path lay before them straight as the horizon, with no curves or detours off into the woods, and seemed to run on indefinitely. Justine noticed that the trail held no tracks from car tires and assumed that any visitors must go by foot, though she could make out no prints in the moonlight. The road was edged with shallow depressions like natural gutters, where organic detritus gathered in drifts and clumps. Most of the matter seemed to be fallen pine needles.

"That's weird," she muttered, and Laura-Lee tossed her an incredulous glance, as if she'd just pointed out the most obvious fact in all existence. "The trees by the roundabout were eucalyptus, right? But these ones all look like some kind of pine."

"You're right. But that's not all. Does that sky look, I don't know... *different* to you?"

Justine could see nothing wrong at first glance, but the longer she looked, the more certain she became that Laura-Lee was right. The night sky above them now carried a purple cast that she'd rarely if ever seen before, and the constellations bothered her in a way she couldn't define. Astronomy was not her strength, but the configurations of stars above seemed subtly *off* somehow.

If what she saw plucked at her nerves, what she heard scraped a rough blade along them. Growing up in a country town, Justine was used to the background sounds of the bush and knew when she was amid nature in its normal course of things, and the ambience of this place felt as alien to her experience as the stars above. She wondered for a moment what denizens might lurk in the depths of these woods, what they might look and sound like, and found herself recoiling from the thought.

"I don't think we're in Kansas anymore, Cho-Cho." Laura-Lee pulled her hand free of Justine's comforting grip and tucked both beneath her armpits, huddling in on herself. "This feels all *wrong*, you know? Maybe we should just jet before things get any worse."

"Hang on." Justine slipped out her phone and opened the camera. Aiming the device down the path, she waited for the image on her screen to stabilise and come into focus—something it stubbornly refused to do, teasing her time and again with the possibility before receding into a dark, grainy blur. She turned the phone toward Laura-Lee, hoping her photogenic features would tempt the viewfinder to display a crisp image, but the girl too avoided focus, reduced to a smear of lighter colours that was soon swallowed up by the black backdrop. With a hiss of frustration, Justine tucked her phone away.

"Fairyland's no fan of Instagram, huh?" Laura-Lee was aiming for whimsy, but the quip fell flat in the heavy atmosphere. "Hey, can I have my cigarettes now?"

Justine had meant that bribe as a joke, but her classmate's pleading look revealed her need for something tangible and familiar. She was used to imagining strange things and stranger places, but this fresh impossibility was playing merry hell with her nerves; she could only guess how hard it would be for someone as prosaic as Laura-Lee to handle such an affront to reality.

"We're not littering Fairyland with durry butts, Walters."

She felt the same mix of atavistic awe and dread that was compelling her companion, but she didn't want to break this spell by clutching at talismans of the mundane. She was impatient to see more, *know* more, even as the very marrow of her insisted that she turn back and remain comfortably ensconced in ignorance. Laura-Lee groaned as her schoolmate continued down the path, reluctant to follow but even less keen to be left behind.

As they walked on, Justine noticed a sinister fog seeping through the trees around them. The further they travelled, the thicker it became, shrouding the gaps between trunks in a dim grey gauze. Already the way back was hard to make out; how long until they were walking blind in a cold, featureless world? She opened her mouth to say something but was oddly leery of adding anything to the soundscape of this strange environment.

Her Docs thudded on the tightly packed earth of the path like beaters against the skin of a deadened bass drum, and her gait settled into a steady metronomic rhythm; she noticed that Laura-Lee, consciously or otherwise, was timing her footsteps to match as though they were treading along to a club track. The subtle breeze winding through the pines seemed almost tuneful, an abstract melody that wound on and on with scant repetition and reminded her of the classical music she appreciated but had never been able to understand. Things that sounded like sly, sour crickets sawed out their stridulant patterns across each other to create low-key polyrhythmic percussion, and clutches of pine needles occasionally fell to the ground below at apposite junctures, punctuating the song-scape like soft-struck cymbals. This arrangement of parts left Justine feeling that she was walking inside a piece of alien ambient music, a sense both alluring and disturbing. She was tempted to slip her headphones back on to block out this sick symphony.

Beside her, pale Laura-Lee peered into the fog ahead and behind. "We should go back," her schoolmate said, her voice adding itself to the backdrop like the beginning of a narration, and as soon as the words were out of her mouth—a cue to the choir—another sound wove its way into the mix.

Justine's first thought was *wolf*, but that descriptor was woefully inadequate. The voice that was rising from the trees off to their left shared some similarities with the lupine howl, but it was warped into a strange melody that seemed right at home amid the hum and hiss of the world around it. The only thing in her experience to which this eerie vocal could be compared was a video she'd once watched on YouTube where a baby's cries had been run through Auto-Tune to create an unnatural keening that set her teeth on edge. Replace the baby with a blend of wolf's wail and slowed-down whale song, and the result might be something like the uncanny voice now ringing out through the woods.

The girls ground to an immediate halt, and Laura-Lee's fingers clutched at Justine's arm.

"Oh geez. Oh wow."

Another howl rose from the trees to their right, joining the first in a discordant harmony that would've had avant-garde composers leaping for a pen. A third throat sounded out a series of three low notes, a batrachian bass counterpoint, and a shudder worked its way down Justine's spine like a silent zither stroke.

"Cho?" Laura-Lee's voice was that of a small child waking alone in a strange place with no succour in sight.

"Yeah. Let's go. *Quickly*."

The girls turned and hurried back the way they'd come. But they were deep in the fog now, and they found themselves striding into a haze that threatened to obscure the woods altogether. Inside a minute, they would lose sight of the track itself and all sense of direction with it. United in this thought, they both broke into a run without a word or glance exchanged.

"Keep going straight!" Justine cried. The warped wails continued to ring out from either side, growing closer and greater in number. "Don't look back!"

That said, she couldn't keep from imagining the kind of things that might make those sick sounds—the mouths that would shape them, the teeth that would ring such mouths—and was desperate to know just how close they were. Anything at all might be snapping at their heels, and in this murk, they'd never know until it took them down. She couldn't even see Laura-Lee anymore, let alone whatever moved through the fog on all sides.

She peered over her shoulder and couldn't spot anything looming through the brume in pursuit. But those terrible howls were growing louder, closer, their mutilated melodies blending into a cacophonic din that somehow still sounded musical, a dissonant horror movie soundtrack played on strings that grew slack or taut with no rhyme or reason. Justine realised that whatever was making those calls would just as likely come at them from the sides as from behind, and as she turned back to face front, her balance wobbled. Her boots clashed and she tripped. For a long moment she felt suspended in space and time, helpless and weightless, and then the hard earth of the trail raced up to meet her.

The impact found its place in this environment's unnatural orchestra, a muted tympani thud. No sooner had she hit the ground than she was up again, racing on, but now her sense of direction was shot, and she couldn't be sure that she was running straight on the path. For all she knew, she'd hear the grit of pine needles beneath her soles one second and meet the harsh bark of a tree trunk the next. She cried out to Laura-Lee, hoping for a return call that she could use to orient herself, but no reply was forthcoming. She couldn't even hear the soles of the girl's glitter sneakers slapping on the path ahead.

Justine nearly tripped again as one foot came down in the natural gutter alongside the track and a drift of pine needles slid away from beneath her boot. She staggered to a halt, peered down through the murk and saw just enough to line herself up with the edge of the trail. If she followed this line, it would keep her pointed toward the way out, and the sound of needles underfoot would tell her if she was going astray.

She was about to hurry on when she heard nearby fallen branches cracking like dry bones beneath the passage of something large and heavy—and then, from the fog directly in front of her, a low and eerie melody unfurled as one of the creatures moved unseen onto the trail ahead.

This close, its voice carried an undertone of glottal moistness like a sick dog singing through a throatful of phlegm, and something about its timbre gave the impression of curiosity, of triumph. Whatever this creature was, it could sense her proximity, and it was *pleased*.

Justine stood perfectly still, knowing it hardly mattered what she did now. She had maybe seconds before the unknown reached out and claimed her. In that moment, her mind whirled away from her to chase insane possibilities, much as it had on the roundabout only minutes ago—and just as it had then, it threw up something ridiculous and implausible. In a heartbeat, she gambled everything on an outlandish hunch.

Justine gasped in a deep breath, opened her mouth, and began to sing.

Back around,
Around, around.
Around, around, around.

The words and melody came without conscious thought, and she cast herself into them with all the fervour she reserved for bedroom performances when her family was out, throwing shapes in front of the mirror as she sang along to The Birthday Massacre or Deafheaven. She couldn't recall the verses of "Walking the Cross", so she repeated the refrain, and then again, expecting at each breath to be grabbed and devoured. And having done so, she fell silent, fingernails digging into her palms, waiting for the unseen audience to respond.

The invisible thing in the fog before her emitted another quiet howl, this one seeming to express hesitation—perhaps even recognition.

Justine held her breath, poised on the brink of calamity.

And then *it*—whatever *it* was—stalked on many legs across the path, into the trees on the other side, and left her alone.

Justine gasped in near-hysterical relief, stunned that her leap of logic had worked again. Then, scarcely daring to believe she was safe even for a second, she hurried on into the grey haze.

Whenever her left foot crunched on pine needles, she adjusted her angle to stay on the track. The warped wails and howls of the unseen things continued to ring out through the woods on both sides, along with the crack and shuffle of branches underfoot, but none drew close enough to challenge her progress. She increased her pace, venturing now to call out quietly to her classmate. She heard no human cries in response, nor any sign that Laura-Lee was still pounding the path ahead.

When she began to catch glimpses of the track before her, she realised the fog was thinning. Daring to hope she was on the home stretch, she broke into a jog, the beats of her boots building in tempo until they matched the pound of her heart. And then, with a delirious joy, she saw that the murk was lifting away to reveal the end of the path, the opening in the trees, the same old boring roundabout she'd taken for granted her whole life until tonight.

She tensed, well-versed in the savage nature of fate and fully expecting some indescribable monstrosity to blindside her at the last moment, and sprinted headlong for the gap.

Justine burst out of the trees, her boots clapping on the cement of the footpath, and stumbled into the road that circled the roundabout. A bright-eyed beast screamed its monotonous call of challenge, and she had a single moment to recognise the sick irony of escaping one death only to run right into the waiting jaws of another.

Then the car was sweeping by just feet away from her, its blaring horn fading as its angry driver directed it through the roundabout and away. Gasping at her close call, she dashed across the bitumen to the paved ring of the roundabout and didn't look back until she'd circled clockwise around the cenotaph and come out on the other side.

The wall of eucalyptus trees to the west stood unbroken, inscrutable.

She was home. She was safe.

Leaning on her knees, panting in exertion and relief, Justine took a few long seconds to remember that she had not walked that fourth road alone.

"Laura-Lee?"

No reply. And no sign of the girl in any direction. She called again, again, but in vain.

She told herself that Laura had made it out before her, had selfishly run off instead of waiting to see if her schoolmate had also escaped. The thought rang hollow, an obvious lie, but no matter what she believed, there was nothing she could do now. Oh, she could return to the path, to that eerie other world that lay beyond her own, but in her terrified relief, that was simply not an option.

Justine turned north and hurried home, not daring to replace her headphones, listening instead to the mundane music of the familiar world around her—a symphony in many pieces that did not lock together, no threat in its disassociation, a comforting ambience of blissful ignorance.

***

One week on, while a hundred candles burned down at the beach in Laura-Lee's name, Justine sat on the bench closest to the roundabout as she had every night since, and she thought of many things. She did not send up silent prayers for her classmate's safe deliverance, considering that pointless and crass... but all the same, she held two cigarettes between her fingers like a promised reward for her return.

She didn't know what strange land she had entered by way of the fourth path, or where it ultimately led, but she kept returning to the fact that she and Laura-Lee had not been the first to discover it. That world was known to others in the Cross—Marjorie Bartholomaeus, for one, and no doubt she was far from alone in her arcane knowledge, for she had taught others how to sing themselves safely along the trail. And what might those experienced explorers have found further into the uncanny woods? What treasures and tales might they have brought back to share behind closed doors, laughing at those who would never suspect such depths lay right at the heart of their little town?

Justine couldn't even begin to imagine how Mare Gilly had found the secret way, how she'd learned to sing the unseen terrors into harmlessness, but she had passed on her skills, and they were known amongst the weird and wise of Singer's Cross to this day. She walked the streets of her town and watched each passer-by with fresh eyes, wondering who knew and how they might turn that knowledge to their benefit. Was a conspiracy afoot? What might these people do if they discovered that Justine knew, too?

When these thoughts grew too much, she thought of Laura-Lee and the many ways she might have evaded those creatures in the fog. The girl could've run off into the trees, become so lost that she couldn't find her way back to the path—and there was nothing to suggest that she might not yet do so. Maybe she'd found shelter, perhaps even a hut or cabin where, as would befit the surroundings, a huntsman might keep her safe from the predators in the woods. And if the fourth road led into a world of fairy tales, she might even find a happy ending there, married to a hunky prince or taken in by a group of friendly little folk whose songs were of a merrier aspect than the ones she and Justine had heard approaching through the fogbound trees.

Popular as she was in this world, she might just find herself a queen in the other.

But Justine had to consider worse endings, too—eager hunts that climaxed in savage feasts, charnel scenes that would be cut from the goriest and most terrifying films for their visceral intensity—deep red things that no-one down on the beach could possibly imagine; no-one, perhaps, except the likes of Marjorie Bartholomaeus, whose fingers had that very night been cradling a dead rose that Justine was sure she had last seen tucked behind Laura-Lee's ear as they walked the fourth path.

She could attempt to discover her classmate's fate, and perhaps she even bore a responsibility to do so—but Justine knew that, despite the rash curiosity that had led the both of them down that path in the first place, she lacked the courage to venture back into that world of alien airs, or even to approach Marjorie Bartholomaeus and ask for clarity. She was ashamed of that, but perhaps this watch she kept was a way of working herself up to such a task. Perhaps one night soon she would walk the Cross once more, alone or with someone wiser by her side, and maybe she'd even come to know those weird woods in a way that few in town ever could. But not tonight.

Tonight, she would simply watch and wait.

And hope.

The long hours passed, and lights went out all over town as midnight approached. Traffic on the roundabout died down to almost nothing, and in homes from one side of Singer's Cross to the other, people sent out wishes and prayers for the safe return of their missing angel. And Justine, who knew better than any of them just how unlikely a boon that was, sat on the bench and kept her lonely vigil regardless—waiting for the trees to part and an impossible path to appear, for Laura-Lee to return like some prodigal princess to a kingdom that had scarcely appreciated her until she was gone.

The Library of Half-Read Books

Norman Prentiss

I should admit upfront that I'll never reach the end of this story.

Everything I read remains unfinished. I own a library of half-read books. Stories begun in earnest—a romance of opposites thrown together; a detective sifting through clues, the murder nearly solved; a future traveler finding a planet similar to her own, welcomed by its inhabitants, then discovering a horrifying secret. Who could resist reading further to find how such plots might resolve: A chance meeting ten years later? The butler? A cookbook?

I'll never know.

***

Let's not attribute it to procrastination or laziness on my part. My mind is always active. I read constantly. But I haven't finished a book in a long while.

If we're honest with ourselves, we're all surrounded by stories we don't follow to the end.

Don't believe me? Try the old game of watching passersby from your seat at a sidewalk café, or eavesdropping on couples at other tables. You think about their lives, imagine where they live and who they love. Remember, you're not allowed to follow them home: all you get is a glimpse as they walk past, or clipped phrases as they stuff food into their mouths. It's always bland comments about their annoying boss or spouse or their adorable pet.

Are we ever lucky enough to overhear someone plan a surprise party or a murder?

"He'll be so shocked," or, "She'll never know what hit her."

***

In a section of a book I sampled recently, the main character strolls past a tragedy.

The woman's walking along a city sidewalk and an ambulance looms ahead, parked at the curb with its motor running, red lights flashing. She was on her way home or headed to a party, so she doesn't really have time to stop, but she's intrigued—as anyone would be. A small crowd has gathered, and she considers asking someone what has happened, but she doesn't want to appear rude.

From the nearby apartment building, a person is wheeled out on a stretcher, and that person is suddenly a local celebrity. Everyone's eyes follow the course of the gurney, and some spectators press forward, nearly blocking the path to the ambulance. One of them has an autograph book open to a fresh page, pen ready; they force their way to the front of the crowd. "I've followed your whole career. I watched you before other people cared, back when you were healthy."

Paramedics act as bodyguards. They push the spectators away. The autograph book falls unsigned to the sidewalk.

After the stretcher goes into the back of the ambulance, double doors shut like the curtain at the end of a performance.

But the story isn't over.

It might be soon, but the book's main character will never know. She doesn't live in this building and has never met the person who's been taken ill. It would be too much trouble to guess which hospital they've been transported to, drive there herself without benefit of speed and siren, head to the Emergency Room, and rush to the check-in desk, frantic.

"That person who was brought in," she might say. "About ten minutes ago."

"Name?"

She tells the receptionist her name.

"No. The name of the patient."

She peers through the plexiglass separator, hoping to find a check-in list, forms or stray wrist labels with names she could attempt to read upside down. "Ten minutes ago. It couldn't have been more than ten minutes."

The receptionist stares at her. "We can only release information to a family member."

She summons an expression of grief and anxiety and concern, and hopes that will be response enough.

"Are *you* a family member?"

"No, I..." She looks to either side, then behind to see if a line has formed. She hoped someone else would come to her defense, but she is alone. "I saw it happen."

"Did you need to report something to the police?"

"I'm just...curious."

"I'm going to have to ask you to leave."

"Can I give you my contact information?"

"That won't be necessary."

"Please." There aren't security guards grabbing her by either arm, but that could happen any moment. "Please. I want to know what happens next."

***

In a story, everything should happen for a reason. If a character sees someone on a stretcher, it turns out to be a friend from her childhood, a former co-worker or lover—someone whose hospitalization will impact her in some significant way.

Maybe she could follow up on the incident, figure out the landlord's at fault for the person's illness. She could Nancy Drew the whole thing, deduce which neighbor might benefit from the "accident."

But that hypothetical scene at the ER reception desk is too much work. It requires too much risk-taking. Too much acting and improvisation.

More likely, after the double doors close, the main character simply watches the ambulance drive away. She lets it go.

The same way any of us would let it go.

***

A few ambulance sirens add some spice, relieve the everyday tedium.

When I read from a piece of realistic fiction, I'm pleased it's not realistic at all. The author has to omit the toothbrushing, laundry folding, or taking the car in for repairs. They gloss over moments when the protagonist waits on hold for customer service ("Your call is important to us. Please stay on the line and we will answer whenever we fucking feel like it," repeated over and over). All the boring parts get left out.

When they call it "slice-of-life" fiction, it's at least an interesting slice.

***

I'm willing to try books from different genres.

This next one's a fanciful romance, set in the past. Or maybe the future:

***

"Dearest, I thought we'd never be alone."

"How tiresome our friends are. If we can count them as friends."

"In these stolen moments, let us not tarry with talk of friends. We must savor precious time together. Car-pay the dee-um."

"But what if we are seen?"

"My manservant is guarding the entryway. We will not be disturbed."

"I shudder at the thought of my father catching us together."

"He'll have to know sometime. We shall soon be married."

"Would that it were possible."

There are many reasons why this marriage couldn't happen. They are too young. Their families are enemies. One of them is low born. One of them is the wrong race, religion, gender.

Species.

"Hold me, my darling."

Their arms intertwine, all fourteen of them.

***

That revelation is a surprise, but it's not an ending. The couple still needs to get married, or not. One of them will inherit money, or die, or shed a few redundant arms.

I stopped reading this story because it was getting ridiculous.

***

The other day, just for a change of pace, I began reading a picture book intended for children.

It was fun how quickly I got to turn the pages.

The little guy or gal is lost in the woods. Night falls and cruel faces stare between tree limbs, red eyes flashing.

"Who are you?" the kid says to one pair of eyes.

No answer.

"What are you?" the kid says to another pair of eyes.

Again, no answer. Because animals don't talk.

"Why are you?"

This time there's a response. A creature steps onto the forest path.

The creature's face looks like a hand. Its raised hand looks like a face.

A mouth opens in the center of the palm. "I'm your new friend," it says.

The kid exhibits perfect manners, bows and says, "Pleased to meetcha."

The forest creature bows in return. The deep bow reveals an additional feature:

a humpback, or

a third shoulder,

or a second head, or

another creature, standing directly behind.

"Your parents should have warned you not to wander far from home," the creature says. "You could get lost."

"I am lost."

"They should have warned you about talking to strangers." The creature wears a large glove over its head, because if it wears one over its hands it wouldn't be able to see or hear or talk.

"But you're my new friend."

The creature moves closer. "Your parents taught you that everything is about love. People care for each other, more than they care for themselves. Your life will be filled with happiness."

The kid nods. "Yes, that's what the world is like. It's why I can wander safely in the woods and befriend marvelous creatures."

The creature laughs. It is always fun to hear laughter, and the kid's laughter joins in. The forest no longer seems as dark.

When they are both tired out from laughing, the creature says: "Your parents have been lying to you. The world is not about love. It is all about hatred and revenge. People care only for themselves. All life leads to disappointment."

The kid nods again, but he is puzzled. He has always believed his parents, but he also believes his new friend. They can't both be correct.

"You now understand how the world really works," the creature says. "This knowledge is a gift. It is a key that will help you unlock the future."

"What is my future?"

In the illustration, question marks appear above the kid's head. Five of them, like the number of floppy fingers projecting from the creature's scalp.

"Let's see." The creature tilts its glove-head, makes jazz hands with its eye- and mouth-centered palms to indicate that it's thinking how to respond. "I know these woods well. I can show you a way out, so you can return to your parents. They will tell you more lies about the world."

"You don't make that choice sound very appealing."

"Or you can stay here with me. Your newest friend."

In the drawing, the question marks over the kid's head have changed to exclamation points. "If you were me, what choice would you make?"

A dozen or more pages remain. Things can happen quickly in a children's story: the kid can follow a path back to civilization, reunite with worried parents, sleep in a soft familiar bed and dream of lies to come; in contrast, the forest choice could lead to wonders, a sky above dark trees turning bright, raining down multi-colored candies, while new companions with shifting silhouettes teach a calming syntax of retribution; or nothing happens, until starvation and night chill pelt the child with stones and needles, and later a small body is discovered half-buried under damp leaves by adults with question marks and exclamation points woven in their hair.

At this point, I snapped the book shut. Even a chance glimpse at an illustration or large-print words on later pages would be enough to confirm the ending for me.

I returned the book to the shelf.

***

A child once asked me: "Why don't you tear out the last pages of all your books, and throw those pages away? Then you won't be tempted to look."

"That's not the point," I said. "The endings must still be there, even though I never get to read them."

I said nothing further, since there are some things a child will never understand.

***

A horror novel would offer the best explanation.

In one story, a married couple has moved to a new city. Both of them have flexible work schedules and can do their jobs entirely online. They were able to live wherever they wanted, as long as the place had a good Internet connection.

They've made the wrong choice.

The new house has a personality. Stairs creak without footsteps. Lights flicker. Kitchen or bathroom appliances turn off during use, turn on when nobody's in the room.

The couple give the house the name of a mutual friend who couldn't seem to do anything right. So when a musky smell inexplicably fills the room, one of them might say to the other, "I don't think Alex has showered today." When an upstairs window seems to slam shut on its own, one of them would quip, "Alex is in a bad mood."

The mood of a house affects the people who live in it. Doors slam on their own, or not. Wood floors snap like slapped faces. Wind through window frames whisper cruel phrases like "You don't understand me" or "You're being ridiculous" or "Be honest with yourself."

Later, in the house alone, one of them delivers a monologue of regret. "I should have been nicer to you. I never realized you were [choose one:]

sick

mentally ill

easily bruised."

At some point, the person is no longer alone. A spirit appears in *The House Named Alex*. The spirit floats closer. As with many spirits, its gossamer body is like a book raised in the air. The haunted person speaks aloud, as if reading from a page. It is unclear if the words are quoted from the spirit's mind, or if they're invented by the haunted reader:

"If you wrote the ending you would know what has happened to me. Yet my fate changes as you read or listen or speak. Here is the page. Here is the written resolution. Read it."

The horrible language is inscribed on the parchment of the spirit's body. Head to toe is a narrative. The transparent face is a text, a grinning skull beneath, a brain cradled under a bowl of bleached cartilage; synapses fire across gaps, typing a Morse code simulation of personality.

Perhaps it is a forgiving spirit. The Occupant of the House Named Alex moistens a fingertip, reaches forward to turn a delicate page.

And screams, turns away. The end is too much to bear.

The spirit says: "I will make you dread any ending, as you should have dreaded the end of our life together."

Several chapters remain in the book. What further horrors could happen? I'm too frightened to continue.

***

We don't need to be scared by a book to stop reading it.

We don't need a haunted house to make us say cruel things to one another.

Sometimes I feel like a child lost in the woods, learning about life's disappointments. Or a star-crossed lover whose own body seems alien. I've had terrible arguments with the person I love the most.

I've followed an ambulance to the hospital. At the reception desk, I was treated like someone who was not a relative or a spouse:

"Please cover your mouth and nose."

Done. "Now can I see the patient?"

"We're not allowing visitors." There was judgment in the receptionist's tone—a suspicion that I was to blame for the illness, or the accident that might not have been an accident. The patient had arrived with a specialized Medical-Alert bracelet: "For God's sake," inscribed on metal, "Don't Let Anyone Into My Room." Small padlocked cages protect crucial wall plugs. They've removed the special smothering pillows from the area.

"It's very difficult for us not to be together at this time. I'm sure you understand."

"Policy. We have to treat everyone the same." The receptionist slides a plastic panel in place, terminating the conversation.

Except, I wasn't in the reception area. I wasn't even allowed inside the hospital, and had to beg over the telephone:

"Please, we've been working from home each day. I'd forgotten what it's like for us to be separated. Can I speak to a supervisor?"

"You won't get a different answer."

"Let me explain." I tried a human approach, an emotional appeal. "I've got this huge library, okay? Any type of story—you name it, there's a book on the shelf to match. Stories remind us of our own lives, did you know that? Whenever I choose a book and begin reading it, I keep turning pages until something hits too close to home. An image, say, like a shard of broken glass reflecting light. A plot device like a late-night telephone call, or an old letter hidden at the back of a dresser drawer. Some echo in a line of dialogue: 'This is the last time!' or 'I'll never feel the same way.' That's when I have to stop reading. It's too painful."

Silence. Then, "We have to keep the lines clear for other calls."

"Do you? I'm telling you about the loss I feel. The haunting that grows for me, the same way that a story moves forward. Shouldn't that explain why you should let me visit? I need to be close to the person I love the most."

"For the safety of other patients, we can't allow that."

"But I have to. I have to know how this ends."
"None of us know."

***

Actually, I didn't get through to a receptionist.

The recording said:

"Your call is important to us. Due to high call volumes, there may be a long wait. Be aware that by order of the Governor, hospital and nursing home visitation is currently prohibited. We recommend that you consult our website for further information."

***

Owning a library of half-read books is like living in the middle stage of a pandemic with a cure endlessly deferred, hope dangled in hypodermics and shifting predictions of herd immunity. The disease narrates a loss that can't be measured, since it has no fixed ending. Banished from the sick room, I imagine conversations I'm not allowed to have in person. Walls and glass and plastic shields separate me from human contact.

I huddle in lockdown, trapped in my home as I wait for an "all clear," for the ending that never comes.

It Only Hurts When I Dream

Lucy A. Snyder

I tumbled down concrete stairs
in college. Afterward, a place
along my spine always aches
when the temperature drops.

I smashed my bike in traffic,
banged both knees, but wasn't
crushed by cars. When it's warm
they crackle like rice cereal.

But ever since I lost you
I cannot pack that wound;
your absence will forever
hurt. Time heals nothing.

Donald, Duck

Peter Straub

They were a rugged bunch, the old originals, Huey thought. You could say those guys wrote the book, invented the rules, laid down the laws, set the mold. For four decades, show biz was their playpen. In the twenties they danced their legs off; in the thirties they did boffo business at the box office; in the forties they got so big the Cagneys, the Grants, the Hayworths, the stars of the other Hollywood, begged for cameos in their pictures; in the fifties, they really hit their stride and got into the merchandising, the theme parks, the licensing business, the stuff that went on spinning off money long after their end of the industry faded away to nothing. *No limits*, that was the deal. Ten-twelve hours straight in the studio, then a little cavorting in their kidney-shaped pools, a few drinks with the girls at their favorite getaways, publicity photos at Chasen's, an assignation in the back room at Musso & Frank's, a quip for Louella at Mike Romanoff's, a cigar at the Brown Derby, a little steam at the Beverley Hills or the Wilshire, a nap and a pick-me-up back home in the Hollywood Hills, then back into the studio for another ten hours of mayhem. Every day a laff riot, every day a payday!

When the industry changed, which was a damn shame in Huey's opinion, and never would have happened if every little project hadn't started costing forty mil and up, the old comic books vanished right along with the cartoons, and a whole new generation came in. Mutants and malcontents, most of them, Huey thought. The ones who managed the crossover into film never panned out; they used violence and darkness as their hooks, but good old Tom and Jerry put violence right in your face and made you laugh at it. Crow, Judge Dredd, the X-Men, what were they but empowerment fantasies at heart? Say what you will about Uncle Donald, he always had the sense to turn his temper tantrums into self-mockery, not bloodbaths. Besides, the new generation got everything wrong from the start—they dealt from weakness instead of strength and got the crossover ass-backwards. Even a banged-up couple of old vaudevillians like Sylvester and Tweetie Bird, a one-joke act if ever there was one, knew enough to start in the movie houses and then go into comic books, not the other way around!

The problem was, no one had ever bothered to think about what these guys were supposed to do when they stopped performing. Of course they hadn't. Everyone imagined they would simply go on forever, rioting through movie houses, across lunch boxes and the funny pages, turning the tap that released a flood of golden coins day after day, month after month, year after year. Doesn't everyone, don't even *people*, think their present conditions, whatever the hell they are, will probably endure and endure... until they get even better? And isn't this dopey optimism endlessly, witlessly reinforced by tv and the movies? Case in point: *All Dogs Go to Heaven*. If that were true, would you want to go there?

Ask a former child star if all dogs go to heaven, Huey thought, and after you hear the answer drive, if you can still drive, over to your local Huey Duck's Ducks Unlimited (one in Century City, one on Hollywood Boulevard, one in Boca Raton, and one in Orlando), slide onto a bar seat, and drink until you forget it. On the menu today: "Goofy's Own Private Mudslide," $5.50, "Minnie's Champagne Cocktail," $7.00, "Beagle Boys Stolen Summer *Weissebrau*," $3.50 the glass, $14.00 per pitcher, plus the usual golden oldies. Never mind that Goofy got so deep into LSD in the sixties that he now speaks entirely in psychobabble; never mind that Minnie died of Alzheimer's; never mind that the Beagle Boys went straight about a million years ago and now serve on the board of the Scrooge McDuck Foundation. In Huey's opinion, his Great-Uncle Scrooge probably came out of the collapse better than anybody—the guy had no family to worry about, and he was old enough to have acquired some sense.

And of the children's generation, he had managed the transition better than most. Some of Huey's peers felt that it was in poor taste, well, appalling taste, for a Duck to own a chain of Duck restaurants, and some were offended by his menu's "exploitation" of the family and their old friends. The first time Dewey Duck had seen the menu, he threw it on the floor, stamped on it in a fit of unintelligible obscenities worthy of Unka Donald at his most irate, and stormed out, swearing never to speak to Huey again, a vow it took him most of a year to break. At the time, Dewey was eking out a living as a street mime, which had led Huey to the conclusion that only the very rich and the very poor could afford to be proud.

The others had adjusted as well as they could, given that most child stars do not make it even to, so to speak, purgatory. Dewey spent the time left over from his telephone sales job on acting classes and auditions, and Louie taught second grade at a small private academy in Santa Monica. Louie's wife, Sharon, always felt a little insecure around Cosima, Huey's wife, but that was mainly a class thing. Although Dewey never accepted his eldest brother's business, Sharon had finally managed to persuade Louie that Ducks were of another species entirely from the creatures they resembled.

Thank God for Sharon: later, she confided that she had simply worn her husband down with relentless questions: *Do those ducks have jobs? Can they talk? Drive cars? Have you ever seen one of those ducks smoke a cigarette, Louie, while you smoke at least a pack a day of Unka Donald Ultra Lights? Ever seen one go to the toilet, Louie? Or pick up a fork? And how about the whole question of food—do you think those birds in the park can eat stuff like chili dogs and steak and asparagus and your own personal favorite, choucroute garni? Well, if they can, why don't people feed them meals like that, instead of lousy old bread crumbs out of a paper bag? And why don't they complain? When some fool comes up to the side of the pond with a paper bag in his hands, why don't they yell FORGET THE BREAD CRUMBS, GO BACK HOME AND GET ME A NICE, JUICY VEAL CHOP? And how come they don't get arrested, going around naked all the time? You would, wouldn't you? They don't even own clothes, and you own five suits and four sports jackets! Your Uncle Donald has six whole walk-in closets filled with suits. But what about those naked lady ducks, Louie—do they turn you on? No? You don't even get a little tingle down there when you see them diving underwater for a bite of kelp? Are you sure, Louie? Yes? Well, if all that's true, what's keeping us from getting a babysitter and going over to one of your brother's restaurants now and then for a free meal that I don't have to shop for, cook, or clean up afterwards?*

A free meal, that was the real issue. Huey had never minded the idea of comping members of his family and others from the old crowd. He even welcomed the Mick's kids and grandkids and let them stuff their faces gratis, although Mick and Minnie had completely spoiled Burlie, Toodles, and Stacy-Wacey. Those three were so rich they bought new luxury cars every time they wrecked the old ones. The fortune that came in from the Mick, why should they sweat over a little thing like a smashed-up Lexus? Mick didn't give a damn, that was for sure. Sour old guy, spent all day shuttling between Palm Springs, the Friars' Club, and the various houses he had bought for his mistresses, still hot to show off what rumor claimed to be the most remarkable endowment since Trigger's. Huey could remember a party at Unka Donald's and Aunt Daisy's house in the late fifties, someone playing the piano, the Mick's bratty kids shoving people into the pool, and the Big Guy motioning him aside, pointing to the area south of his big white buttons, and saying, "Well, Huey-baby, I know you've heard about it, but how'dja like a little peek?" When Huey declined, the Mick waved him away, saying, "In my day, people were gracious enough to show a liddle *cur-ee-oss-iddy.*"

Which, at least in Huey's mind, demonstrated another important point about the entertainment industry, namely that the same people who expected things to get better and better always felt as though they were getting worse and worse—day by day! Huey had put in enough schmooze time at the Friar's Club to know that if you were in the mood to listen to a world-class whiner, all you had to do was sit down next to someone like Dick Tracy, that poor shlub. Every single time Annette Bening pops another kid, he sends her a dozen long-stemmed roses, good stuff, top of the line, but does Warren Beatty ever take a minute to call?

***

Most of Huey's time in the Friars' Club barroom had been served in the year after Aunt Daisy's unexpected departure for a better world, wherever that was. One day a hacking cough, the next day a raging fever, a night in the Danny Thomas wing at Cedars, and before you know it, you're slipping the preacher a couple of Franklins and thanking him for giving such a beautiful eulogy. That's how it went with Daisy Duck, one, two, three— the cough, the fever, the funeral service. Caught Donald completely by surprise, caught him flatfooted, knocked him stupid with surprise. No time to prepare or learn his lines, bang, deer in the headlights time. We're ready for your closeup, now do grief. Do mourning. Do heartbreak. Give us your pain, baby, you're an old trouper, give us your tears, your sleepless nights, your aimless days. If your dead wife doesn't do it for you, think of your dead puppy—you an innocent six, him a bloody smear on the highway. *That's* the heartbreak we want, the dead-puppy heartbreak, the I'm-all-alone-in-the-world-and-I'll-never-be-whole-again shtick. Your family, your friends, they all have these demanding expectations, they want the dull eyes and the unwashed hair and the unmatched socks. At the same time, and here comes the old double-shuffle, these very same characters, who of course happen to be your nearest and dearest buddy-roos, suppose it your duty male and female alike to overcome your personal and individual sorrow for the sake of the social tone that prevailed so happily in the days before the unfortunate loss, for it was that very tone that defined your relationships with these characters, and without it you risk being considered a loser and schlemiel, the kind of guy who won't let *you* get over *his* unhappiness.

In the above circumstances, a place like the Friars' Club barroom naturally comes into its own, you might say, being a convivial yet highly protected environment on its good days practically bulging with cynical hardcases and skirtchasers firing off their best, roughest, most heartless lines at one another in a perpetual atmosphere of masculine cameraderie, and Huey never minded, at least not much, the implied obligation three or four days a week to drive his grieving uncle over there for lunch followed by half a dozen afternoon Bombay Sapphire martinis in the form of three doubles. In the figurative embrace of his fellow-originals, Donald found it possible to relax. When the Mick, the Big Guy, turned a rheumy, reptilian eye on him and growled, "Sorry about Daisy, kid—best piece of Duck's ass I ever had," and reliable old Porky, sweetest guy in the world, chimed in with, "Wrong, you asshole, you're th-thinking about her m-m-mother," Donald could breathe easy.

When had Sylvia Duck first entered the scene? Huey had never been able to pin that event to a specific date. Sylvia Duck had first appeared as a kind of sexual radiance, an erotic shimmer glimpsed in the bandinage at the Friars and on the fairways of the clan's favorite golf courses. She had come in from Aspen, New York City, and Nice, where she owned houses; a marriage to an obscure Midwestern Duck had left her with a modest fortune and a beautiful daughter, Lizzie, for whom she might almost be mistaken; her father, Gaylord Duck, a figure of immense rectitude in his mid-nineties, continued in his lifelong capacity as lawyer and financial manager to several unnamed but fabulously wealthy families located in the Boston area. Huey first heard the old hardcases and skirtchasers begin to gossip about this mysterious creature nine or ten months after Donald became a widower. She had emerged from Aspen, New York City, and Nice to attach herself to a friend and distant cousin of Donald's named Myron Duck, a retired doctor, in whose infatuated company she was seen, though never by Huey, at many and many a party and charity event. The old boys adored the new arrival. Sylvia made them think of Cole Porter lyrics. She was a Bendel bonnet, a Shakespeare sonnet, she was.... "Hell, I wish she *was*," Huey heard the Big Guy mutter to poor old Joe Palooka one dim afternoon at the club, "I'd spend the whole day trying to figure out which to grab first, my tits or my ass."

In his role as his uncle's grief counselor and support system, Huey was privileged to overhear step-by-step reports on the progress of the great Myron-Sylvia *amour*. Myron had proposed, and Sylvia had rejected him; they patched things up at a resort on Virgin Gorda; they spent Christmas in a suite at the Crillon; Sylvia had taken over Myron's exercise program, and had him playing tennis twice a day; with the aid of a humungous diamond from Tiffany's, they were at last engaged; the awesome Gaylord gave his blessing; the lovebirds sailed first-class to Europe on the QE2, the wedding date still up in the air due to the conflict between Sylvia's desire for an appropriately lavish ceremony in a suitably *luxe* venue and certain unfortunate business obligations of Myron's. Then came news of the tragedy, which took place on a tennis court in Jerusalem on a blistering afternoon just as the prospective and still-overweight bridegroom blundered toward the net to hammer the pro's diplomatic return of serve.

Sylvia flew back alone and sequestered herself, apparently, in her father's mansion. As no one in the group knew Gaylord's address or telephone number, both of which were of course deeply confidential, likewise the same information for his great business enterprise, her whereabouts were uncertain. In the old boys' tasteless jokes about "Jewish tennis," many of them based on the vaudeville turns they had witnessed in their youth, could be detected a strain of melancholia distinct as—as the Mick put it—"the kiss of a four-bit stogie."

A month later, Donald dropped into Huey Duck's Ducks Unlimited for lunch on a day when Huey was out shopping for a heavy-duty insecticide, and who happened to be seated alone at a booth in the back corner, perusing the menu with the aid of a Minnie's Champagne Cocktail, but the ravishing Sylvia Duck, his sister in grief, the all-but widow of this widower's distant cousin? Five weeks after that, Donald called Huey to inform him that the thrice-weekly visits to the Friars' barroom and the six Bombay Sapphire martinis in the form of three doubles were a thing of the past. "Kid," his uncle said, in the Borscht-Belt rasp that is the trademark of the show-biz original, "much as I love ya, there are certain needs common to a Duck of my age and position in the world that no nephew, no matter how great he is, and you are, kid, you're the greatest, could never in his whole entire life supply the answer to. Let's put it this way, all right? You with me? Let's put it like this—I've never exactly been a god-fearing Duck, but right now at this point in time I am almost tempted to think that cousin Myron, may he rest in peace and all that, died for my sins. Because from the way I'm feeling, I guess I musta gone to heaven." Sylvia Duck had moved into the quirky old house in the Hollywood Hills.

So that was what happened to a guy like Uncle Donald when he had to stop performing. He lost his mind and fell in love. You could read that sentence the other way around, too.

Donald, Duck

***

It was only a short time after the conversation in which Donald spoke of Myron dying for his sins that each of the nephews received a call from their famous uncle inviting them up to the house on King's Road to meet his beloved and, he wished them to understand, bride-to-be. Cosima, Sharon, and Pinkytoes, the wives, were invited, but Wolfgang, Truffles, and Afterburn; Acey-Deucey and Trinkle; and Botswana-Infidel, the children of the three couples, were not. Sylvia had let it be known that, generally speaking, she found children unbearable, except of course for her darling daughter, the incomparable Lizzie, who so greatly resembled her.

At 6:30 pm on the appointed day, Huey, Louie and Dewey, side by side with their respective wives, appeared at the charming house on King's Road, Huey attired in a dark grey wool-silk blend from Armani, Louie in an only slightly chalkstained old tweed jacket with reinforced elbows from the more respectable end of his closet, Dewey in black jeans, a black T-shirt, and a black leather jacket from Melrose Avenue that went nicely with his piercings. The ladies also had dressed according to their conceptions of suitability, with Cosima dignified and stunning in a little black Chanel, Sharon maternal and sensible in a pretty Laura Ashley dress, Pinkytoes sultry and disdainful in what appeared to be several layers of undergarments.

A glowing Uncle Donald in a brand-new smoking jacket answered the door and embraced them each in turn. This was great, the whole family together again—apart from the children, Huey silently noted—just wait until they met Sylvia, she was the best thing that could have happened to him, honest to God, sometimes you just got lucky, yep, he was a new man, on top of the goddam world, felt thirty years younger. Daisy, God bless her, woulda wanted him to have this happiness, didn't they agree? Hell, what were they doing standing around outside, let's go in so they can meet the goddam light of his life, and he meant that sincerely. He led them through the door and halfway up the hallway, bawling his beloved's name as if he suspected her of having fled from the room where he had left her.

But there she was, safely ensconced in the curve of the old Art Deco sofa with her ankles prettily crossed before her, her back ever so slightly turned to the decorative but unnecessary blaze in the fireplace, above it the impressive portrait of Daisy specially commissioned from Mr. Carl Barks and the urn containing her ashes on the mantel. White-gloved fingers held her place in a little book and her lovely profile gazed through the great wall of windows upon the hazy panorama of greater Los Angeles. She seemed lost in her thoughts, these perhaps occasioned by the contents of the little volume, which, Huey observed, was the *Selected Poems of Emily Dickenson*.

The sense that this tableau was all too literally a "scene" and had been stage-managed for maximum effect vanished the moment Sylvia turned her charming head, took in the company before her, and gave a palpable start of surprise. In Huey's breast, and no doubt in those of his brothers as well, happiness for his uncle's good fortune struggled against a primal form of envy—Sylvia was radiance itself, a creature seemingly made of sea-foam and moonlight. Unlike the commanding beauty portayed by Mr. Barks, she seemed inherently fragile, in need of protection from the cruder, more vulgar world lurking without. Her voice floated on a gasp of wonder: were these three handsome fellows actually the wonderful nephews of whom she had heard so much? And Huey, of course, she recognized him immediately, he who had done so much for dear Donnie in his time of need.

Donnie? Huey asked himself.

The question disappeared before the spectacle of Sylvia Duck drifting up from the Art Deco sofa in an extravagant tumult of ruffles and drapery that yielded a momentary glimpse of a tender leg and a sumptuous bosom. Huey felt as if he were levitating a few inches off the ancient Kirman rug. Like his brothers, he was infatuated on the spot.

It was to be the last time he took her at face value.

Sylvia deposited the book on the end table with a pat of fond regret. Surely, this was a moment worthy of celebration, was it not? A beaming Donald, or Donnie, rushed off to fetch a magnum of Dom Perignon, and while he was gone his heart's darling made a comic complaint of such a show-biz legend doing his own fetching and carrying. Yes, the boys agreed, that was the silliest thing, it was indeed, when "Donnie" could so easily afford a manservant, not mention a cook. Growing up in Gaylord's great manor house, the child-Sylvia had enjoyed the attentions of four fulltime servants, yes, those were the days, darling, no one expected such treatment now, but surely the boys thought it absurd that a figure of "Donnie's" stature should, at his age, have to carry a heavy tray laden with drinks all the way from the pantry, or the scullery, or whatever that odd little room off the kitchen was called? In Dewey's hesitant affirmation Huey thought he saw a trace of concern for little Botswana-Infidel's eventual inheritance. Well, *Donnie* had millions, didn't he?, literal millions, truth be told thanks to licensing agreements more millions even than his Uncle Scrooge, and Huey had no fears for the financial security of the next generation, even if Botswana-Infidel's bohemian father displayed more interest in spending money than earning it.

The sleeves of his jacket slightly dusty from the wine cellar, Donald returned, staggering only slightly under the weight of the silver tray, on which rode the huge bottle within a huger ice bucket, eight champagne flutes, a bowl of yummy salted almonds, a double Bombay Sapphire martini on the rocks for the host, a bottle of Rolling Rock beer specifically requested by Pinkytoes, and a crystal ashtray roughly the size of a manhole cover. The question of who might use this last item, since Mr. and Mrs. Huey did not smoke, neither did Mr. And Mrs. Louie, and Mr. And Mrs. Dewey, as far as one knew, smoked only those exotic cigarettes made from a forbidden weed, was answered when the panting Donald, "Donnie," thrust one hand into a pocket of his splendid new garment and produced a pack of Pall Malls, one of which he tucked into his bill and another into his sweeheart's, then ignited both with a pass of a slim golden lighter. The old legend grinned at his dumbfounded nephews and their spouses. "Before Sylvia gave me this smoking jacket, I hadn't had a puff in forty years," he said. "But I don't want my honeybunch to smoke alone, do I? And at my age, it's like Sylvia says, you gotta give yourself all the treats your heart desires."

That afternoon, Donnie's honeybunch regaled the nephews and their mates with piquant tales from an adventuresome life: she had grown up in Boston and Paris, gone to school in Switzerland, and spent a few years in her late teens as a starlet in the Roman film industry, now a wisp of its former self, so sad, but as a result her French was *fantastique* and her Italian *molto bello*. She had married young, but the marriage didn't have a snowball's, the two of them being babies still finding out who they were. Soon after sweet darling Lizzie's birth they parted never alas to meet again, for the bereft hubby came to a mysterious end in Calcutta she thought it was, and with the kindly aid of his estate, mother and daughter travelled the world, never failing to appreciate the finer nuances and subtler tones. Oft had they wintered in delightful little Aspen, CO, where the amusing in fact highly amusing actor Jack Nicholson many times squired them down the expert's slopes and feted them with his home-made spaghetti bolognese and garlic bread; in Palm Beach, they had been houseguests of the dashingly handsome, tragically misunderstood George Hamilton, who was *so* much cleverer than anyone gave him credit for.

With all her experience of the world's rarest textures and fabrics, Sylvia had of course been asked, as a personal favor, to decorate if not virtually to design a great number of splendid houses and apartments owned by aristocrats, financiers, and film royalty, work which had brought her if she might be permitted to say so herself a nice degree of acclaim, of recognition, which is all we *really* need, isn't it? Oh yes, she had turned professional, all her friends had insisted on it, and by then it was time for darling Lizzie's education in Switzerland, so Sylvia had accepted the challenge, what a whirl, Paris Bonn Dallas New York Seattle St. Moritz Cannes Frankfort Singapore Denver Boston Tokyo, heavens, a girl had to get off the merry-go-round and find some peace and quiet in her *own* space or just go crazy, and that was when she met the divine Mr. Myron Duck and thought he was meant to be her salvation, but it turned out Myron had another role entirely, one which he performed beautifully, like the gentleman he was.

"Don't laugh, now, you little pricks," said Uncle Donald, lighting another Pall Mall and inhaling to a luxuriant depth, "because what I'm about to say is a spiritual kinda thing. You could call cousin Myron, who was a guy I never paid a lotta attention to when we were coming up, if you want to know the truth, you could call him our Cupid. Sylvia's and mine. He was our god-danmed Cupid, that's what he was, and I pray that he may rest in peace, and all that good stuff."

A huge, transparent tear with the density of glycerin stood at the outer corner of each of his darling's rapturous eyes.

The impression Sylvia made on her fiancee's family was neatly summarized in the remarks uttered by the nephew's wives as the visitors passed through Unka Donald's gate and hesitated a moment before separating into pairs for their homeward journeys.

Cosima said: "She's at least forty years younger than he is!"

Sharon said: "And she isn't trustworthy!"

Pinkytoes said: "And on top of that, she's an evil bitch!" From Pinkytoes, this may have been a compliment.

***

Two weeks after Sylvia had made her great impression upon the women of the middle generation, Huey's uncle called him with an unusual request. It seemed that the awesome Gaylord, informed of his daughter's desire to remarry, had refused to grant his approval until he could "Look the fellow square in the eye," as he put it, and "judge the cut of his jib." The provenance of this last phrase was more financial than nautical, for by it Gaylord Duck had expressed his insistence upon reviewing his prospective son-in-law's account books, brokerage statements, income tax forms, and the like. He wished to do so in the privacy of the suite he had reserved at the Bel Air Hotel, and he wished to do so alone. Gaylord was to arrive late that afternoon, and Sylvia had borrowed Donald's car for the purpose of driving to the local Mercedes dealership, there to purchase, as a kind of pre-wedding present, an appropriate means of transportation for herself. Would Huey be so kind as to pick up his uncle, drive them both to the accountant's offices on Wilshire Boulevard to collect the crates of documents, then deposit them at the Bel Air?

A series of interlocking obligations involving an ineffective exterminator and a harshly worded document from the Health Department delayed Huey's appearance at the house on King's Road until nearly 4:00, and when he pulled up in front of the gate he noticed a For Sale sign half-way up the path to the front door. Half-crazy with impatience and anxiety, his uncle came rushing through the door, too rattled to say any more than that Sylvia could do nothing with his funny old house, nothing at all, it seemed the house had long ago outlived the charm of its eccentricities, and both he and his darling girl felt she deserved a canvas more worthy of her magnificent talents—that is, a house large and luxurious enough to bring out the best in Sylvia. Somewhere in Beverley Hills, they thought, something a bit off Mulholland Drive, on or near the crest of the hill. But couldn't Huey please concentrate on what they were supposed to be doing and get to Wilshire in less than, say, an hour, or was that too much to ask?

Stung, Huey raced like a madman to the accountant's office, where three large cartons filled with documents awaited him. Two of the cartons filled the trunk, so the third rode on the back seat as Huey shot down the crowded avenues and by-ways that took him to the serene world guarded by the gates of Bel Air. His uncle kept glancing at his watch and firing off colorful obscenities. Huey's attempts at reassurance backfired, badly. When he mentioned that all of this seemed entirely unnecessary, since Sylvia's first husband had clearly left her a good deal of money, Donald groaned and said he was all wrong. The first husband, that bum, when he had that funny accident in Calcutta, or wherever it was, he had betrayed both trusting Sylvia and her doting father by leaving an estate half the size he had claimed. Damn near left the poor kid and her little girl without a dime to her name. Huey'd heard about the house in Aspen, the house in Nice, that apartment in Manhattan, hadn't he? Too bad, they were long gone, no more, kaput. Why did Huey think that the father was taking such pains now? Was Huey a *complete* idiot? And when Huey pointed out that Donald after all possessed one of the world's best-known and most famous faces and had amassed a great fortune besides, his uncle's scornful respose silenced him for the rest of the careering journey.

Ducks like Gaylord cared nothing for fame, didn't Huey understand even that much? Ducks like that thought fame was vulgar. They thought fame was a *disgrace*, those old-time New England Ducks! They'd rather be caught *dead* than have their pictures in the paper. Geez Louise, didn't kids know anything any more, were they all blockheads? Gaylord and the Gaylord-clan, they represented culture, good breeding, good manners, hell, they went to the top schools in the country, and Donald had never actually gone to school at all, had he? Out there busting his gut to get a laugh more or less from the moment he was born, how could he know anything about art, like paintings and statues, which were ordinary, everyday things to Gaylord and his pals, who had so many statues they used the small ones for hat racks! And when it came to money, Huey had it all wrong, kiddo, he had it arsey-versey, because Gaylord and those type of guys, money ran down the street just to jump in their pockets.

So on the one hand, Sylvia could barely afford her next six ounces of caviar; and on the other, she couldn't put her hands in her pockets without pulling out a fresh wad of bills. Huey supposed his uncle had good reason to be worked up.

Then catastrophe, or what seemed to be catastrophe. A uniformed driver was opening the rear door of a black limousine as Huey pulled up in front of the hotel, and from the dark interior emerged an elegant, white-haired, beautifully-attired Duck with an aristocratic profile and a cultured New England bearing. It could have been no one but Sylvia's regal father. "!#@&!," Donald muttered. The immensely uniformed doorman was already gliding forward; an eager bellhop followed the chauffeur to the back of the limousine and began stacking up a great number of suitcases. Uncle Donald slid down in his seat and peered over the dash until the doorman had safely escorted the gentleman inside.

Huey asked his uncle if he wanted to turn around and come back later, maybe.

For a short time, Donald muttered to himself, throwing in an occasional !%&! Then he straightened up, said, "No East Coast snob is gonna intimidate Donald Duck," and was out of the car before the doorman returned. Huey explained that he and his uncle were dropping off some documents for Mr. Gaylord Duck, and while the doorman and a second bellman unloaded the boxes, he rushed inside to witness the awful donnybrook.

No curses or sounds of fisticuffs came to him from the reception area; no feathers floated in the air; no security men were hurrying toward the desk. All had the calm of a Christmas carol: the attractive young men and women behind the long desk, the upright, attentive figure of the concierge; the two elderly Ducks engaged in friendly conversation beside a cart piled high with luggage. In fact, Huey noted, the great, the ideally handsome, ninety-year-old Gaylord Duck appeared to be no more than sixty-five years of age. A smiling Uncle Donald beckoned him forward and introduced him to the great man, who displayed no irritation whatsover at the last-minute appearance of the documents he had requested, who in fact regretted the necessity for such measures and hoped his new friend and future son-in-law would understand that in these sorry times it was a father's unfortunate duty to ensure his only child's marital well-being, especially since they had been so horribly misled on a previous occasion not to be mentioned again. And would these two fine chaps join him a drink perhaps in that nice secluded corner of the lobby perhaps?

What seemed to Huey a great number of bills were distributed all round, and the three of them repaired to the secluded corner, where they were promptly joined by an obsequious waiter. Drinks were ordered and, with fawning servility, delivered. The ageless Gaylord revealed his admiration for Donald's splendid career, and over several Bombay Sapphire martinis in the form of half as many doubles the charmed Donald was induced to impart some of his favorite tales of his industry's glorious Golden Age, along the way and for the benefit of his new pal making clear that successive tidal waves of moolah had washed his way, can you say halleluiah? The afternoon drifted into evening; the ever-more worshipful waiter glided back and forth from the bar; successive parties of guests checked in and out of the hotel. Gaylord Duck, who nursed two small glasses of sherry throughout the entire conversation, expressed himself overjoyed with his daughter's good taste and good fortune, which of course would be confirmed, he had no doubt, by a jiffy little ramble through the papers now in his suite. To Huey, who drank only club soda, the great man's voice seemed now and then to wobble off its New England axis and tilt in a more westerly, Chicago-ish direction, but he was in the food business and could not entirely trust his ear for regional accents.

Only a single discordant note entered the long conversation, and only Huey seemed to remark it. It was not Gaylord's suggestion that Donald might perhaps entrust him with the handling of a portion of his holdings, specifically the money frittering itself away in mutual funds, for the purpose of investing it in places no less safe but from the financial viewpoint far more exciting. After a couple of hours, Donald had offered a clumsy hint that he would be open to just such a proposition. And Huey supposed that Gaylord Duck knew what he was doing when it came to investments, even if his streetcar to Boston had experienced a long layover by the shores of Lake Michigan. The dissonance Huey thought he had perceived came in when the great financier asked his future son-in-law, the world-famous comedian, if he ever enjoyed the sport of hunting.

Hunting? Huey said to himself; and his uncle said, "Hunting?"

Didn't everyone know that characters like Donald Duck and the Big Guy and their companions at the Friars' Club never went hunting? They played cards, they sometimes still rolled dice; they meandered across golf courses and played a little tennis. In pools, they floated rather than swam. Most of them disliked any activity that brought them out into actual daylight. *Jeepers*, Huey remarked to himself, *this guy doesn't have a clue.*

"Hunting, yes, of course," Gaylord said. "Fellow like you, fellow with your experience, could handle a shotgun like nobody's business. Great fun. Get up before dawn, get rigged out in the proper gear, spend a couple hours banging away in the blind. I have a little place in Virginia. You ought to join me there sometime."

"A blind?" Huey asked. "Like a duck blind?"

"That's the only kind I know," said the financier. "Tell you what, whatever we shoot, we give to you. Serve 'em as specials in one of your restaurants. You have wild Duck on the menu now and then, don't you?"

Huey shook his head. "I get my Ducks from a farm on Long Island."

"Better taste, wild ones," Gaylord said. "Tang of genuine game."

Huey's old enemy, heartburn, geared up to do its work.

***

A week after Gaylord Duck left town in possession of a handsome check representing the value of Donald's mutual funds, Sylvia called everyone with two exciting bits of information. She and her honey-bunny had decided to skip all the fuss and bother of a big wedding and had been married the day before in a quiet civil ceremony at the LA County Courthouse. She was sorry none of the nephews had been invited, but they hadn't missed much, since the wedding had taken less than five minutes. And one family member had witnessed the event—the witness! At Donald's insistence, her daughter Lizzie had flown in from Hawaii to have her baby where her mother could look after her.

Sylvia must have been guarding her daughter's health with the ferocity of a wolverine, for none of the nephews so much as glimpsed her until after the birth of her child, which followed the wedding announcement by two weeks. During those weeks, Donald and Sylvia were preoccupied by some mysterious errand, some unspecified task that occupied most of their days and evenings. Huey left half a dozen messages on their answering machine, none of them answered. On the fourth day of silence from the newlyweds, Huey took a break from the restaurant and drove up into the Hollywood Hills to see if some disaster had occurred. He feared that he might come upon a smoking ruin, or three corpses eviscerated by wandering madmen.

On King's Road, the house stood intact, altered from his last visit only by the absence of the realtor's sign. Donald had talked his bride out of selling the place, anyhow, good news to faithful Huey, who loved the funny old house and saw no reason why his uncle should spend upwards of five million for a place off Mulholland. Mel Tormé used to live up there, but Mel Tormé was dead, and why would you want to live in his neighborhood anyhow? Huey rang the bell, pounded on the door, peered in through the windows, all to no effect. One car, a two-seater Mercedes convertible, was visible through the windows in the garage door, but not his uncle's old runabout or Sylvia's new Mercedes sedan. That night Chewie called and left another message. Late the next afternoon, Louie telephoned him at the restaurant and said that he, too, had driven up to the house and found it empty. At a family dinner the following evening convened expressly to discuss the Donald problem, the three brothers were startled by the vehemence of their wives' dislike of their new aunt.

Cosima said: "She's a goldigger, and I don't trust her for a second."

Sharon said: "She's a goldigger and a conwoman, and I don't trust her father either. He's supposed to be ninety years old, but didn't Huey say he looked sixty-five? I bet he isn't even her father."

With her usual candor, Pinkytoes said: "She's a golddigger, he's a conman, and do you think that this Lizzie is really her daughter? They've already stolen something like half a million in mutual funds, what's to stop them from killing Donald to get all the rest?"

Two days later, Uncle Donald strolled into Dewey Duck's Ducks Unlimited and apologized for having dropped out of sight. He looked healthy, serene, and in a blissful mood. Dewey could have kissed him on the spot. Oh, Donald was sorry if the kids had been anxious about him, but they oughta loosen up, y'know?, oughta get some fun outta life insteada worryin' about an old coot like him night and day. Hell, the old coot was having the time of his life, no kidding. Sylvia, his bride, made him happier even than he had been in the days when everybody made a living outta going crazy. Couldn't believe his luck. Do anything to make that woman happy.

Huey's heartburn kicked in again. What had the lovely bride required to make her happy over the past two weeks?

The darling kid was never happy in the old house, Huey knew that. Forget about it being too higgledy-piggledy to allow the girl to express her natural talents, how could she ever be happy there, how could she feel at home? If he weren't such an insensitive old fool, he'd of understood the deal right away— you can't expect one woman to live in another one's house. So, like Huey knew, they put the old place on the market. Whaddya know, sold right off the bat. And the very next day, their realtor had shown them the perfect place. No kidding, perfect. Square feet up the wazoo, lotsa wall space, billiard room, library, four bedrooms, four baths, tennis court, big big pool, and best of all, the same great view he had before but even better. Amazing! Where was it? Oh, that was perfect, too. Just off Mulholland

Drive, Drake Lane, on the crest of the hill. Mel Tormé's old neighborhood, did Huey know that?

"I hope you'll be very happy there," Huey said.

Happy? If his bride was happy, Donald was happy. She *loved* the new place, walked around all day with a grin on her face. The kid loved decorating, and that's what had kept them so busy over the past coupla weeks. In and out of furniture showrooms, design centers, rug warehouses, art galleries, the studios of guys who made stained glass windows and marble mosaics and art plumbing fixtures…. Did Huey even *know* there were guys who made art plumbing fixtues? Of course on toppa all the decorating, she had Lizzie's baby to perk her up. Her first grandkid! By the way, Lizzie flipped when she saw the new bunkhouse. Got her room already picked out, and it'll be ready by her next visit! He hadda say one thing, Sylvia was right when she said her daughter was a beauty, that was for sure. Those two, you could almost mistake 'em for sisters. And Sylvia said the funniest thing when Lizzie had her baby. They walked into the room, see? About half an hour after the birth, this was. Well, Sylvia goes up, kisses her daughter, and picks up the little baby. Then she says—get this—she says, *You know, I've never seen one of these before.* With her own daughter lying right there in the bed!

"That's funny, all right," Huey said. "Uncle Donald, why didn't you invite us to the wedding? We would have loved being there."

Oh hell, there was hardly enough room in that judge's little chamber for Lizzie's belly, much less the three nephews and their wives. And they had to have Lizzie there, poor kid was only days away from the big event, and no insurance, of course, because kids never had insurance these days, they couldn't afford it. So Donald was happy to cover the medical bills. What was he supposed to do? Let the kid give birth in an Emergency Room? A man has responsibilities, after all. That's why he put the new house in Sylvia's name.

Reeling, Huey barely heard his uncle say that he was sorry to break up the happy confab, but he had to pick up the girls and the baby and drive them to the airport. Lizzie was going back to Hawaii on the afternoon flight.

Were there afternoon flights to Hawaii? Huey said his car was bigger than Donald's old runabout, and it was parked right out in back. Could he spare the time? Of course he could. In fact, he had to leave the restaurant anyhow—a new, nearly radioactive roach powder had come on the market, and Huey wanted to see if it worked as well as it was supposed to. Donald said, Great, this way you get to meet Lizzie. Whatta peach.

On the way to the old house, Huey realized that he had no idea if the baby was male or female, or what its name was.

"Uncle Donald, what name did Lizzie give her baby?"

Donald wasn't sure if he'd heard the baby's name. On the whole, he didn't think so. Maybe Lizzie hadn't named it yet.

"Well, is it a boy or a girl?"

Donald wasn't certain he'd heard that, either. It was one or the other, though, that was for sure.

When they pulled up in front of the house on King's Road, Donald jumped out of the car and ran up the walk before Huey's feet hit the asphalt. Huey came around the car and started up the walk toward the open front door. He could hear his uncle calling his wife's name, as he had on the afternoon when the nephews and their wives had been introduced to her. Huey went through the doorway and stood in the hallway, listening to his uncle yell "Sylvia!" from the direction of the kitchen. He walked into the living room where Sylvia had so becomingly adorned the Art Deco sofa. Today the sofa was empty, and no fire burned in the fireplace. Above the mantel, a pale rectangle showed where Aunt Daisy's portrait had hung. Quick footsteps began to mount the stairs in the hallway. Donald yelled "Sylvia!" again. Huey's eyes moved back to the mantel—her ashes were gone, too. What had happened? He banished his sudden vision of Sylvia throwing the portrait into a blazing fire and following it with her predecessor's ashes.

From upstairs came a clamor of voices that quickly softened into whispers.

Sylvia's voice called out, "Huey, are you here, darling?"

Huey allowed that he was there.

"And are you really going to be a sweetheart and drive us to the airport? You don't have to, you know."

Huey insisted on driving them to the airport.

He went out into the hallway and looked up the staircase. A low rumble of conversation came through the door to the guest room. The door flew open, and Sylvia came rushing down, followed by Uncle Donald and a slim young woman carrying a baby basket. Sylvia ordered him out of the way. The plane took off in an hour, they had to get out there right away, so get in your car, Huey, and show us how fast you can drive. Huey jumped aside, and Sylvia hurtled past him and out the still-open front door. Donald came rushing after, a small overnight bag swinging from his left hand. Lizzie flew past so quickly he hardly took her in: he had a blurry impression of gypsy-ish hair around the hard but attractive face of a woman not far from thirty. He could not see the baby at all.

Sylvia and Lizzie had climbed into the back seat before Donald was finished locking the door. Sylvia motioned them forward with a furious wave of her hand.

For the first ten minutes of the journey to the airport, the two women huddled together and spoke too softly to be heard. Donald told a long, pointless story about Joe Palooka, that poor bastard. The baby did not utter a peep. Looking into his rear-view mirror, Huey saw the two heads, blond and dark, move apart. Sylvia leaned forward and patted Huey's shoulder with a delicate porcelain hand. It was so nice of him to do this, wasn't Huey being sweet, Lizzie?

"We better get there in time," Lizzie said. "You know what I mean."

Huey asked about the baby's name.

"It doesn't really *need* a name yet, does it?"

He asked if her husband was picking her up at the airport in Hawaii.

"*Hawaii?*" she asked, then immediately said, "Oh, yeah. No, he's not. He can't. The stupid jackass is dead."

When he found her face in the rear-view mirror, it was shadowed by her dark tangles of hair.

"Fell off a mountain, the dope," said Sylvia. "Right outside Calcutta. Calcutta's where the bad husbands go."

For the rest of the journey, Donald rambled cheerfully through memories of the golden days. The child never made a sound.

Huey pulled up in front of the enormous terminal and began to open his door. Again, Sylvia's slender fingers tapped his shoulder. No, he shouldn't get out, he'd done enough, she would just run Lizzie to her gate and say good-bye, don't be a silly old silly.

Protesting that at least he had to give a proper farewell, Huey ignored the grip on his shoulder and got out of the car. "Me, too," Donald said, and got out on the other side.

"As long as you're out there, hold this." Lizzie thrust the baby basket at him through the open door. Startled, Huey looked down into the depth of the blankets and saw a pink, immobile face that might nearly have been made of plastic. Lizzie scrambled off the back seat and snatched the basket away from him. Then Sylvia was before him, giving him an air kiss. She gave another to Donald. Her head turned toward the glass doors, Lizzie stepped sideways. Huey moved with her and again peered into the baby basket. A wide blue eye stared upward, though not, apparently, at him. Very slowly, a broad pink lid swam over the blue iris and swam back up.

"Nice to meet you, I'm sure," said Lizzie's voice. The blue eye, the perfect skin, and the blankets disappeared. He straightened up to see Lizzie's back fleeing toward the glass doors, her mother hurrying along in her wake.

***

The new, radioactive insecticide worked like a wonder, but for two days after it was administered, every Duck that came out of Ducks Unlimited's kitchen tasted like a chemistry set. Huey was forced to go on the Internet. He consulted search engines and searched for newsgroups that might discuss his problem. Alt.restaurants.infestation sounded promising, but turned out to be a forum in which food service personnel griped about their customers. Alt.burningcockroaches.zone, which he tried on a lark, brought a loose, baggy critical perspective to the problem of head lice. Alt.foodies and alt.kitchens missed the mark completely. Huey spent so much of his evenings at his computer that Cosima grew sulky and the baby, Afterburn, screamed when he picked him up.

He was just investigating a group called alt.insects.demonic.entities when he answered the telephone and heard Sylvia's silken voice, beginning as usual without preamble, telling him something about travel plans. He wanted to hang up;

he wished he could find a newsgroup that would tell him how to rid the world of Sylvia; what he said was, "Excuse me, my mind was wandering. Could you repeat that?"

This was three days after Lizzie's typhoon-like exit from Los Angeles.

Huey should really take something to aid his concentration, Sylvia said, but all right, she would start over. Without Lizzie around, the house in the Hollywood Hills seemed intolerable. She was sorry, but she couldn't stay there another day. Sylvia's mental well-being, in fact, the state of her health in general, compelled her to go off on a nice little journey somewhere until the house on Drake Lane was ready for her "touch." Some distant cousins in the Cotswolds had been literally begging her to come for a nice long visit, and she thought this was the perfect time to answer their wish. Donnie understood completely. He *wanted* her to go. Well, Huey knew how his uncle Donnie felt about family. It was *everything* to him, simply *everything*. But Sylvia could not help but feel guilty anyhow, leaving Donnie all alone like that. Would Huey please look after the darling, would he try to keep him entertained in the absence of his honeybunch? She would also call her father, the splendid Gaylord, to see if he could think of some little project the two of them could do together. Wouldn't that be the sweetest thing, Sylvia's two darling men having guy-type fun together? Anyhow, Sylvia wanted Huey to know that she had booked a flight to London for the afternoon of the following day, so maybe he could be a very, very good boy and invite his uncle for dinner tomorrow night?

"Sure thing," Huey said, and went back to his research. By the time he came across alt.bugs.goodriddance an hour later, he had forgotten all about his promise. The things he saw as he wandered through newsgroups blotted out everything else, and he did not get to bed until two in the morning.

Soon after he arrived at the restaurant the next morning, he saw something disappearing under his gas range that made him want to turn around and walk back out. It could not have been a roach; although he had never seen a rat that large, there was a faint possibility that it was a rat. A rat the size of a border collie, with insect-like hind legs. Wishing that he were holding a .357 Magnum, Huey got on his knees and looked under the range.

Donald, Duck

The thing had gone somewhere else, perhaps into the walls. He could see no big holes or openings, but a thing like that probably had the power to slip through cracks. For some reason, he remembered the expressionless blue eye that had winked at him from the depths of the baby basket. For a moment his head swam and his stomach threatened to turn inside out.

He stretched out on the floor in front of the gas range, breathing in big, noisy gulps. The dizziness and nausea passed. He got to his feet and went to the front of the restaurant, where his manager was punching figures from an account book into an adding machine. Huey told his manager to call the staff and tell them not to come to work for three days. Then he told him to go to the discount store and come back with a dozen boxes of the radioactive roach killer. The manager said Huey looked sort of funny, was he feeling all right?

"Not really," Huey said. "Get that stuff, okay? Buy their whole stock. Buy every box they have."

His manager told him he ought to go home, and not to worry about the radioactive bug powder. He would put it in all the right places, now you go home, Boss, you look like you need some rest.

Huey saw that mechanical eye, winking up at him.

Uncle Donald!, he thought.

The manager picked up the telephone and began speed-dialling the chef and the headwaiter, who would then notify their men of the three-day closing. Huey waved a sketchy good-bye and went back through the kitchen, being careful not to look too closely at anything, through the rear door and into the alley, where his car baked in the sunlight. When he drove into the street, he took his cell phone from his pocket. Uncle Donald picked up on the second ring.

"Uncle Donald," he said, "I just remembered that I talked to Sylvia last night, and she wanted me to ask you to dinner. Why don't you come over about six? Cosima's always asking about you, and the kids would love it."

Well, said Uncle Donald, he'd love it, too, but he was afraid he couldn't make that night. As a matter of fact, he was going to be out of town for the next four or five nights. That Sylvia, she was really something. You'd think a guy was in danger of falling apart, the way she worried over him. So she gets up and goes to visit her cousins in the Cotswolds, so what? Is he going to break down and go nuts just because he's on his own for a coupla weeks? Does he need babysitters now, do people have to put him to bed at night? It was ridiculous, but he loved her for it.

"Uncle Donald, it's just an invitation to dinner," Huey said.

Yeah, but see, here is Sylvia coming at him on two fronts, get the picture? Not only does she call his favorite nephew, she also goes and calls her daddy, good old Gaylord, and whaddayaknow, Gaylord loves the idea, he got right on the phone with him, worked out all the details right there on the spot.

"What details?" Huey asked.

For the trip, dummy. What did he think, a man could get organized without making *arrangements*? Gaylord got his plane tickets, set up a car to take him to the airport. Actually, the car was due now, that's why he picked up so fast—he thought it might be the driver. Everything else he needed, Gaylord would have waiting for him.

"You're going to Boston?" Huey asked. "You're going to stay with Gaylord?"

Hell no, Boston? *Boston*? Gimme a break. This was gonna be an adventure, what kind of adventure could you have in Boston? No, Gaylord was in *Virginia*, he was inviting him to *Virginia*, where he had this like duck-hunting camp or something, been in his family for like three generations, everything first class, no discomfort, even the Ducks are like trained to fly where you aim the shotgun, piece a cake. Just the two of them, the dogs, and the Ducks, plus a cook who comes in at mealtimes.

"Uncle Donald, I don't think you should go," Huey said. "I mean it. I don't even think Duck hunting is legal in Virginia." But he heard no companiable hum in the receiver; his connection had been severed. When he redialled, Uncle Donald said, "He . . . Huey? . . . darn phone . . . hate these blasted . . . Hey, the driver's here."

The line went dead.

Disremembering Me

Christopher Sartin

Do you know who I am?
Perhaps, an acquaintance
Perhaps, an old friend

Maybe, someone you've passed?
Along the street
Amongst the sea of people
The shuffle of hurrying feet

Please, look closely!
You may find something you recognize
Something in a motion
A glimmer in the eyes

Listen to my voice
Is there something that's unique?
Some rhyme or cadence
A rhythm in my speech

Do you see anything?
Any sense of familiarity?
Please, say you do
For it's all lost to me

Drink, Drink from the Fountain of Death

Eric J. Guignard

I worked over thirty years in purchasing for a company out of Manhattan that replicated antiques and heirlooms around the globe into home décor pieces and showroom designs, museum accessories, elegant toys, seasonal ornaments, and other high-end *objet d'arts*. To say I was well-travelled would be to say that a bird knew clouds. I was the Jacques Cousteau of back alley bazaars, the Magellan amongst dealers of knickknacks. And over those years, amongst those travels, I was ever attune to peculiar ideas, superstitions, fables and legends, tales of the grotesque or of the wonderful. My business, after all, was not just replicating antiquities, but of crafting the stories that went along with them.

Of all that I've been told, of all that I've seen or experienced, of all I've learned of the peoples of this planet, this following episode, occurring in my own country, is perhaps the most hideous and unbelievable.

It was late October, and rainy that year in 1987, when myself and a friend, Ray Prince, travelled along the southeastern seaboard of the United States on one of our famed buying expeditions. Already I'd procured botanical art and porcelain whimsy; stainless steel mobiles; art deco bowls; polished bronze sun dials; insects in Lucite; gold dinnerware; tea pots and mariner wheels; and more. More, more, yet always I wanted more. *We* wanted more.

We were driving a rental station wagon down Interstate 95, having left Jacksonville en route for St. Augustine, the oldest occupied city in the U.S. and a hotbed for Spanish colonial ornamentation. Ray had a giant map unfolded on the dashboard of the car, when he said, "Let's turn off here, Jim. It's a shortcut."

Famous last words.

We ended up on a winding, rough slit of road that seemed nearly to drown in the surrounding swamps, which Florida is so well known. After thirty minutes and the beginning of an argument as to whether we should turn back, inexplicably the road opened up from more than a single dirt path to something of a two-lane asphalt byway, of which I was entirely grateful. Old barns came into view, fruit stands, and possibly more rustic antique shops than I've ever seen grouped together in one locale.

"Dare I say, mother lode?" Ray grinned under the suspicion his shortcut would prove to be a great success.

At the time, I couldn't help but agree. "You're a divining rod for yokel treasure."

Our shared laugh was a comfortable moment, and from there we spent the remainder of the day ransacking and plundering as our credit cards would allow. Yet even amongst such riveting and endless novelties and heirlooms, I found myself growing apathetic to stuffed alligator luggage, cannon balls, and collectible cigarillo boxes.

"Is it just me," I asked, "or does this town seem like the lost graveyard of conquistador armor dupes?"

"If there's ever a run on those things, we'll know where to go."

It was getting to be obnoxious, pushing through shops overflowing with conquistador shields, helmets, swords, and all their knock-off ilk. Just how many antique-crazy shoppers came out this way with an inextinguishable compulsion for collecting Spanish-American exploration of the 1500s?

By the twelfth shop, a converted outbuilding named by a weathered oak sign as *San Giblets*, I added, "And paintings of

Ponce de León. In every one, he looks to be suffering consumption."

"It's the statues of him that bother me more," Ray replied, as we descended into the shop's cavernous basement of maritime kitsch. "They're creepy, pointing a finger off into the unknown. I find myself turning to where he's looking, wondering what it is I'm not seeing."

Incredibly, what awaited us at the bottom of the stairs was the exact subject of Ray's distaste: a life-sized figure of the famed Spanish explorer, carved of wood and, admittedly, painted in remarkable detail, wearing a sleeved doublet of golden thread overlaid by a cuirass armored breastplate. Ponce de León stood aside two glass cases of intricate sailing ship models, one arm casually affixed above the hilt of his sheathed sword, while the other arm was raised, gloved hand pointing to a place directly behind us, which was nothing but laminate planking of the stairwell.

"Ha," I laughed, "it's a warning for visitors with little self-control of their wages to stay away from the overpriced merchants of this town—"

My voice dropped as the joke went flat, for I realized I didn't know what town we were even in, and then, further, I was interrupted by someone from behind who'd overheard us.

"There's been great debate over it," the person said quite seriously. Turning, I saw it was an unsmiling man, tall and lean, wearing a Panamanian-style white linen suit. The man continued, "Some people contend the pointing hand is symbolic of Ponce de León's discovery of this land, first sighting what he would later name La Florida from the bow of his ship *Santa María de la Consolación*."

"Illuminating," Ray said flatly.

"And the rebuttal of those debates?" I inquired.

The man gazed almost longingly into the painted eyes of Ponce de León. I followed his regard and felt almost mesmerized by some trick of light or passing shadow into seeing a flickering within the statue's pupils.

"What others believe—" the man said, "what I believe—is that Ponce de León is pointing the way to the greatest fountain of all time, the Fountain of Youth."

"Indeed?" Ray was amused. He looked at me, while I felt only inexplicably agitated.

The tall proprietor—for I took him as such—nodded. "There are many tales, ship logs and diaries from his crew, and accounts passed down from the native Calusa people, describing certain details proving Ponce de León's discovery."

"St. Augustine," I said. "That's where the legends state the Fountain of Youth to be."

"Oh, please," the proprietor said, rolling his eyes. At last he'd given an expression to his otherwise waxen face, although the act made me only want to slug him. "As Barnum said, 'There's a sucker born every minute.'"

"So the sucker is he who believes the fountain is in St. Augustine," Ray asked, "but *not* the person who claims the fountain is real, but existing elsewhere?"

"It's real, all right, and it's out there. Whoever locates it will become rich beyond their wildest dreams!" The proprietor's eyebrows rose, waggling in a manner that reminded me of a dying Groucho Marx. "Ponce de León points the way."

Ray rubbed at the stubble on his narrow jaw, ran one finger across the thin mustache he kept groomed like an Errol Flynn movie extra. He looked almost to laugh. "I've seen about a thousand of these statues in your town, and they all point different directions."

The proprietor shrugged. "You won't have to worry about finding it. Tradition says that if you're chosen, the fountain will find you."

Now Ray's laugh did come out. "Well, that's helpful."

I gazed again into the carved figure's eyes and felt the unnerving sense of it gazing back.

"You look like serious collectors," the man said, relaxing. "Tell you what I know, the fountain is said to be northwest of here, in the swamps, as indicated by the original statue. I'd say around Deep Creek, off the St. Johns River."

"The original?" I asked. "Where's that?"

"You're looking at it. This original statue was carved out of a boat's mast taken from Ponce de León's fleet. Happens to be on sale, too. Half price, great bargain."

At that, I quietly joined in with Ray's laugh. We declined the offer and left *San Giblets*, the first store all day we'd exited empty-handed.

"Creepy," Ray said, and I agreed.

Dusk settled in around us, the Florida sky reflecting the great Atlantic overhead, but reversed in hue and design, slow moving waves of irradiant pink and molten bronze and the shadows of lavenders that portend night's dreams to take rise. It was beautiful and opulent, and I felt that moment itself to be the realization of the Fountain of Youth, for time seemed to stop and magically infuse our being with the splendor of our ever-present universe.

Yet like life, the moment passed. We decided to get a motel for the night, one of those cheap motor courts that barely survived the decommissioning and now molder languidly under growing threats of mold, dust, rodents, and debt. I still didn't know what town we were in. There was no phone book in the room, just a pad of stationary from the State Tourism Department and a Gideon's Bible in which someone had crossed out the first page and scrawled, *Satan slept here* and below that, *Winky too*.

"This motel," I said, "Odd, it's at the end of the road we drove in on."

"I noticed that," Ray said. "What kind of town only has one way in?"

I took a bite from my take-out sandwich. "That shortcut was supposed to cross straight through to St. Augustine, right?"

"Sure."

"Wherever we are, this place isn't shown on the map."

Ray shrugged. "Eh, we'll ask in the morning."

***

In sleep, I had a nightmare of Ponce de León pointing at me, his consumptive face waning to something skeletal. Laughter sounded, but it seemed not to come from him, instead surrounding me as an enveloping fog. Though not seen, I imagined it as coming from the tall proprietor we'd spoken with earlier. Ponce de León's arm lengthened, his pointing hand drawing nearer, nearer to me, and I unable to move, watching his gloved finger grow larger by perspective, as if soon to impale me like a lance.

He turned, and one half of his face was of flesh, the other half skull, wet and glistening with vines and gray moss. The eyes were wooden, those of the statue. His other hand released the sword at his hip, and lifted a goblet, beautifully jeweled by smoky pearls, rubies shaped like falling tears, and cut diamonds as blue as the ocean becalmed.

The liquid inside the goblet began to overflow, as if a valve turned from within, and it became a great pool of crystalline water surrounded by a perfect circle of ancient stones and toadstools that were as immortal as the legends.

Ponce de León spoke, and his voice was my own. "Drink, forever."

***

In the morning we breakfasted and checked out.

"What's the way to St. Augustine?" I asked the motel clerk, an elderly woman with long grey hair and a quiet, dreary sort of countenance.

"*Weeell*," she said, apparently thinking vigorously on the matter. "Y'all oughta take the 95, head down south and that'll get you near enough."

"We *were* on the 95. Map showed a shortcut coming through here."

She sniffled. "Nope."

"No shortcut?"

"Like I said."

"So we need to backtrack to the 95?"

"That'll do you."

"Huh." I watched a horsefly the size of my hand buzz languidly around the counter. "Weird, the map doesn't show you listed, no markings of any town out here."

The woman swatted at the horsefly with a half-hearted disinterest. "Map's outdated, I'd say."

"Sure," I politely agreed. "By the way, what's the name of this lovely burg?"

She just chuckled. "Now you're gettin 'uppity."

With that, I took my cue, and Ray and I left the strange little town, our purchased treasures packed down tight in the back of the rental.

Ray returned the map to its berth, unfolded across the dashboard. "Back the way we came."

"Easy enough," I replied.

It wasn't.

Imagine the tributaries of a watershed feeding into a larger river, or the shape of a chevron pattern with mirrored forty-five-degree angles abutting a central line. Following configurations such as this going one way, against the angles, is a perfectly obvious route; each junction seems to flow into the road behind you, all apparently leading toward the same location. However, changing direction and travelling the opposite way leads one to see every crossroad as a choice to be made, the branching of a letter Y, requiring the traveler to veer left or to veer right.

At first we deduced to follow the asphalt, which at times turned one way before swerving to turn the other, but always seemed the obvious choice to alternative roads that were not much more than muddy trails. However, as I'd remembered from driving in the day prior, the asphalt soon petered out into a single dirt path, so now at each crossroad one direction looked as equally uninviting as the other. From a bird's eye view, the choice may have appeared obvious, but from our perspective the passage evolved into a labyrinth of wild hedgerows.

The ground grew rougher, rockier, while wetter, so we bumped over large stones one instant and splashed through puddles the next. Trees grew in closer together, and lack of sunlight caused them to appear wan, as if wasting from some disease. My watch showed an hour had passed although it'd felt to be three.

"We're lost."

Ray was beside himself. "There's not a single sign anywhere! What kind of a podunk corner of Hell is this?"

For the hundredth time, he balled the map up, then smoothed it back out onto the dashboard. "The road," he said. "It shows only two intersections along here. We've passed at least three dozen."

A movement outside the window caught my notice, and I thought I glimpsed a figure through the trees pointing away, but then dismissed it for shadows as Ray admitted, "We need to go back to town."

As I reluctantly agreed, Ray grabbed my shoulder and shook. "Jim, the gas. Look at the gauge, it's on empty!"

I don't know why, but my only reaction was to laugh. "Lewis and Clark, we are not."

It was at this point the sickening comprehension of a terrible predicament began, for even after fifteen minutes or getting the giant station wagon turned around on that narrow path, and descending back the way we'd just come, we realized this particular road had also a vast number of crossroads branching off, identical thin trails snaking through dense undergrowth as if we'd become firmly entangled in the center of a mesh web of gossamer, where sticky lines seemed to radiate in all directions.

"This is bad," Ray whispered.

I stopped, and we got out to gaze at our verdant prison. The ground was soft, viscous, every tree wrapped in fat, ropy vines. Looking up, the forest canopy reminded me of the steep angles within a vaulted ceiling, while thin patches of daylight filtered down through their dark branches to reflect luminescent orange and white fungi spreading from beneath rotting bark.

"Our tire tracks," Ray said. "Look."

I didn't understand until he explained, "The ground is muddy, it keeps our prints. See the tracks behind us, driving this way? There are no other tracks in front of us, which means we didn't come this direction. We took a wrong turn in circling back."

"Ponce de León will be forgotten," I laughed with relief, "in the stead of discoverer Ray Prince's navigational brilliance!"

We got back in, and I turned the ignition, but the car would not start.

"That's it," Ray announced, unnecessarily.

Dark clouds rolled in, and it began to rain. We cursed and tried to get the car started, but to no avail.

"Should we wait out the rain?" I asked. "Follow the sun?"

He didn't answer, and we stared out the windows, glumly.

"I think we're going to have to hoof it out, Ray. No one's going to come looking for us out here."

He agreed, even as the rain worsened. We'd be able to walk back to town if we could find the paved road, which we should be able to locate by following the tire tracks. So we layered our clothes, brought out jackets; took off our shoes and rolled up pants to walk through the wet, and we left the station wagon. We followed Ray's idea, reversing direction along the dirt road, my feet recoiling at every step through the gelid, clingy mud. We went on like this for about two hundred feet, the rain plodding off our backs, the insects around us chirping and crikking and screaming in some orchestra of delirium, until I found where we'd missed a turn that had previously been made in the car. A shout of triumph went up that we'd ultimately escape this mess with little worse than loss of a few hours time and the addition of blisters and some new gray hairs to our coiffures.

"Just keep following our tracks, and soon we'll be back to the asphalt," Ray said.

And that's what we did, successfully for about twenty more minutes. At that point, as we came through a clearing, we found the road in front of us—split by yet another crossing—to be flooding with rain water, erasing the tire tracks.

"Damn this place, this entire state..." Ray groaned.

Suddenly I felt as if someone was watching us, some *thing*, and the cacophony of insects quieted. We decided the asphalt couldn't possibly be much farther ahead, so we chose the direction seeming most reasonable and tramped through the deepening mud, desperately hoping the paved road would return to sight at any moment... and then the path ended. We realized we were well and truly adrift in the swamps of eastern Florida with no sense of where to go. Visions of stalking pythons and monstrous alligators took hold and, as the daylight faded, I found my earlier fortitude to be a sham. I looked to Ray, and he was in equal spirits. We rushed back to find safety in the car.

Only the car could not be found. There were more crossings, smaller trails leading off from larger ones to turn small again, paths that could not be seen one way, but revealed themselves from the other direction, seeming to promise only immediate escape, but leading instead to darker dead-ends.

Soon night fell, and the rain continued.

Drink, Drink from the Fountain of Death

It was the longest night of my life, and I dreamt terribly again of Ponce de León. By morning the rain had not slacked, and our surrounds were seriously flooding, water having risen already above our ankles at every step. We spent another day and night, then day again, wandering the swamp, drenched and shivering, frightened of every sound, cursing every insect bite... and suspecting some presence to be watching us, following us, something made of gauntlets and arm guards, gorgets and doublets.

We quite reasonably began to speak of impending death. I'd known of men who could survive worse environments for longer periods of time, but neither of us were of that ilk. Every step was agony, the onset of a coronary. We were slowly freezing, yet still perspiring, starving, gasping, crying, and bereft of hope. I tripped over the root of a mangrove and injured my leg.

"Jim," Ray panted, "Jim, what is that?"

I shook my head without looking, examining my leg to ensure nothing was fractured. Ray walked away.

"Jim," he repeated, "I see something ahead. Light..."

Now I glanced up and saw a glow through the trees, a splendor faintly pulsing. Ray trudged toward it, then I got up to follow, limping behind. The glow became brighter, the air warmer.

"It's help," Ray said. "Someone's there."

An ethereal light shone from the distant vision, a light that seemed to have no source, for storm clouds above blotted out all else. A waver shaped the air, as if a ripple across reality, and I caught glimpse of a beautiful pool of crystalline water as pale blue as Mayan opals. The pool was surrounded by lush glades bordered by a perfect circle of ancient stones, ringed throughout by toadstools glowing fluorescent orange, pink, lavender.

"My god," I heard Ray shout, his voice moving farther away, "the fountain... it must be... it is the Fountain of Youth!"

I only stared as Ray broke out in a run, splashing through the swamp, shouting, "We'll be rich!"

I called to him by impulse, "Wait, it's a mirage, a rainbow after a storm—"

The rain hardened, another ripple seemed to radiate outward from the pool, and Ray was momentarily obscured. I wiped the water from my eyes, blinked, pushed onward and saw him nearing the strange sight.

"Ray!"

I saw then also the nightmare that will haunt the rest of my days, for in the center of that pool, standing on its surface, as if Jesus Christ walking on water, was Ponce de León in all his glorious conquistador regalia.

By what trick of perspective I know not, he seemed as near to me as to touch at arm's length, which caused me to shrink back. Beneath his feathered morion helmet showed a face no older than my own. He appeared healthy, vital, filled with prowess, yet it was the eyes that betrayed him; they stared out as fixed and unblinking as the statue we'd observed in the antique store. Ponce de León gazed upon Ray and pointed with a gloved hand, beckoning him forward.

How could de León still be here, looking the same as he did five hundred years ago? The riddle came to me all at once: *How does a person stop aging?*

And I knew there was only one certain answer... "Ray, come back!"

He was too far gone by then, either by distance so as not to hear my warning or by mania, caught in a dream of riches and immortality. He crossed the ring and stepped into the glimmering water where he would age no more.

I saw then there were others, hundreds more, also in that pool, flashing in and out of view: conquistadors, Native Americans, pirates, trappers, fishermen, tourists, all the seekers of agelessness, all the discoverers of death. The sparkles, the glimmer of the light around them were beings too, flying creatures like fairies, made of teeth and delicate wings and glowing fungi, the same bioluminescent attraction of lanternfish swimming forever in deep water brine.

Ponce de León's phantom wrapped around Ray like ropy, strangling vines and sank into the Fountain of Youth, pulling my friend down with him. "Drink," de León said, "forever."

Ray struggled and cried out for release, but he was gone in a flash.

I watched all this in horror, in the span of mere seconds, frozen by shock, by numbing disbelief.

By the time Ray was gone, Ponce de León's wooden gaze shifted to me. He pointed, gesturing me closer... all the hundreds of other ghosts in that pool pointed, gesturing me closer... Ray Prince rose back up, fixed in age for the rest of eternity, and pointed, gesturing me closer.

I turned and ran.

I wandered in the swamp for days more, fighting hypothermia, starvation, illness. I followed roads and paths that led nowhere, that led everywhere. At every juncture I saw the fountain, its distant pool of lights, watching me, following me, rippling nearer and nearer, if ever I stopped in one spot for too long.

By the most serendipitous of luck, a hunter and his dog were out tracking wild hogs and found me stumbling past. I told him what all had occurred and he nearly laughed.

"You use drugs out here, some hippie commune?" he asked.

"Please," I cried, "help me, we must get away!"

"Sure, but you say your friend is out here too, drowned?"

"de León... the fountain..."

"Fountain of Youth," he muttered. "If I had a nickel, every treasure hunter—"

"No," I interrupted, "the fountain, it's found us. There!" I pointed toward a pool of ethereal light, appearing from behind a stand of nearby cypress trees.

The hunter looked, let out a little gasp, grabbed me by my arm, turned us to run...

But the path he'd come up now appeared split into fourteen different directions, each obscured by rising mud.

He gaped. "What the shit—?"

We were trapped together, as I'd been trapped already. The bell jar of such horrors and strain of the past several days finally crushed me under its vacuous pressure; I surrendered, crying, willing existence to simply end quickly so I'd suffer no more.

The hunter's grip tightened on my arm, and he yelled at me to get up, while I mumbled there could be no escape.

He whistled to his dog, some type of hound with small bloodshot eyes and a fat, lolling tongue. "Pointer, home!"

The dog sniffed around, then by scent moved to a path veering toward the right, and the hunter followed, dragging me along. Soon the mirage of the woods dissipated, and we were upon a main road running along the St. Johns River.

***

The police never found Ray's body. They never found the station wagon either, nor the town we'd visited, although I've come to learn there are numerous small hamlets existing in isolation up and down the Florida byways, and it could have been at any of them we'd stumbled across that "wish to retain their own way of living."

Now, decades later, I still don't know what to make of all that transpired, but I think often of my friend Ray Prince, his ghost having found its own grim timelessness in never aging again…

He still looks as he did the day he died, for every so often I catch glimpse of him reflecting back to me in lone pools of water, his pointing finger turned beckoning, inviting me in for a drink.

Lost

Jason Stokes

I'm lost. I have no idea where I am. Well, not entirely. I'm in the woods. Deep in the woods. The Appa somethings. That's what daddy said. I guess that's where this is. I'm not really sure what that word means but it's in a park, deep inside. There was a big sign when we came in and it said State Park on it and that same word daddy said. I remember staring at it through the car window, so many trees reflecting on the glass it was difficult to read but it said State Park and had a symbol on it, like a police badge almost but different. It looked very official.

That was yesterday. It feels like more. Like several days now.

I've been walking for so long I can barely feel my legs. I know I can't stop. I don't even know if I could, but I want to. Every step takes me deeper, I know that because the trees are getting taller. They're much taller in the middle of the forest but I can't go back and if I stop… I can't think about that. Not right now.

Everything in here moves like it's alive. I tell myself it's squirrels, birds on branches but there's something else, something bigger and it's right behind me. Even though my legs shake and feel like they may collapse under me, I keep going. My feet catch on rocks and roots, causing me to nearly fall flat on my face so I focus on just staying upright, moving as fast as I can. There must be another way out.

I meant to ask what it meant, the symbol on that sign when we came in but then the car stopped, all at once and jerked. Mama made a gasping sound like something caught her throat. She does that a lot when Daddy drives but she wasn't upset this time, not like usual and she was whispering. I thought at first because of Davy... my brother, but she was talking to me and she looked excited.

"Angie, look."

I pressed against my seatbelt, but I couldn't see good past the front seat and daddy's wide shoulders, so I craned my neck, sticking it out like a giraffe. I did see it then, standing in the middle of the road, staring right at us. It was a deer; I remember its eyes were so big and black, but she looked at us and I thought I could see something so deep it was like staring at the sky at night. She was amazing and calm like she didn't care that we almost hit her while she was trying to eat. She just stared at us, still as a statue, like she wasn't alive at all but like one of those in the gas station we stopped at on the way up. Then, after a minute she just walked away. Slow so I could see her pass by my window. I knew she was a girl because the boy deer had big antlers and she didn't have any at all, but I thought she was the biggest deer I'd ever seen even though that wasn't too many and the boy ones must be gigantic.

"That was pretty cool, huh?" Mama watched me from the front seat, a huge smile on her face and I smiled back.

"Very cool," I said, twisting to see the deer launch up and over a row of bushes and disappear into a small patch of trees near the only building out there. Its tail flashed white and then it was gone.

My ankle is swollen, I can feel it through the sock and my legs hurt. They've never hurt this bad before. I'm afraid if I stop walking, I won't be able to get up again. I know I can't. Daddy wouldn't let me; he'd tell me to just push through it. Just keep going, try not to think about it. It'll hurt later, I know that but right now, I have to find a way out and it's getting dark. I think maybe it's always dark in here, it's cold too. Much more than the campground where we set up our tents. It was warm there, even this morning when the sun was barely up before anyone else came out of their tents and there was fog everywhere. It surrounded us like a magic mist hiding everything. I've never seen anything so... I don't even know the word for it. It was incredible. Not like anything at home. We live in a small town, not in the city but... not like this. That's why I got up before anyone else. That's why I wanted to go walking through the grass, letting the water soak my socks and cling to my legs. It felt itchy but also kind of cool.

I walked a long way this morning, keeping the camp to my back. I didn't want to go too far, where I couldn't see the tents anymore but when I got to the edge of the woods they were already so far, and I wanted to see what was in there. So, I put our tent to my back, walked in a straight line so I could find my way back again. I broke branches on the way to mark my path like I'd seen in videos online and I looked back every few minutes, making sure I knew where I was. Even out here I didn't think Daddy would get up early, not that early anyway. At home he always slept until the sun was fully up. It was still a little dark when I started, the morning sky growing a brighter and brighter blue way up above the crisscrossed branches and barely visible through the wide, green leaves. Birds chirped and sang in the trees as I went.

I counted in my head, keeping track of steps or anyways I did until something caught my attention, made me freeze in my tracks. Where I walked was a path, dirt, but not wide like the ones we had taken to get to the camp. They were narrow, with bushes and leaves covering in some parts and moss growing on rocks along the side. Sometimes my feet disappeared beneath the thick leaves, crunching twigs and pine cones as I walked.

When I heard something snap, like a twig but much bigger I stopped, still as that deer and I held my breath. It was close, I knew that because it had been loud, but I didn't know exactly where it had come from until a few seconds later when it happened again, like a large branch, snapped in two. Looking around without moving, I turned at the waist, still holding my breath. If it was another deer, I knew I'd run. In the car she had been beautiful but out here, alone, my leg jerked, anticipating the need to move faster than I ever had before.

The next sound didn't make me think of a deer, it sounded more like a moose or like a really big dog. Grunting, deep and heavy. When I was little, we had a golden retriever and it sounded like that, only a lot bigger. I kept twisting, this way then that but I couldn't see where the sound was coming from and there was a high spot to my left, a few feet higher than I was and I thought it must be coming from up there. The grunting sound was quieter but only a bit, like whatever it was there was moving away. I had to see it, even though I was so scared I could barely move, I knew I had to climb up there before it could get away.

In here. In here it's always dark with a light way up in the sky, so I know the sun is still up but it's fading. It's been getting darker and I tried walking towards it, towards the light, like maybe just going in one direction might help. Like I'd have to run out of trees eventually but there are miles of it. It never ends and the light faded so much I can't even tell where it's coming from now. Twigs crack under my feet and I keep thinking someone is following me. I know that's impossible. I'm alone. All alone but I pull my collar up, hugging the jacket tight. It's too big, hanging off my arms so I have to roll the sleeves back, but I prefer it to being cold.

It's like a kind of armor, protecting me from whatever might be in here with me. When it starts to rain, I'm glad I have it even more. It's thin, not made for wet weather but as the droplets fall, pinging off leaves nearby at first, landing around my feet as I push further, I can feel them hitting the material and rolling off. Soon it's not just a few drops but thousands, maybe millions of them slapping against the trees and leaves and my jacket so fast you can't make out anything but one constant sound. The steady rush of water as it pours from the sky. I slip in the mud and fall sideways, grabbing out for nothing and land hard on my side. I kick twice before I manage to get up again and the rain is coming so hard. I have to pull the hood up, but I still can't see. Rain has run into my eyes; it drips from the hood so fast I can't make out the trail in front of me. I manage to find a tree, one of the biggest I've seen so far, and I nestle up the to the trunk, trying to find shelter under the gnarled low hanging branches but the rain funneled off the bigger branches and broad leaves overhead still pummels my head and already the ground has turned to thick black and brown muck, a small pool has formed where my shoes sank into it, a dirty brown color. I look back down the trail and I can't see anything more than a few feet. Which is good. If I can't see them, maybe they can't see me. The jacket is brown, it'll blend in good against this tree, so I pick my legs up and tuck them as tight as I can, pushing against the tree trunk, trying to become as small as possible while rivers of rain pour from everywhere. My shoes are soaked, my shorts too so that it makes me shiver and even with the hood enough rain got down my back that I can feel it tracing a path down my sleeve.

I look down and I see that it's not rain that's running down my arm. A river of light pink and red snakes around my wrist, between fingers and to the tips trembling as I hold my hand out shivering but not from the cold. The red drips from my fingertips, splashing into the mud below. I scream but before I know it a hand clamps down over my mouth, shutting off the sound before it even begins. It's my hand. Still red with blood. I can't scream. I can't stop. I have to keep going. The blood is coming from the sleeve, I hadn't even realized it was there until now and now I have to try and forget about it. I push myself up to wipe my hands on my shorts. A new stream makes it way down my arm, replacing the old one as soon it's gone. Keep going. There has to be a way out.

I wonder which I'm more afraid of, that I'm really alone, and don't know how or if I'll ever get out . . . or if he's out here too. Every time I stop, straining against the roar of the rain and squint into the mist, different than this morning, thicker, I see something, but I can never put my eye on it. It moves too fast, a shadow that's probably not even there. The path is washed out, it's barely there anymore and I have to walk slowly to keep from falling. Which is good because I'm getting tired. I know I can't go on like this much longer.

I had climbed that rise this morning slowly, carefully, like a game hunter or one of those guys on tv. I crouched down low and tried not to make any noise as I poked my head over the ridge. At first, I didn't see it. I scanned the underbrush but couldn't locate what was making all that noise because I was looking too low. When I raised up, I saw the biggest animal I'd ever seen in my life. Way bigger than the deer though it probably would eat her if she were here, me too if it knew I was standing there, knees trembling, eyes wide as they could get. It was a bear. A big brown bear with huge paws and long claws sticking out of one that it was using to dig in the ground. My throat went dry and I swallowed hard. My heart was beating so fast I was afraid it would hear, and I made some kind of squeaking sound that was lost in the crunch as the big animal put its weight on an old limb, snapping it in two, crushing it to splinters. The scene was so mesmerizing I didn't notice a second, smaller shape until it was so close, I thought I could smell its breath. The cub was little but still a lot bigger than me.

    I don't know why I did it but after a few minutes, when they started to move back, towards where we had set up camp, I followed them, staying as far behind as I could and not be seen.

    Limbs smack me in the face, wet thick leaves sticking to my face and I feel like I'm running blind now. Even though I'm going slow it wouldn't take any effort at all to catch up from behind. The path winds and snakes around trees like it wasn't put here by the park rangers but walked over and over by something or someone with no aim or direction. It's so cold I put my hands in the jacket pockets, wrapping the material around me tight, ducking whenever another branch appears from the mist to try and knock me down again. There's something heavy in the pocket and immediately I know what it is. I wrap my fist around its shape, and it helps me feel just a little better.

    I followed the two bears for a while until we reached a clearing. I figured it couldn't be far from the camp site and it was still pretty early so I wanted to stick around awhile. The huge mama bear was digging around the edge of the forest, staying out of the tall grass beyond and the cub was running around, sticking its nose into everything, knocking over rocks and small tree trunks that had fallen, mimicking the behavior of its mother. Quietly, I found a tree with a low branch and climbed up it, putting myself at least twice as high as I thought the mama bear could reach, hoping she wouldn't notice me up there. I stayed a long time, watching before I saw the movement on the other side of the clearing. Immediately I felt my heart clench as Daddy appeared, pushing through the tall weeds, Mama close behind. She had Davy, my brother, in a little backpack, like a passenger on their morning hike. I couldn't make out what he was saying but I knew he was calling for me. They knew I'd left without permission. I wanted to call back, but the mama bear was too close. I didn't want her to know where I was. I shifted in the tree, the branches creaking under my weight, deciding what to do and I thought she must have heard me because her head shot up and she made a weird noise, but a second later she was loping fast back into the woods, the little cub trailing close behind. By the time she was out of sight Daddy had already crossed the field, stepping into the shade of the forest not far from where the bear had been. He probably couldn't hear me, so I pushed carefully off the limb to start down.

I was so excited to tell him about what I saw, and I thought maybe, if we were real quiet, they might even come back so he could see her too but then everything happened at once and before I could reach the ground, the whole world stopped. I was looking at Daddy, he had stopped under the trees and he was taking off his jacket. A brown and green, windbreaker kind of thing. He had his arms up, lifted over his head and I had my mouth open to shout to him, to say I was coming and to look, look there was a bear. I remember I looked down, my foot slipped, and I had to look down and there was an explosion. It was so loud my ears rang and I jerked, missing my footing. I fell, straight down and landed hard on my ankle. It twisted and I wanted to scream but the fall knocked all the wind out of me, and I was just lying there, shooting red pain firing up from my leg and I knew it was broken. It had to be. I wanted to cry for my daddy, to help, to come carry me but my ears were ringing, and I could hear something else. Someone else was screaming. It was the most awful noise I ever heard, and I knew immediately who it was. Mama was screaming so loud it made my blood turn cold. I tried to get up, but I couldn't, and no one would have heard my calls for help over Mama's screams so I forced myself up on one foot, the pain exploding in my ankle and leg so bad I almost fell down again. I thought I may just curl up and cry but I had to know what Mama was so upset about. Where was Daddy, what was going on?

When I got up, I saw a man running across the field and I could see Mama where she had been before. The man saw her first because he stopped in his tracks. I couldn't see his face real well but I could tell he had a bright orange hat, and he had a gun in his hand that was pointed down. When Mama saw him, she stopped screaming. Then she started again, shouting help, over and over again. She just kept screaming at that man to help but he didn't move. He stared at her and then I heard Davy, wailing. He must have been crying all along, but it was hard to hear him over everything else. I put some weight on my ankle and knew it wasn't broken but it hurt so bad I couldn't barely move. I started to walk towards Mama, slow, hopping on one foot but then she stopped screaming for the man to help and I looked, and he finally moved but all he did was raise that gun slow and he pointed into the woods near where Mama was. I thought maybe he saw the bear too but then I saw Mama run, like that deer yesterday, she ran as fast she could straight into the woods but before she could disappear another explosion came, and she fell into the dirt. My legs gave out and I fell to the ground.

I didn't know if he'd seen me, but I knew what had happened as soon as he started walking towards the woods. He crossed the distance faster than I could imagine and I saw him stop where Daddy had been, just for a moment and then keep pushing into the trees to where Mama was. I couldn't hear Davy crying anymore and I tried not to think about that. I was so close, if I had moved, he would have seen me. But I didn't move, I didn't even breathe. I watched as he passed and as soon as he was far enough away, I scurried along the ground, crawling on my hands and knees, the pain in my leg fading but still making me want to cry out every time I twisted it.

Daddy was laying in the dirt when I found him. The jacket he was wearing on the ground next to his body. He was staring up at the sky, eyes still, glossy so I could see the reflection of the trees in them. His mouth was open, but it wasn't moving. Somehow, I knew I was shaking but I couldn't make sense of it. I couldn't think of anything. I couldn't do anything. I clutched the jacket in my fist, pulled it off him so I could see the giant red wound in his chest. Then I put it back. Covered the mess so I didn't have to see it. It smelled terrible and something inside of me was lit up like a wire, something that wouldn't let me stay, that made it impossible to think. When a limb crunched, I didn't look up, I didn't wait to see the man in the orange hat or whether he would point that gun at me next. I just ran.

There's a clearing up ahead. I can see it, there's a break in the trees. It's almost completely dark now. The rain has let up a bit, but I can still hear it falling around me and it's gotten a lot colder than before. I don't think I've gone in a circle because I don't recognize anything here. The trees are huge and wide, not like the narrow ones where we camped, and this clearing isn't big. It looks like a little strip cut out of the forest, I can already tell there's even more trees on the other side, more running. I haven't looked back in what feels like hours. I don't need to know if he's back there. I don't care if he is, I just need to keep going. I need to put space between me and what happened. When the trees end, I don't find myself at a river like I expected, a thin strip of water winding its way through the deepest parts of the forest, but it is in a way. It's a strip of asphalt, two lanes wide, it appears in the distance around a curve too dark to see the end of and keeps going in the other direction. I don't know which way is which so I pick the right and start down the shoulder, keeping my head low and staying in the shadows near the forest, so I can run back in if I need to. After a few miles, I find a bridge and the river I had expected before. It's long enough I can't see the other side in the dark, so I crawl up under the concrete awning and pull my legs in. Wherever this road leads it has to reach a town eventually. It has to come out the other side. I don't know how long I've been walking but it'll be night soon. I can hear the bugs starting to make their noise for the night, a constant buzzing sound that seems to come from nowhere and everywhere all at once. I don't want to walk at night. I'll have to stay here but I'm starving and there's no food anywhere. I know you can't drink the water, or it'll make you sick. I press up under the bridge, the dripping sound of rain echoing and bugs buzzing and that goes on for a long time until something else deep, loud. My eyes jerk to the forest, expecting to see the mama bear, tracking me down all this way but then it changes, and I recognize that sound at once.

    Crawling out from under the cold stone I can make out the pinprick yellow lights as they cut through the falling darkness growing wider as they get closer. The rumble and knocking grows louder and I can tell this is an old truck, driving slow, maybe looking out for deer. I wave my hands in the air, one covering my eyes as the yellow lights grow so big and bright, I can barely see. When they pass by, I'm blinded and I think they must have went on except the growling of the engine, the deep belly roar of that old engine is louder than ever, and I can smell the filthy exhaust. I blink into the darkness, regaining my vision and a rusted old pickup waits, windows rolled up because it's the kind you have to do by hand and a tarp over the bed that's soaked through with rain. I try peering through the glass but it's no use and I know I don't have a choice. The engine roars like someone hit the gas so I place a trembling, frozen hand on the old worn handle and lift up. It's harder to open than I expect, and I regret it immediately as cigarette smoke pours out from the other side.

"You lost?" I don't answer for a minute. I want to cry, to scream, to run away.

"Yes sir," I say, not knowing what else to say. I'm not lost, not really, but I don't want to say anything else. Not yet.

"Get in 'fore you catch yer death out there."

I hesitate and I can tell he sees it. I shouldn't and I know it. Daddy would be so mad, but I have to. I look back towards the woods, nothing but a wall of darkness that seems more dangerous than it did before. I can't go back in there.

"Come on, I'll take you to town. Your parents nearby?"

That's all it takes, and I close my eyes, jump in and slam the door.

I don't speak. I don't want to and after a minute the man just shrugs, puts the truck in gear and starts driving. It stinks in the truck; I think I smell beer but I'm not exactly sure what it smells like. I look in the mirror to keep from looking at the man who I know has looked at me twice already. I don't know what he's thinking but I don't like it. The tarp flaps in the wind as we drive and the taillights get bright when we go around turns, illuminating the rusted side of the bed. It's blue in some places, white in others and on top there's a thick coat of red.

"Your folks camping near here?"

I don't look at him. Instead, I examine the cab, the faded seats with holes in them, one of which scratches the back of my leg. A couple of shiny things in the space between us that I think must be bullets but small ones. Like a handgun. A pack of cigarettes sits on the dash underneath the mesh of a bright orange hat.

We're not driving fast. I look at the speedometer and a little white needle points to forty-five.

"Ya get lost, separated from yer parents?"

I nod. Looking over my shoulder, the endless line of trees against the sky fading into a solid black wall. The taillights come on again but we're not in a turn. The tarp flaps in the wind and I see a black space underneath it as well.

"Y'all camping?"

I nod again. My leg is shaking, I want to run.

"What site?"

A shrug. I put my hands in my pockets. My fist closes around something small, metal. I feel safe.

"I bet you're at the State grounds. That sound right?"

I think of the sign yesterday when we arrived. The deer, Mama's excited face. Davy. My fist closes tight, so I almost can't open it, but I know I have to. I nod, yes.

The needle on the dash moves to thirty. In my fist I run my finger along a smooth narrow strip of metal with a notch cut into it. I've never held it, but Daddy always kept it in his pocket if we went camping. Sometimes he'd take it out to cut an apple for me or shave the bark of a stick. I push against the notch and the metal opens, revealing a sharp edge.

"You been lost all day, haven't you?"

I look up at the man, he's dirty and I can make out a streak of dark red across his forehead.

I don't answer him.

The truck comes to a stop. He doesn't bother pulling off the road. The taillights light up red and stay that way.

"You've been running all day, haven't you?" His breath stinks and I know it's beer I'm smelling. I can hear him breathing, his mouth open but there's foul air coming out of it. Air that smells like when Daddy died.

He doesn't hear the click of the blade locking in place. I clench my fist tight and slide my hand out of the pocket.

Lost in the Forest of My Mind

Hannah Elizabeth

Lost is a feeling of not knowing where you are
Lost is a feeling of nonstop confusion and panic
Lost is walking into a dark forest and losing your way out
Feeling alone and deserted
Terrified of what will happen when night falls
Trying to build a fire and find shelter but giving up
Silently praying and saying goodbye to those you love
Hugging yourself as your last resort for warmth
Crying and silently regretting every wrong choice and bad decision you have made
Until suddenly you get a spark of hope
Voices boom nearby sending you springing to your feet to rush towards them
You drag your sleeve over your face to dry your tears
You are stumbling over tree roots and fallen branches
Trying to get to the voices as quick as possible
But then they start to fade
They are leaving you
You start to shout after them
Your legs speed up in attempt to catch up to them
When finally, you see the white light of flashlights

Lost in the Forest of My Mind

You start to make out the figures of people in the distance
They start to shout at you letting you know they see you
When you reach them, you are breathless and filthy
They start asking you if you are ok
But before you can answer darkness clouds your vision
You feel grass and leaves gliding across your back
A few moments pass until you are lifted into a vehicle
You feel bound up by your feet and wrists
You start to internally panic when
The vehicle stops moving
The doors close and a door opens
And suddenly you are drenched in ice cold water
Cascading all over you and making you feel breathless once again
You jolt awake startled and terrified
Your captors lift you up snickering and talking
But you ignore it, fearing what is to come
They drag you to the edge of a cliff
Down below is a raging river
Moving at a rapid pace, almost like it is angry
You try to back up further from the edge
But before you can move, they toss you over
You are falling for what seems like days
Trying to calm down and collect enough air to give you a fighting chance
But when you hit the water you release all the air you collected
The air is frigid and dark
Sweeping you away while you sink
Slowly to the bottom
You try to fight against your restraints
Until a terrible realization dawns on you
You are lost once again
Except this time there is no being found

Step Right Up to Marcy Lynne's Amazing Wunderkammer!

Gwendolyn Kiste

An antique metal Folger's can

It's the first item you see when you walk into the room, clinking at your feet when you step forward. You hesitate, gazing down at it. There's rust around the rim, but the label is still intact, red as a freshly pricked finger, and inside, there must be more than a hundred quarters.

The coffee can sits on the floor in front of a knickknack cabinet, the kind you could pick up at a church lady's yard sale for a dollar. It's no more than waist high, with a line of little compartments running up and down, a few of the shelves recessing into darkness. You can't quite see what's on the shelves. You're not sure you want to.

The light in the room shifts, and you seize up, not quite remembering how you got here. You must have passed through a front door, traipsed across a shag-carpeted hallway, and opened the door to this room. Except you can't recall any of that. The last memory you have is standing alone, halfway down the block in your own empty house.

Step Right Up to Marcy Lynne's Amazing Wunderkammer!

But even though your memory is gauzy as frosted glass, you still recognize this bedroom, as if from a long-ago dream. There's a stained mattress on the floor and a couple posters fastened to the wall with yellowed tape. And when you look again at the knickknack shelf, you know what this is too.

A cabinet of curiosities, a young girl's wonder room. You also know who it belongs to.

"Hello," a small voice whispers, and that's when you see her. Marcy Lynne. She's tucked back in a corner, sitting cross-legged among the shadows, her dark hair slung over her eyes.

The house settles around you, and beyond reason, you already know you and Marcy Lynne are the only two people here.

"Where are your parents?" you want to ask, but these days, you hardly remember your own family, so it doesn't seem right to ask about hers.

Through the narrow window behind her, you see a line of drowsing houses, identical as Stepford wives and just as vacant. There's nobody left in this neighborhood anymore, but if someone asked you where they all went, you wouldn't know what to say. If someone asked you how long you'd been left behind, alone and bewildered as a ghost, you wouldn't know what to say about that either. Time is at a standstill on this street, as though the hands on the clock simply shrugged and refused to go on.

But Marcy Lynne isn't so easily deterred. Out front, she left up her splintered wooden sign scrawled with Sharpie-red letters, the same sign that led you into this house years ago.

Marcy Lynne's Amazing Wunderkammer, 25 cents

Something in the air murmurs to you, and the memories seep back into you slowly, like ink blotting on a page. You almost laugh aloud, remembering how Marcy Lynne used to charge you and the other kids to see inside this cabinet.

"That's only fair," she'd say, twirling a thin strand of hair around her finger.

Fair. As if a single thing that happened to her had ever been fair. Marcy Lynne was the same age as you, but you barely knew her, barely knew how to look her in the face and fathom that much loneliness, all the secrets she had to keep since nobody ever listened anyway.

Still, that didn't stop the neighborhood from staring. It didn't stop you either. You and the other girls would sneak into this house, into this room, and you'd each drop your quarters in that old rusted-out Folger's coffee can.

Then with your heart fluttering in your chest, you'd peek inside the cabinet and gape at the revolving door of anomalies, treasures scrounged from around the neighborhood, the things that nobody else bothered to see.

There were only ever a few items at a time, so it took no more than a moment to get your quarters' worth, but Marcy Lynne didn't care about any of that. She always invited you to stick around.

"For a sleepover maybe," she'd say, brightening. "Or for my belated birthday party."

Smiling, she would put out her hand, but nobody would take it.

"Not today," the others would say, turning away, and they wouldn't even wait until they reached the hallway before they rolled their eyes at Marcy Lynne.

"What a weirdo." They'd giggle, and your cheeks would burn with shame.

"She can hear you," you'd whisper, but that's about all you did. You never told them to stop. Nobody ever told them to stop.

"Marcy Lynne will be fine," the parents always said with a wave of their hands. "Besides, there's nothing we could do for her anyway."

Not that they ever tried to help. They were far too preoccupied with themselves to bother with the girl in the oversized sweater, huddled alone on the sidewalk, her gaunt figure blighting the landscape of the neighborhood.

Now alone in this room, you watch her, and she watches you too.

"They're waiting for you," she says, motioning to the exhibits. Inside the cabinet, something whispers to you. Your body goes numb, and you want to run, to be anywhere but here. Only that's not what you do.

Instead, you take another step closer and peer inside.

Two Empty Cicada Shells

Step Right Up to Marcy Lynne's Amazing Wunderkammer!

You can barely see these specimens at first, hidden away in a narrow compartment at the bottom. But then you move a little closer, breathing in a mouthful of mildew, and there they are, the shells practically trembling in front of you. So delicate, so detailed. At once a membrane and a memory.

From the hollow imprint where their eyes used to be, they seem to stare back, and for an instant, you're sure they're alive. With unsteady fingers, you pluck one shell from the cabinet and hold it in the center of your palm. It's the color of dead leaves, of seasons withering, of things long past. You clutch it tighter and feel the emptiness there.

Marcy Lynne rocks back and forth on the floor, her knees pulled into her chest. "They came the year I was born," she says, "and when they return, I'll be seventeen, maybe old enough to go with them this time."

Her eyes flickering, Marcy Lynne gazes at you, and it seems like she really believes that. But the two of you linger in this room that looks like yesterday, and you think how it's probably been a very long time since a single hour has passed here, let alone a whole year. The world has decayed around Marcy Lynne, but her patience is infinite. She'll wait, even if waiting does no good.

You're waiting for something too, though you aren't sure what it is. You don't know why you stayed behind after the others went away. No one is making you remain in this place, certainly not Marcy Lynne.

Growing up, you'd always see her around the neighborhood, darting between houses, hiding in culverts, picking through torn Hefty bags deposited curbside. Anywhere she might find something that someone else discarded.

And there was plenty to discover in what this street cast aside. They threw away appliances that still worked and clothes that still fit, and when it suited them, they threw away each other too. You learned at a young age how people have a tendency to get restless, to want something different, something better. They'll surrender the whole world on a whim.

Of course, that was a long time ago now, back when there was still a neighborhood, back before everything went away.

"Where do they all vanish to?" you ask suddenly, and your voice sounds miles off. "The cicadas, I mean. They come for a summer, but then where do they go?"

Marcy Lynne shakes her head. "It doesn't really matter," she says. "All we need to know is they're not here to stay."

At this, the cicada shell crinkles against your fingers. Shivering, you put the husk back at the bottom of the cabinet, but even when you look away, you can still feel it crawling in your hand.

A Small Fetus, Suspended in Liquid (Animal Unknown)

You lean closer to this specimen, curled up in an Erlenmeyer flask, floating there in yellow liquid, suspended for all eternity in the dark.

"That one isn't mine," Marcy Lynne says, fidgeting on the floor, and you believe her, since none of these things are really hers. She's only a collector, spinning your neighborhood's garbage into gold. But if this isn't hers, you have to wonder who it once belonged to. Or what it even is.

It could be the runt from a litter of lost rabbits. Or a Barnumesque sideshow hoax made of wire mesh, crafted by a devious hand. Or maybe it's something else, something you'd rather not think about.

Your jaw clenched; you decide not to ask any more questions.

Instead, you settle down on the floor next to Marcy Lynne, so close to the cabinet that you could reach out your arms and embrace all these treasures at once.

"I'm glad you came," she whispers, and outside, a streetlight flicks on. In its jaundice-yellow cast, the rows of abandoned houses look frail as brittle bone, their outlines like cheap movie sets built of cardboard and ready to collapse at any moment. Somewhere that's not real, that's never been real.

Marcy Lynne exhales a thin laugh. "It's been quiet for so long," she says. "I was starting to worry that I never existed at all."

At this, you say nothing, the weight of her words prickling your skin. You wonder if you're the last person in the world to remember her.

You also wonder if she's the last person to remember you.

A Leather Sack of Human Fingernails

You don't have to reach for this one. It tumbles off the top shelf and nearly falls into your lap. The drawstring opening has gone slack, and all the fingernails spill out in front of you. You recoil, wanting to flick them away, but you can't help yourself. You silently count them, taking stock of each variety.

Fingernails that are trimmed and clean. Like a doctor's or a businessman's.

Fingernails that are long and gnarled and calcified at the edges. Like someone who'd grown too weary to bother filing them.

Artificial nails lacquered in shades of red and blue and silver. Like the kind your mother used to wear. *Exactly* like the kind she always wore.

You don't remember when she left. You don't remember when any of the families started to slip away, dissolving like spring mist. Your parents and the other parents never talked about where they'd gone. It just didn't seem like the polite thing to do.

"Some people aren't meant to last," your father said one night at the dinner table, as though that was enough of an answer.

Marcy Lynne's family went too, vanished into the night. Which night in particular nobody knew, because nobody on the whole block ever really cared about her sallow-eyed parents who shouted long after midnight, once the hope and the propriety and the bottom-shelf whiskey ran out. It didn't take long before the mail started to pile up in little yellowed stacks, and the grass decided to do whatever it pleased.

Every day on your way to school, you loitered on the sidewalk out front and stared up at the windows of their house. Like everyone else, you figured Marcy Lynne disappeared with the rest of her family. You kept thinking that until you went walking alone one Sunday night and nearly stumbled right into her. You were meeting up with the other girls on the block, a pilfered pack of your father's Marlboro Lights in your back pocket, an offering that you hoped would make the girls like you.

That's when you saw her. Marcy Lynne just sitting there on her crumbling backstep, a ring of shadows embracing her, her gaze on the earth, her calloused fingers digging into the soil.

"How are you?" you asked, practically blurting out the question, but she only shrugged.

"I'm still here," she said, and you were curious if that was a blessing or a curse.

Because you didn't know what else to do, you offered her a cigarette. She shook her head and kept scrounging through the dirt, pulling up small flecks of something right out of the ground. Your vision gauzy, you edged forward until you saw what it was.

Fingernails. Dozens of them.

If the other girls had been there, they would have screamed. They would have wept until their complexions went red and then they would have run home and told their parents all about it, all about how that strange girl that nobody liked had upset them again.

Not you, though. You kneeled next to Marcy Lynne.

"Where do they come from?" you asked, and her eyes flicked up at you.

"From us," she said. "From what we do here. To each other. To ourselves."

Your head went foggy for a minute.

"This neighborhood will devour us whole if we let it," you said, and the words sucked the breath right out of your chest. It was the first time you ever admitted it aloud.

Marcy Lynne was still looking up at you, and you felt caught under the weight of that lonesome stare.

"We should run away," she whispered. "We should run *right now*."

Her eyes bright, she reached out her hand to you. Your guts twisted, and you almost reached back, almost pulled her out of the darkness, almost imagined how the two of you could escape this place, racing as fast as you could, so fast it would have felt like flying.

But you didn't do that. From the sidewalk out front, the other girls called for you, their giggles harsh as steel wool, and all you could do was turn away from Marcy Lynne. Just like everyone else.

"Besides," the parents always said, "there's nothing we could do for her anyway."

Step Right Up to Marcy Lynne's Amazing Wunderkammer!

You never agued with them about it. You never argued with anyone. Back then, you used to think it was the things we did wrong that were most worth regretting. But standing again in this empty house with this abandoned girl, you're starting to think it's everything we don't do, especially when we know we should.

After that night with Marcy Lynne, you waited at your window every evening. Your throat tightening, you'd stare out onto the street until it was too dark to see, trying to guess who would disappear next, fearing it would be you.

Only your time never came. It was the next-door neighbors on both sides, and the so-called nice family across the street, and even your own family: a mother and a father and maybe a brother or sister whose name you no longer recall. But it was never you. You stayed behind, even if you never knew why.

And so did Marcy Lynne.

A Heart-Shaped Bottle of Pale Sand

This is the prettiest specimen in the cabinet, so lovely you're almost convinced it's some kind of trick. You creep closer, and squinting, you see it's filled with tiny seashells, collected from oceans Marcy Lynne never had a chance to visit.

"They must have been beautiful," she says, as if there are no seas left on earth. Part of you fears she might be right.

You pour a bit of sand into your palm and hold one of the pale shells up to your ear. You expect to hear the melody of salt waves, of Atlantic darkness at midnight, but that's not what's waiting for you. You hear the whole neighborhood instead—sparklers sizzling in the Fourth of July sun, sprinklers hissing over glistening lawns, block parties that never stop.

They're calling to you. This cabinet is alive, and if you closed your eyes, you could tumble into it, as easy as falling into a looking glass.

"Go ahead." Marcy Lynne flashes you that quiet smile that reeks of heartbreak. "It only takes a moment. That's all it ever takes to disappear."

You exhale a small wheeze, as you finally understand: she's done this before, so many times she's probably lost count. The whole neighborhood, all the families who vanished before you. When they tired of this street, they found their way out through her. This place is a blinking red exit sign, a steppingstone, and Marcy Lynne is the gatekeeper, the Charon of forgotten suburbia.

"Why you?" you ask, and she shrugs.

"Why not?"

Outside, the streetlight on the corner flickers out, and you realize that with no one around to fix it, it will never light your way again.

Marcy Lynne starts to say something else, but you can't hear her, not with your family and the rest of the neighbors murmuring in refrain. Though you can't see them, you can tell they're smirking and chortling where they are now, at their backyard barbeques that never end. A place with no rainy days, no responsibility, no problems at all. Maybe Marcy Lynne could be happy there too, but it doesn't matter. It's a universe closed off to her. She's not welcome, and she knows it.

But you're welcome there. These whispers are an invitation. There's still a quarter in your pocket, heavier than it has any right to be. This is the cost of your future, your fare across the River Styx.

Only you aren't quite ready. You haven't seen everything in the Wunderkammer yet.

With a familiar ache in your belly, as hollow as a cicada shell, you breathe in and lean close to the final trinket in the cabinet.

Prince Rupert's Drop

You learned about this one in science class, maybe the same class that Marcy Lynne sat in the back row, invisible as a ghost, her hair in her face, her eyes seeing things the rest of the universe couldn't fathom. Maybe that's where she found this specimen, pocketing it from the lab after the bell rang, after all the kids went home and never returned.

A Prince Rupert's Drop. It's an odd little artifact, molten glass dropped in cold water, crystallizing into the shape of a tadpole with a long, spiderweb-thin tail. A paradox, the glass so strong that the elliptical end can outlast a bullet, but so delicate that just a flick of that tail will shatter it into dust. It's both indestructible and impossibly fragile.

And this is it—the final treasure, your final moment here. At last, you've overstayed your welcome on this street.

Step Right Up to Marcy Lynne's Amazing Wunderkammer!

You take the coin from your pocket, and with your heart in your throat, you deposit it in the rusted-out coffee can. It plinks against all the rest, and Marcy Lynne gazes at you, her face fading to gray.

"Thank you for coming," she says, and this will be the last time she ever says that, because you're the last one. The rest of them are already waiting for you. Everyone is waiting, the Prince Rupert's Drop glinting back at you. You see them swirling in the glass, your parents and the other parents and the girls your age, their murmurs rising like an uncanny aria from the seashells, their hopes crinkling in the husks of long-forgotten cicadas. The tug of something new, something you could call home, brims inside you. All you need to do is reach out, and you'll never be alone again.

But your body goes numb again, and you seize up in this moment, between the here and there. Her eyes dark, Marcy Lynne regards you, almost as if she were expecting this.

"It's okay," she whispers, and she's right. You've always known exactly what you needed to do, even if you told yourself you didn't.

You smile, and with the air shimmering around you, you extend your hand. Not toward the Prince Rupert's Drop or the cicada shells or any of the treasures perched on shelves.

Instead, you reach out to Marcy Lynne.

Except she doesn't reach back. Her face pinched, she recoils from you, as though this might all be a trick. You suddenly can't breathe, everything in you convinced it might be too late after all. You might have waited on this street for a thousand lifetimes. You might have waited too long.

Then the earth rumbles around you, and she moves closer. "Are you sure?" she asks, entwining her fingers with yours, and you laugh, since it might be the only thing you've ever been sure of.

Your eyes clear at last, you guide Marcy Lynne to her feet, and without a word, the two of you start toward the door. The voices in the Wunderkammer, sharp as broken glass, call out for you, and when you reach the hallway, you hesitate, a final whisper boiling in your ears like blood. It warns you not to go. It tells you that past this broken street, there might not be a world left anymore. But you grin, because that doesn't matter. Oblivion is better than staying in this room.

The others have already chosen their way out. Now you get to choose yours.

Giggling, you and Marcy Lynne skip down the narrow hall, lightbulbs bursting in their sockets, the carpet turning to ash beneath your feet. You'll have to be quick, or you won't outrun it. Outside, the overgrown grass is slick, and the two of you pass Marcy Lynne's crooked sign, the one that brought you here so long ago. Together now, you keep going, the pavement crumbling away, everything you've ever known crumbling, making room for something new. You pass by all the empty houses evaporating into dust, and if you looked back, there would be nothing left. No Wunderkammer, no bedroom, not even the echo of the families who thought they owned the world.

But you don't look back, and neither does Marcy Lynne. Your past fades like static into the night, and smiling, you tighten your hand around hers.

And you don't let go.

Ocular

Mick Garris

I recognized Givens even through the exaggerated lens of the bottom of the shot glass, even after Number Six, where things looked kind of watery. He was a little guy, with that jowly, hangdog, drooling St. Bernard expression that introduced him. I emptied the glass and motioned him into the booth. You're not really supposed to drink at Schwab's, but I was a pretty damned good customer, and if I had my nipper in my pocket, they'd bring on the glass and look the other way. And the way my career was going at the moment, I needed a few shots of liquid courage before facing my esteemed representation.

Even if you'd never met him before you'd peg Givens as an agent on the skids. His suit was noisy, the tie deafening, and the collar a little frayed. I'd have given anything to jump ship back to the Morris office, as if they'd have me at this point. The days were blurring now that glory was hanging in the closet of the past. I'd done that Lancaster picture back in '44 or '45, but you know, it was the end of the war and even a lot of good pictures got swept under the rug back then. Burt was a handsome guy, and a hell of an athlete, but not what you'd call Academy Award material, not back then. But I got a hell of a performance out of him, and we both got some pretty nice notices in the trades. Of course, he's a movie star now and I'm… well, I'm having lunch at Schwab's with Bert Givens. I was still doing the studio stuff in the forties, the glory days, you know, not this independent bullshit. Hollywood is changing, and not for the better. If you ask me, this whole anti-trust thing is killing the picture business.

And once Wasserman finagled that piece of the profits for Jimmy Stewart on that cowboy picture… well, the end is nigh, my friend. The end is nigh.

Givens sighed in concert with the red Naugahyde booth as he took a seat and signaled the waitress. She saw him and smiled that phony waitress grin, said "Turkey croquettes?" and took his nod to the kitchen. I don't know what he saw in those fucking croquettes, but he ordered them every time. They made me gag. They broil up a pretty nice little skirt steak at Schwab's if you ask for medium rare. But again, one look at Givens and you'd take him for a turkey croquettes kind of guy. Which is no compliment.

A little teddy bear grin lifted the corners of his jowls, and I knew right away something was up. I waited, but he stayed clammed up.

"Please, Bert," I pleaded. "Don't make me play I've Got a Secret with you. Garry Moore you ain't."

It was still early for lunch, barely noon, but Schwab's was filling up. It never ceased to amaze me how many guys from the Business lunched here. Of course, if you were nooning at Schwab's, you weren't working. And if you weren't working, you were looking for work. And maybe Schwab's was not the best place to be so obviously looking for work. The aging, balding, expanding actors were the most pathetic because they were, well, so public.

"I got a nibble," Givens said, barely able to conceal his gnome-like glee.

"So go to the doctor and get a shot," I said. I didn't mean to be mean, but Jesus, with six belts of Vat 69 simmering through my vascular system I wasn't going to be Amy Vanderbilt.

"I'm talking about work."

"I'll tell you again. I don't do television. All those live cameras going on at the same time, it ain't like directing a picture. Give me one camera at a time, if you please."

Givens was ready to hop up on the table like an organ grinder's monkey, he was so excited. "It ain't television," he said, "it's a picture!"

"A picture?" I asked. "Which studio?"

He settled down then. "It's not one of the majors, but it's a good picture, Lee. It's independent money, but they say Aldo Ray is interested."

"Aldo Ray couldn't get a table at Dino's on a Monday night. Aldo Ray couldn't get arrested."

"Aldo Ray gets them release in England, Germany, and Italy. It's a good picture, Lee. And with you directing, it could be a *great* picture. It's not an offer yet, but if you play your cards right and do a good meet and greet, I think I can make it one."

I hadn't done a picture in a couple years, just that episode where I filled in for John Newland on *One Step Beyond* when he got sick, and that had gotten some pretty nice notices, too. Not that anybody ever gave me credit, but good notices are good notices. "Tell me it's not an oater."

"It ain't a cowboy picture, Lee, this one's right up your alley. It's a *scary* movie."

"Like a Hitchcock?"

"Yeah, just like a Hitchcock. But… with a *monster*."

My gut sank, and it wasn't the steak. A monster meant no money, no good stars, no respect. And more likely than not, a shitty little paycheck. And Aldo Ray.

"And what's the name of this little Hitchcockian opus?"

"It's just a working title; they're not married to it." Givens was starting to squirm.

"Oh, boy, this is going to be good. Lay it on me, Bert."

Even Givens couldn't say it with a straight face. "*SHE CREATURES OF MORA TAU REEF.*"

"A.I.P? Allied Artists?"

"It's a new company. Regal, Royal, some fancy-pants kind of name. But they got the money in the bank, and they got Aldo Ray. And if they play their cards right, they got Lee Benton."

"I don't know, Bert, a monster picture? I mean, I never heard of these guys."

"They're new. Just meet with them. And do I have to say you need this picture?"

There it was, the salt in the wound, the finger in the eye. But he was right, I needed this picture. And if I could put my own stamp on it, who knows? It might lead to something better. And if the script were even remotely interesting…

"So, Bert, have you read it?"

"I'm halfway through. It's a good read." I nodded, dreaming desperate dreams. "And one more thing." Another big grin, like this was the icing or something.

"Thrill me." I knew it wasn't going to be something to celebrate.

"It's in 3-D."

Oh, hell. It just kept getting worse.

"Jesus, Bert, it's the year of our Lord 1959! For crying out loud, it's going to be a new decade in a few months. Oboler made *BWANA DEVIL*, what, '51, '52? *HOUSE OF WAX* was a long time ago. They don't make 3-D pictures anymore, and for a good reason! You ever see one of them things? I've *still* got a headache from that goddamned Rhonda Fleming *INFERNO* thing."

"Well, Royal or Regal is making this one, and it comes with a paycheck. Somebody's going to direct this picture, and it may as well be Y-O-U."

"I can spell, Bert. Remember, I did a season of *Romper Room*."

"And they'd like you back."

"Thanks but no thanks. I fuckin' hate kids." Even my own, but I didn't need to tell him that. And besides, I haven't seen them since they moved to Westwood with their mom and that B-movie actor. I should talk; here I am pinning my hopes on a B picture, myself.

I sighed and filled my shot glass again, downing it just as my steak was delivered. A good thing; I needed the protein right about now. Bert's eyes were wide, patient, expectant. What the fuck, it could be a good picture. Goddamn it, I could *make* it a good picture! And what else was I going to do? Keep bullshitting my Guild buddies over lunch at Schwab's?

"Get me the meeting, Bert. The Seduction of the Innocent has begun."

***

I should have felt good about myself and my future as I stepped out onto Sunset under the harsh light of the midday sun. If I played my cards right and kissed the right hiney, I had a movie to shoot. So it wasn't for Universal-International or Paramount or Warners. It was a movie, and God knows I needed a movie. It's not just the money, though, of course, that was part of it. But a man has to have a little self-respect. And with a picture spattered with a handle like *SHE CREATURES OF MORA TAU REEF*, the self-respect generated was guaranteed to be teensy.

Traffic was heavy at the intersection of Sunset and Crescent Heights. Across the street, the Garden of Allah apartments baked, the palms sagging overhead like the old Russian broad that ran the place, who was out in her *schmatte* with a turban wrapped around her collapsing skull, raking the sidewalk. I watched Bert pull away in his little Italian sports car and choked on his fumes. As the cars and busses and trucks rolled by, something in me wanted to step out into their path. Don't you ever feel that way? I mean, I'm not a suicidal kind of guy, but there's some kind of little devil in my brain that just wants to tug me into oncoming traffic. I never really succumb to its pull, but I always feel like I could. I just wanted to step out into the path of that big two-tone Caddy with the perky little brunette behind the wheel and be crushed by it. I really wanted to be pinned to the grille of that Chrysler Imperial and dragged down the Boulevard. I didn't want to die, but it was hard to keep from stepping into the roaring street. I could actually see the red skid marks in my wake, which shook me from this morbid reverie.

I looked up and saw my own reflection in the picture window at Schwab's, and I was shocked by what looked back at me. There was a middle-aged guy there, a spare tire hiding the belt, three days of out-of-work Gabby Hayes chin whiskers, an off-the-rack Robert Hall suit going shiny with age and mileage, and a vacancy behind the eyes like you'd see on one of those guys on a street corner downtown selling pencils. Speaking of self-respect… I vowed then and there to get a haircut and a shave, a new suit, and spend an hour a day with Jack LaLanne.

***

Surprisingly, it was a pretty happy set. Cramped, yes, hot and sweaty in the little east Hollywood Boulevard garage they tried to call a studio, but not unhappy. Aldo Ray turned out to be a pretty decent guy when he wasn't on the sauce, and we even got John Carradine to play the scientist (yeah, *that* was a stretch) and got Mara Corday fresh off her Universal-International contract for the ingénue. Her husband Dick Long said he'd do a bit, but I knew they'd never let him take time off from *77 Sunset Strip* to do SHE CREATURES OF MORA TAU REEF. We had an eighty-grand budget and a thirteen-day schedule, so I was feeling pretty good... I mean compared to what this thing could have been. Of course, the 3-D camera was five times the size of what I was used to working with, and the technicians who aligned the lenses were as slow as Chaney the Second as Lenny, but it was okay. I didn't want to go too far into the cornball with the trip into the third dimension—you know, paddle balls into the lens, shit like that—but I wanted to make it active. I kept trying to think of ways to use the tool, rather than exploit it. But hell, with a title like SHE CREATURES OF MORA TAU REEF, perhaps subtlety was not the best artistic choice. What I wanted was to get Mara Corday's tits right up into your face so you felt like you could slide a greedy hand right into her cleavage, but I knew I'd never get past the Hays office with that one.

And speaking of cleavage, Mara turned out to be a pretty slick little actress. She was game for anything. Hell, she even played second banana to THE BLACK SCORPION, though I fell in love with her last year in GIRLS ON THE LOOSE. Aldo was always trying to pull some of that Method shit on her, but I think it was his way of trying to make time with her. She seemed too smart to fall for that baloney. I hoped she wasn't too smart to fall for mine. Hey, the divorce has been final for eight months now. Mine, not hers. But we could work on that.

Well, the Ron-Del Studios were palpitating with the summer heat, as well as Mara and the other She Creatures. We rounded up some models and strippers and put them in the skimpiest little French bikinis that we thought we could get away with, and when they converged on Carradine's lab and everything got wet, well, my temperature sure went up, I can promise you that. The girls all had rubber fins glued to their backs and the backs of their arms, and little rubber gills on their necks that opened and closed with the pull of some fishing line. So, in our little opus, there's a fire breaking out in the lab, and the girls are gasping because they can't breathe out of the water, and Carradine's spouting scientific mumbo-jumbo like it's fucking *Henry V*, and the air is starting to get pretty thin.

Ocular

Suddenly the flames are reaching high up to the ceiling, well over the top of the set, and the effects guy's face just goes as white as a mayonnaise sandwich. Blaisdell the monster guy starts shrieking like a little girl, or like a dying kitten, running for the doors. Well, he's pushing when he should be pulling, and everybody's starting to panic as the place fills with smoke. It's a dog-pile of fish girls in the little tinderbox stage, and some of them are starting to drop from the heat and the smoke. Carradine actually starts to cry, which didn't help at all. Aldo, well, Aldo didn't seem to notice. He probably thought it was in the script. Again, he's a nice fella, but I don't know if he was all there that day.

So it's screaming and sweating and crying and basically just all hell breaking loose. Nobody was doing anything productive, so I just played director, and shoved everybody away from the door, heaved against the heavy door plunger, and got the thing open. But that was just a box within the box. The whole building, which looked like it had once been an auto repair shop, was filling with roiling clouds of movie smoke—the worst kind, if you ask me—so I headed right to the thick glass window, which had been painted black and covered with a layer of asbestos, ripped off the fire retardant, and chucked a trashcan through the glass.

The smoke raced for the gaping hole in the glass like an escaping convict, as clean air—well, as clean as Hollywood air gets in 1959, which isn't very—tried its best to replace it. As cast and crew made their way off the stage and onto the shabby eastern end of the Boulevard, gasping and choking, I stood hypnotized by the jagged mouth of the glass opening. The shards were like teeth, calling, beckoning me. What would it be like, I wondered, if I had been thrown into that glass? What if I had made an Olympian Weissmuller dive right through the center, and one long, jagged tooth slid right down the length of my neck? Would I have even felt it, or would it just have slid through my flesh like a breath, opening my carotid artery like a whisper? Would it have continued to travel down my torso, gutting me like a halibut, dumping my innards out of their flesh closet like so many dumplings? Would I feel it? Or would it just be a big red secret between me and my body? A crimson river ebbing with my life…

I was being stupid, and I knew it. But the wicked grin of the broken glass would not let me go. I looked down at my arm and saw the faint pulse of the veins beneath the skin. Daylight hit the glass and painted a prismic pattern on my pulse, calling to it. I held my arm over the blade of glass, just wondering. Again, I wasn't going to do anything about it, but what would happen if I did? I wanted to just lower my wrist down onto the window and pull it down and across, gently, almost lovingly. I didn't want to die, but I could not evade the pull of the hungry glass.

I brought down my arm, and the glass gave it a gentle kiss. It could slice through my skin like a gift. It was so insistent; it wanted me so badly. It's not that I wanted it back, it's just that I felt, hell, I don't know, *compelled*.

The screaming siren that announced the arrival of the fire engines pulled me out of that compulsion and brought me back to the real world. Well, back to Hollywood Boulevard, anyway. I walked away from the shattered window, backwards, watching it recede with its own siren call fading into memory. I joined the crowd on the sidewalk, and stated the obvious: "I guess that's a wrap on the lab."

Carradine was already walking down the Boulevard, loudly rehearsing tomorrow's speech to himself. Aldo asked me if I wanted to join him for a drink, but I begged off. I slid over to Mara, who sat on the curb in tears, and draped a comforting arm on her shoulder. She looked up at me through a lens of tears, and I swear to God, they collected a prism of their own when they hit just the right angle of the sun, and it sparkled my shirt with bright, late afternoon color.

"Are you okay?" I asked her. She sniffled and nodded in the affirmative. "Anything I can get you?" She just took my hand and cracked a brave little smile.

"You're sweet," she told me, and I would take that to the bank. I was working up a line of credit.

America deserved Mara Corday in full 3-D.

***

The producers and the brass at Regal or Royal were in a tizzy. We could do without anymore lab footage, and the fire looked pretty spectacular on film, but we lost half a day. There was no choice but to pull pages; there was no way they'd go over the Lucky Thirteen. It was up to me to make the cuts, and there was some agony in that. You know, the man-woman, touchy-kissy stuff is the easiest to shoot in one of these pictures, and it's the stuff that puts the patrons to sleep. Aldo Ray smooching with Mara Corday is only going to be interesting to Aldo Ray, to be honest. Especially in 3-D. You go to a picture called *SHE CREATURES OF MORA TAU REEF,* it ain't to see Aldo Ray in a clinch, that's for sure.

The big love scene had to go.

I was afraid to tell Aldo, but as it turned out, he didn't give shit one. To tell you the truth, I don't think he ever read any of the pages until the night before each day's shoot. He probably didn't even know what the goddamn picture was about. And though Mara acted disappointed, she wasn't so great a thespian that I couldn't see the relief in her eyes.

I drove the Edsel (unjustly maligned, in my humble opinion) home over Laurel Canyon to the little cottage where I was hanging my hat in Studio City, when I decided to clear my head a little with a side trip down Mulholland Drive. Even as evening was falling like a closing night curtain, the temperature still hovered somewhere in the low nineties. I pulled my tie off and threw it over onto my hat in the passenger seat as I drove, seeking beauty anywhere I could find it.

I pulled over at a gravel overlook and watched the lights blink on like little eyes through the coffee carpet of smog. In spite of the heat it was turning into a nice night. The grid between the orange groves was coming gently to life, and it beckoned to me, called me into its heart. The scent of oranges drifted up through the cruddy fumes of internal combustion like fingers, finding me and caressing me. On the radio, Julie London was singing "Cry Me a River" as the river of Laurel Canyon Boulevard sliced through the San Fernando Valley below.

It was my own personal drive-in theater. I sat in the Edsel, the engine idling its gassy breath into the night air as Julie kissed my ear and the scent of orange tickled my nostrils. Lights below throbbed like a heartbeat. This vast silver screen beyond was calling out to me. I wanted to dive into its heart.

I dropped the transmission into gear and inched the front tires right to the precipice. The Edsel shivered as it stood at the brink, idling in Drive. My right foot suddenly weighed a hundred pounds, and it was sheer will that kept it from dropping to the floor on the accelerator. I put my left foot on the brake and my weighty right foot goosed the engine a little. The Edsel wanted to roar, it wanted to take its 300 horsepower and launch into space as I rode it straight down into the middle of Ventura Boulevard below. Only that damned left foot kept it from charging ahead... and it was getting tired. It wanted to fall to the floorboard and relax, while Mr. Right Foot wanted to slam to the floor.

I lifted the gearshift into Park just as Right won the war. As my foot dropped to the floor, the engine bellowed like a hungry beast, but the Edsel remained trembling in place at the lip of the Mulholland turnout. I was perspiring profusely now, giant pools of sweat darkening my Arrow shirt below the armpits. I climbed out of the car and lit up a Lucky, contributing to the many aromas the night sky had to offer.

I knew I was only Clark Kent, but I wanted to be Superman, leaping from the brink of the Santa Monica Mountains in a single bound and flying through the air. My landing would be less elegant than George Reeves', perhaps, resulting in a pile of mangled flesh and shattered bone, but it was my party and I could fly if I wanted to. And at the moment, I wanted to. Or rather, the beckoning San Fernando Valley laid out before me wanted me to.

A car pulled up and broke the spell: teenagers, looking for a spot to neck, and they were so hopped up they didn't think anything of pulling up within sight of another car. I tossed my Lucky butt to the gravel, stomped it into lifelessness, climbed back into the Edsel, and backed away from my perch at the edge of the world. I peeled out, headed back down home, and went to bed.

***

The next morning was like all the others. I woke up feeling like I was being born all over again. Not like a spiritual rebirth or reawakening or anything like that. Just like I was starting over every day, like I had no history, like I had no center. I felt like a puppet just going through the moves. I was overwhelmed with passivity, too laden with ennui to offer self-propulsion. When I was shooting, I was somebody: a director, a filmmaker, a guy who called the shots. When I was in between jobs, I was unmotivated, whiskered, an unidentifiable unflying object, glued to the Motorola television from *The Early Show* to *The Late Show*, chasing the classics and eating my heart out. Unloved and unloving, poor me. Glad I had a job to energize me, I rose at dawn, shat, showered and shaved, and drove off over the pass to Zuma Beach for our first day of location shooting.

The drive over the mountains to the beach was inspirational. As the sun rose through the hazel morning scrim, I felt at the center of a three-dimensional world. The Edsel and I passed through it like a pinball; it surrounded me, swaddled me, put me at its center as I slid through it. Through the expansive windshield, billboards and trees and houses and overpasses enveloped me, and the sensation of approach and departure had new meaning. The changing depth of focus stimulated my visual senses as I drew closer, then farther, from everything. My peripheral sight was filled with passing fancy, and I took it to the beach.

I had seen before, but today I had vision.

Aldo was already sitting on the sand in his chair, happily nursing his third orange juice of the morning (surely enhanced with Smirnoff), his eyes shaded by heavy Foster Grants, when I arrived. The girls were still in makeup and Bill Thompson was lugging the giant 3-D camera from his station wagon.

"What's the plan, Lee?" he asked me.

"I'm glad you asked," I said. "Let's see what we can do with this 3-D thing. Let's make some magic."

Inspired, even electrified by the morning drive, I got inventive. We lugged the camera under the lifeguard tower, using the legs as foreground. I pictured every shot through a window, taking full advantage of the possibilities of three dimensions. Hell, maybe I could even talk the mucky-mucks at Regal/Royal into mixing the soundtrack stereophonic. I felt like a kid, I felt like I did on the Lancaster picture—energized and creative—as I walked Bill through the day's setups. He was even older than me, and not used to working up a sweat, but I could tell my enthusiasm was catching. We planned the day's work, with wild, Dutch angles, moves between the legs of the terrified beachgoers, a traveling, chest-high shot of the blooming bodices of our beach girls. Feminine pulchritude may well be the cheapest, most satisfying special effect, and we had plenty of it.

I even had him whip together an underwater housing so we could get some shots of the creatures swimming at, past, and around us in all their distinctive dimensions.

I smiled as the girls came out of makeup. Even in fin and gills, these ladies were sexy little numbers, hell, maybe *because* of the fish parts, I don't know. Their bikinis were teeny, their bosoms anything but. When these luscious young lovelies came bouncing out of the surf, the global temperature was sure to rise.

The setups came a lot slower in 3-D than on a conventional picture because the camera was so damned big and so hard to lug around. I tried to talk the powers that be into another day or two so we could shoot some more moving shots—movement being where you can really *do* something with 3-D—but they were businessmen. They had no vision. They were paying me, sort of, for mine, but not letting it off the leash. I did what I could, and to tell you the truth, this was coming together a lot better than anything called *SHE CREATURES OF MORA TAU REEF* had any right to. I wasn't even going to mind putting my name on this little ugly duckling of a picture.

I started to wonder what Busby Berkeley would have done with this technology. Can you imagine what he'd have concocted in your face with all those kaleidoscopic shots and his dozens of dancing doyennes in three dimensions? That inspired me all over again, and I had the grips whip up a high tower to shoot directly down on the She Creatures as they emerged from the water. I had them construct a rope pulley system that allowed me to drop down and in on them: a poor man's stage crane, right out in the middle of Zuma Beach! I knew this shouldn't have been so much fun, but, against all expectations, I was having the time of my life. I felt like a juvenile delinquent. All I needed was a ducktail.

The sun began to drop, and I wished we were able to shoot in Technicolor. The sunset was downright breathtaking, a palette of reds and pinks and purples I had never seen before. The sun's last grin on the horizon spread out over the Pacific Ocean in a glorious yellow-orange ripple. We'd put in a pretty damned good day, and the cast and crew were justifiably tired, but still smiling.

As the thespians and their drones loaded up for home, I stayed behind, dazzled by the purple fall of evening, needing to see the full spread of night smother the coast. Before long, it was just me and my new best friend, the Vast Pacific, sending in its tide in hungry little waves. I was hypnotized by the deepening waters, entranced by the foaming little crests that lapped lazily at the shore. The sirens of the night were calling my name.

The sea settled as the moon and its attendant stars emerged, reflected in the newly darkened waters before me. For the first time, life itself seemed three-dimensional, and in 360 degrees. Little fingers of salt water tickled my feet through my Florsheims, but I didn't give a shit. Soon, it was covering my shoes, threatening to climb up my pants. I didn't give it the chance. I stepped out into the water, relishing the little chill against my skin. My pants sucked the water up through the gabardine, and they stuck to my legs. I stepped even deeper into Mother Ocean as she tugged me to her breast. I felt the need to nurse from her. Deeper into the water I stepped, coming to a stop when it reached my waist. The briny scent surrounded me with its tang. I looked all around, tempted to let it pull me out into its vastness and have its way with me.

I was at peace, and so was the sea, becoming so calm that its surface was turning to glass. If I so chose, I could just lie down on my back and let it float me to Hawaii. I wanted to be cast adrift. I wanted to be claimed by the water. I felt so, I don't know, *fetal* or something. I just wanted to go back into the amniotic fluid of the sea and return to the place of my birth. It would be so calm, so gentle, so simple, so utterly without stress. I almost gave in to my ultimate passivity, eager to swim with the fishes, when I simply turned my head and changed my mind.

What the fuck was up with me? Was I trying to kill myself? This was one happy goddamned day, and I don't get too many of those anymore. Things were looking up. What was the attraction to my own demise? They talk about this subconscious psychological mumbo-jumbo all the time, but you know, like Freud says, sometimes a cigar is just a cigar. Hell, maybe there's something to this headshrinker stuff. I thought that tomorrow I'd put in a call to Dr. Michaelson and get a recommendation.

But for now, I was all wet, so I climbed out of the sea like that lady on the clamshell, and headed for the Edsel. By now, the traffic to the Valley was light, and my drive home to Studio City was uneventful, and scored by Peggy Lee, Perry Como, and Mitch Miller.

***

I called it home, but it was just a rental. Comfortable, even if anonymously furnished, the little hillside bungalow was just a place to flop and make plans. It seemed particularly lonely that night after the flurry of activity and the sudden family that is a film crew. I missed my wife, at least until I thought about what that meant. I missed Mara. Hell, I guess I even missed Aldo. The starburst wall clock above the faux fireplace ticked loudly through the otherwise silent room. Jack Paar was on the TV with the sound off as I sat working on my notes for tomorrow's work. But the pad on the card table before me was blank, and I tapped on it with my ballpoint, trying to work up an idea. Shecky Greene was Paar's guest, and he must have said something awfully goddamned funny, because Paar and the audience were in tears. I stared at the screen, which cast a blue corona of light across the wall-to-wall carpet. I wanted to laugh, too, but I just couldn't work up the energy to cross the room and turn up the volume. So I pulled my attention from the cathode ray eye magnet and back to the page before me. I hadn't noticed, but I'd been doodling right in the center of the page: a great big spiral. It was one of those *HYPNOTIC EYE* type things, you know, just circling and circling and circling.

As I went over and over the spiral, the end of the pen nearest me did a little circular dance. I didn't know what my hands were doing; I was entranced by the pen's little Terpsichorean movement. The pen was expensive for a ballpoint, a little thank-you gift from John Newland for helping him out. It was buffed, shiny Tiffany's silver, sleek and dagger-like, gleaming under the harsh light of the pole lamp that stared down from over my head. I lifted the pen, and could actually make out my distorted, elongated reflection in its surface. I turned its point to face me, wiping off the little glob of ink that had collected there.

I drew the pen close to my face, then closer.

What would happen, I wondered, if I just kept bringing it closer? I held it an inch in front of my right eyeball. What would happen if I pulled it in, through the retina, entering the bull's-eye of the pupil, and eventually into my own brain? Would I hit a tickle center, and start to laugh uproariously? Would I release an aqueous sense of humor to gush across my face? Or would it be unbearably painful?

I held the pen still, just half an inch from my retina, amazed at how steady my hand was. It didn't jiggle a jot. I drew it even closer, and I swear I could feel the chill of the silver. I wanted to inscribe something on my own eyeball, but I didn't know what. Hypnotized by the gleaming pen, I wanted penetration.

Suddenly, the light from the television changed, and Jack and Shecky had given way to the test-pattern Indian chief that signified that Channel 4 had gone off the air for the night. I dropped the pen to the table and stared at it in horror.

Jesus, how long had I been holding it there?

I looked down at the spiral I had drawn on the pad on the card table and realized it was time for bed. I had to be up at dawn for work. Hell, I could suss out the details on the set; all those directors on the high-priced studio pictures seemed to. One more belt and I was fast asleep before I could even bother to brush my teeth.

***

Back to the beach. Craft service had lugged in the requisite doughnuts, and I staked a claim on the lemon-filled. Aristocracy on the film set has its privileges, even on a Royal or Regal set. I was alive even before the usual three cups of high-test black coffee, and was stalking my shots even before the first A.D. got there. Some rock'n'roll combo was going to be setting up to play on the beach in our big scene: my first musical number! She Creatures and some Negro singer I never heard of called Chubby Checker (I guess they couldn't afford Fats Domino, of whom I was an enormous fan) with something called "The Twist". We would test the artistic boundaries of 3-D technology today, that's for sure.

We spent a luxurious three hours choreographing and rehearsing the band, the dancers, and the She Creature attack, and frankly, I tried to work in some of that Busby Berkeley magic with our rope pulley and a jury-rigged dolly that could carry the immense camera. I got as fancy-schmancy with the setups as I could on this tight schedule, but if you don't mind my saying so, I think it was going to be a pretty impressive number. Maybe we could show Arkoff a little something about how to stage one of these teenager monster pictures.

It was all going swimmingly (sorry). Chubby's song turned out to be a pretty nifty little tune you could dance to; maybe they could even get some airplay with it. If his little dance caught on, it would be good for the picture. The girls were stunning, fins and all. We had a bunch of local kids there to dance, and they seemed pretty happy so long as we kept the hot dogs and root beer coming. They seemed to get a charge out of the music, too. I decided that I had to ride the beast myself. I hadn't operated camera since the turn of the last decade, but I was having such a good time that I had to climb back on the horse. Spirits were high and the music playback was loud. Surrounded by all these kids and their music, it felt like *American Bandstand* on the beach.

It took two dolly grips to shove me and the camera through the dancers and past Chubby as the amphibious girls broke out of the waves and charged into the routine. They were troopers, these chicks. Casting had recruited them from the burly clubs on the Strip and a couple of the shadier modeling agencies in town, but they were game and beautiful and weren't afraid to show a little skin. Or a lot.

So I was charging through the action, my eye pressed against the viewfinder, when the glamorous Queen of the She Creatures, Miss Mara Corday, emerged regally from the depths of the sea, trailing seaweed and webbed feet, and it was quite a sight: creepy and sexy at the same time. Her remarkable breasts were holstered by a seashell brassiere, and her stride was slinky, confident, even a little sinister.

She approached the camera as the camera approached her, her eyes pinning the lens and catching the light just so. And then, the jack-in-the-box moment; just as she filled the frame with her magnificence, the Sea Beast sprang up behind her, a giant, green, fang-filled fish head with scaly claws and a mighty roar. There wouldn't be a dry seat in the theatre. It even made me jump.

Ocular

Unfortunately, Janos, the guy in the rubber monster suit, was not known for his grace. As he rose from the brine, one scaly, finny foot slapped onto the other, and he went tumbling fish-head first into the delectable Miss Corday, snagging her delicate seashell holster and popping it free of her notable assets, which in turn came crashing into the giant camera. She shouted as she fell against the machinery titty first, leaving an unmistakable nipple print in the center of the lens like a kiss.

She shouted and I screamed. You see, Janos fell into Mara who fell into the camera, which crammed the viewfinder deep into my eye socket, bursting the eyeball and sending its liquid center down the right side of my face like a wash of tears. I pulled away from the camera with a wet, smacking *pop*.

I'm told that Mara kicked Janos right in the jewels, she was so furious, but I was preoccupied. I could see the deflated white sac of my eyeball—or what was left of it—dangling innocently from the viewfinder. I spun around, not knowing where to turn or what to do. The eye was obviously beyond salvation, but there was no pain. It was just the horror of it, the old E.C. Comics-style injury-to-the-eye motif. But worst of all was that hideous *pop*: wet, sharp, gelid, and instantly deflating.

It took a while for anyone to notice. The scene was rowdy to begin with, with that Twist music and all, and the kids were really hamming it up with the dancing and the cutie-pie fish girls. What with Mara and then the Monster, well, it was all pretty cacophonous. There were screams aplenty before I tossed my own shriek into the mix. Maybe they thought that was direction or something.

But while everybody was huddled around Mara, tending to her delicate situation (or more likely trying to catch a peep of her suddenly uncensored display of pulchritude), I was left to my own cyclopean devices.

At least for a while.

I held my hand against the newly vacant socket, the tip of my little finger accidentally dipping into the evacuated orbital cave like a nacho into salsa, and it was at that point that I lost our lavishly catered lunch.

Suddenly, Janos seemed a lot less than scary. His phony-baloney fish suit just seemed silly on the klutz; you could even see the goddamn zipper, for Christ's sake. No, clarity of vision was foisted suddenly upon me through one eye. I stood at the center of the maelstrom like the star of a Bert I. Gordon picture, and it wasn't pretty. There was a long, loud *screeeeech* as somebody knocked the needle across the record we used for playback, and the mob went quiet when they saw me drop my gore-soaked fingers from my face, only to see the gaping red and black hole where my eye used to be. I stood dazed and confused in the center of this Clearasil ad, striking terror into the hearts of the kids who were our future.

I was about to win the sympathy vote.

***

I woke up in an eighth storey room at St. Johns in Santa Monica, thick gauze bandages covering my eye. Mara was there, a single, gentle tear clearing a line of pale white flesh from under her foundation. Bert was there, too, looking pale and horrified. They tried to offer me a brave smile, but I could see the horror, distaste, and pity beneath it. A paunchy, silver-haired doctor, all in white like the room itself, gave them a private nod, and they left me to face the music alone.

I was a little loopy from whatever medications had sent me flying, but I was calm, too. I knew what had happened. "Well?" I said.

The doctor took a deep, theatrical breath. "I'm afraid you've lost an eye, Mr. Benton."

"Like hell," I told him.

"I beg your pardon?"

"I haven't lost a damned thing. It was hanging right there on the viewfinder, like the morning laundry."

He didn't know how to react, but I let him know that it was okay to smile. So he did. But it was fake, and didn't look very good on him. I think he preferred the grave, professional look.

Despite the new hole in my head, I felt okay. I mean, it was no treat to only see from one side of my nose, but I could live with that. I asked him to send in Mara and Bert, in that order, preferably, and they came in sheepishly, not knowing how to act. I wanted to put them at ease. I guess it's just a holdover from the job: I was the patient, but I wanted them to be comfortable.

"I'll tell you something: I'm not getting one of those Sammy Davis, Jr., glass eyes, that's for sure. I don't want anybody trying to figure out which eye to talk to. I'm just going to wear a patch, like a pirate. Maybe get a little of that John Ford respect, what do you think, Bert?"

Mara and Bert exchanged a look; this wasn't going to be as difficult as they thought.

"That's right!" Bert said, his drooping jowls lifting at the corners. "I think we can make this work for you! You even got into this morning's *Times*!"

"Front page or Metro?" I asked.

"Metro."

"Well, it's better than a poke in the eye… oops." Too meaningful. It wasn't what I intended, but I'll take a joke wherever I can find one, even if I made it myself.

Mara came over and gingerly settled her petite kiester onto the corner of the bed. She laid a delicate, porcelain hand gently on one of mine, and asked, "How do you feel?"

"A hell of a lot better now," I told her with a smile I hoped she wouldn't consider hungry. "Don't tell Dick how much better I feel." I knew she wouldn't.

"Naughty!" She lightly slapped my wrist.

"It's the pills talking." She took that for an answer, for the time being at least.

I saw a figure flash past my newly abridged peripheral vision, just to the right of the mountain of my nose. I turned, but didn't see anybody.

"Who was that?"

"Who was what?" Bert said.

"I just saw someone over in that corner."

The three of them looked at each other like in an old Laurel and Hardy short.

The doctor, wise man of science that he was, said, "It must have been the shadow of somebody walking past the door." That worked for the moment. There were more important things on my mind.

"So Bert." He raised his brows in anticipation. "What's the company doing with the production?"

The jowls dropped again. "Let's talk about that a little later. Let's get you back in peak fighting form."

"They're not taking an insurance claim, are they?"

"What insurance would that be? This isn't a studio picture, Lee."

"Are they going to wait for me?"

Mara was getting exceedingly uncomfortable now, and thought she could buy me off with a goodbye kiss. Well, she was right. She leaned over me, offering me a glimpse of her Himalayan beauty, and painted a blood-red tulip imprint on my forehead. "I've got to go now, Lee. I'm glad to see you're doing okay." Her face flushed a bit, she hurried out of the room.

I looked back at Bert, who was squirming. "Are they replacing me?"

Bert nodded. "Replaced. Past tense."

"Already? Jesus, it's barely been a day!"

"I did what I could, but this is a low-budget thing, Lee. They can't afford to lose a single day. They're shooting now."

My single eye was unblinking. "Who'd they get, Bert? Who's replacing me?"

"They got some guy who really loves the spooky science fiction stuff. Fella named Eddie Wood. They say he's good with a nickel. Turns it into a quarter."

I sighed, my good humor evaporating. "I think I'd like to get a little rest now."

"Lee," Givens whined, "you can't direct a 3-D movie with one eye!"

"It ain't the job, Bert," I told him. "Just allow me a few moments of solitary, meditative depression, would you?" Both doctor and agent were happy to leave me alone in the room.

It was all white, like I said. Even the sunlight flooding the room was a harsh, smoggy white. It all seemed so flat, so utterly without contour, shape, or subtlety. Then I remembered that I was seeing it through a single eye. Of course it was flat. I could only see in two dimensions now. It was at that moment that I realized how I'd spent my life seeing in two dimensions, an entire lifetime of viewing life through the lens. It took the removal of an eye and the third dimension to allow me to see.

Oh, Christ, the irony.

And there he was again. That was no fucking shadow this time. I whipped my head around, but the dark whisk of a figure was nowhere to be found. And he'd be easy to spot, even only in height and width.

But he was gone.

I stood up from the hospital bed and almost collapsed as the blood rushed from my cerebral cortex. I grabbed onto the bed rail as my brain whirled like a merry-go-round. Maybe I wasn't as okay as I thought I was.

As horrible as it sounds to lose an eye—and don't get me wrong, it's pretty fucking awful—recovery time, at least in my case, was not that big a deal. The eye had come out in a clean pop, breaking free of the ganglia with a clean rip. Not a whole lot of nerve endings there, at least the kind that give you pain, so the doctor and the Funk and Wagnall's tell me. Sure there was the danger of infection, but they'd gotten to it quickly and efficiently, and I wore my patch with pride. Maybe I could get some dime store Picasso to paint a nice blue eyeball on it or something.

After a few days, I went home to convalesce in my little Studio City bungalow, just me and my remaining eyeball alone in front of the television. I wondered what this Wood character was doing with my movie, how he was surely fucking it up. I'd actually worked up a good deal of enthusiasm for our little cinematic mutt, and now it was smoke. I had mixed feelings about the movie: I wanted it to be good because of all the work I'd put into it, but I wanted it to be a piece of shit because this new character they brought in *the next day* to replace me had surely botched it beyond redemption. I wanted Regal/Royal to notice the difference. Hell, I could have finished the picture; they could have pushed a few days. I was up to it.

I fell asleep in front of *SANDS OF IWO JIMA* on the Philco, the painkillers I thought were unnecessary having sung me a lullaby.

I woke to the "Star Spangled Banner" pronouncing the end to another broadcast day, and my entire head was throbbing. A shot glass was gripped tightly in my hand, but it was empty. It was time for bed.

I headed into the bathroom and brushed my teeth, the Ipana sickeningly sweet through the scrim of bourbon. As I spat into the sink, there it was again, over the bridge of my nose: a man, or at least his silhouette, and it looked like he was standing in the shower. I snapped my head around so fast I could have sued myself for whiplash, but when I faced the tub, there was nothing there but a cake of Dial.

"Who's there?" I shouted, knowing there would be no reply. And I was right. The little house on the hill just sat there in silent defiance. Unnerved, I finished my evening toilet, and headed for bed. I climbed under the covers in my undershirt and BVDs, but there was to be no sleep for me that night. Even under the influence of the painkillers and half a fifth of bourbon—and it was good Kentucky stuff, too—I spent a watchful night awake.

Shadows from the jacarandas outside reached across the bed and onto the floor like spiny arms and spindly fingers, but that was not what I saw. I saw a man, and damn it, I knew it was not a hallucination.

Just as I rolled over onto my side and was about to drift off to a slumber I was eager to embrace, I spotted him again in my periphery, sitting in the chair opposite and watching me. I sat up with a jerk, just like in one of those cheesy dream sequences that are getting so popular and overused these days.

You've got it figured out by now, and I don't need to state the obvious. Do I really have to tell you there was nothing there?

But this was the weird thing. Now that I've got one eye, everything looks like a movie to me: just flat and without shape. I mean, I can *see* the shapes, but it's knowledge of how the physics of form function from years of experience. But it's like a movie, or a photograph, and there is no true depth. In other words, it's easy for me to bump into things, and I do it all the time.

But this guy, whoever he was, had form and shape and three goddamn dimensions. But I wasn't seeing him with my eye. I saw him with the eye that's missing, with the socket that used to have an eye. He was only in my peripheral vision, like through my *psychic* eye or something. Because when I turned to see him with the eye than could see, the solitary orb still connected to my brain, there was no trace of him.

Hell, I say *him*, and I sure thought it was the same guy every time, but perhaps I was wrong. Maybe there was an entire world on the other side of my nose that I was not aware of, like another dimension—a fourth or fifth?—or something that was calling out to me. If that was the case, however, they were doing a pretty lousy job of it; this fellow or these fellows kept slipping away each time I tried to see them.

Of course, it might have been my own fault. I was trying to *see* him when he couldn't be seen in the traditional sense. Maybe there was a better way to communicate with him, if there was a *him* in the first place.

***

The sun rose, and I was cooked for the day. I don't sleep easily under the best of circumstances, and this was among the worst. Once the sun was up, sleep was beyond my reach, and I was doomed to a day of wakefulness. The morning heat predicted that the sun was to be brutal that day, and a box of light scorched through the little cottage through the picture window. My eye was bleary and bloodshot and my brain throbbed. The vista between the bridge of my nose and the grand view to its right was bleached bright, and my head listed to the side to support it. It's a good thing I never shot a picture in Cinemascope; I'd have to constantly be turning my head from side to side just to see the damned thing.

I stumbled into the bathroom and soaked my head under the cold-water faucet. That woke me up, but it didn't stop the throbbing. It also did not discourage fresh appearances by my new best friend.

It seemed that he was now at every corner, a dark shadow at every juncture, waiting to share a secret with me. But at each and every turn, he vanished. Of course, he couldn't vanish if he was never really there, could he?

I stepped out onto the porch and picked up the paper, and there he was, just outside the door. I took the *Times* into the kitchen and started some coffee brewing, and there was a glimpse of him just behind the refrigerator.

"Tell me what the fuck you want!" I screamed at him, but there was no answer. Not that I really expected one.

I threw the paper down on the kitchen table and opened it up to the crossword puzzle while I waited for the coffee to brew. As I looked down at the puzzle and started to fill in the little letter blocks, I could sense his shadow and shape standing over me, just to my left. This time, however, I did not look up. His shadow blocked my puzzle with darkness, and with throbbing head and shaking hands, I closed my eye in fear and gripped the pencil tight.

I could feel his presence hovering over me as I baked in the window of sunlight that slowly crept over me. My heart was pounding like the score to BEN HUR. I could barely take a breath. I could feel his heat emanating, he was so close.

I gradually lifted my head, never daring to open the eye that could see.

Through my closed eyelid I saw moiré patterns, rushing blood cells, little bursting sparks of brightness in the red-blackness. But beyond that, I saw a man. Though I could not see the kitchen, its walls, the refrigerator, the oven, the sink, or even the windows, my closed eye was filled with summer sunlight. And in front of that eyelid-diffused light, the man still stood.

He appeared as a silhouette at first, even through my closed eye, swaddled in the sunlight. His shape was sharply defined. He was about my height, it seemed, and appeared to be going to paunch. As I adjusted to the sunlight, his features became clearer under the hat that shaded him. His face bristled with several days of neglect; his posture was tired but needy. I could make out his mouth; he was trying to speak to me.

Soon, a light bloomed around him, and the mallet of realization clobbered me with its full force. It was like staring into a mirror. Except for the two cool blue eyes staring beseechingly at me, the man was *me.*

Was he my ghost? Had I died during the night? Or even earlier?

I knew if I opened my eye, my contact with my doppelganger would dissipate, so I dared not. I clenched my eye tighter, and he became clearer. He reached toward me with his hands as he spoke, but it was a silent as a Buster Keaton two-reeler.

What the hell was I trying to tell me?

The me with two eyes, the one standing over me casting a shadow which would disappear if I opened my eye, really needed me to hear what he had to say. He was shouting, but there wasn't a sound coming from his mouth. And I was a lousy lip reader. I could tell it was important, that I was being beseeched. What was he trying to tell me? From the looks of the other me's expression, it was a matter of life and death, something I direly needed to know.

He (I) knew something I didn't know, and my heart began to pound. I felt that I beheld the secret of life and death, or that I was on death's boundary. My two-eyed guide was reaching out to me, begging me to hear him. Maybe he knew what this whole veil of tears was about; perhaps he could help me find meaning in the five decades that had made up this thing I called my life. Or maybe, just maybe, he stood on the threshold of another world, a fourth dimension, one you couldn't enter just by wearing funny cardboard glasses.

He pointed down at my hand with his, but I didn't see anything at first. I thought maybe there was a message in the crossword puzzle, and I asked him if that were the case. He shook his head, violently, but just kept pointing, saying something I just could not hear.

Then, the curtain parted as I looked down at the pencil gripped tightly in my right hand. I looked up at him and he smiled a smile that reached both his eyes. I lifted the pencil and he nodded, slowly at first, like one of those phony birds that dips his head into a glass of water, but then more forcefully.

I stared at the pencil, finally figuring it out. If I could only see him, or me, after losing an eye, I knew what I must do to hear what he—or I—was so desperate to tell me. I had to hear what he had to say; I had to take that step into what lay beyond the silver screen of Hollywood vision.

I slowly lifted the pencil up, then, with all my might, slammed it deep into my right ear. The sound was deafening.

Wide-Shining Light

Rio Youers

I wouldn't have gone to the school reunion but for the fact that Lorna had left me three weeks before, and I felt resentful and disillusioned, and yes . . . in need of company. Perhaps not the best state of mind with which to revisit old acquaintances, but in the raw weeks following a separation – particularly one as volatile as mine and Lorna's – a person will often feel that they are drowning, and at such times will cling to anything. Thus, I treated myself to some new clothes and a haircut, assumed a brave face, and attended the reunion at the Bellston Mark Hotel (three miles from our old school, but with the distinct advantage of being able to sell alcohol). I had hoped to rekindle a friendship, or, better yet, discover a thread that I might weave into a new beginning. I clung to this possibility as the cold water lapped first around my waist, then around my shoulders, then around my face. It covered my mouth, nose, and eyes, and just when I believed my lungs would burst, a hand reached down and pulled me free.

"Martin? Martin Sallis?"

It had been twenty-five years since I'd heard that voice. I turned, drink in hand, and looked at the man who, as a boy, had been my best friend through primary and secondary school. He'd lost most of his hair and gained a paunch, but his voice –

other than it being deeper – was the same. That familiar inflection, and, unmistakably, the interdental lisp, turning the sibilants in my surname into "th" sounds: Thallith. His eyes were the same, as well. Light brown with delicate orange flecks. A person can change stature, hairstyle, even face shape, but their eyes will always remain the same.

I didn't need to look at his nametag. I offered my hand.

"Good to see you, Richard."

We shook emphatically. Red wine spilled over the rim of my glass, onto my hand. The following morning, I would find maroon stains on my shirt cuff.

He grinned. "It's been a long time."

"It has."

"You moved to . . .?"

"Thame."

"That's right. I knew it was somewhere in Oxfordshire."

A pause while we looked at each other, smiling. Richard patted the top of his head. "Sunroof," he said, and I told him he looked good for his age, which wasn't entirely true, but he nodded gracefully, enquired into my line of work, and from there we fell into easy conversation, with much laughter, and I felt the years receding like waves having already crashed.

Even then I thought it peculiar how we opened up to one another. The previous twenty-five years had, in effect, rendered us strangers, yet we forsook reticence and shared like . . . well, like old friends. I found it refreshing. Liberating, even. So much of my life with Lorna had been spent behind a wall. One that she had built. Perhaps it was the occasion (or more likely the alcohol), but I relaxed into a space where before there was impediment and felt that Richard did the same.

Our former classmates danced unabashedly to songs that topped the charts when we were at school, but neither Richard nor I – in keeping with our younger selves – joined them; we had never sought the limelight – were content, both, with our roles of little remark. This reserve was one of many reasons for Lorna's discontent. My "spectacular nothingness," she called it. I preferred Richard's term: under the radar. However viewed, it suited me – suited *us* – and we sat while the music played. Not that we weren't enjoying ourselves; the discourse flowed as readily as the alcohol, and, in timely fashion, we switched from

Zinfandel to Glenfiddich as our conversation turned to matters of the heart.

"How long have you been married?" Richard asked, indicating, with the rounded base of his tumbler, the ring on my finger.

"Seven years," I replied, and sighed. "I should probably take this off, though."

"Oh?"

"We're recently separated," I said. "It's too long a story. One for another occasion, perhaps. Suffice to say our accord has . . . faltered."

Richard's light brown eyes gleamed. "Do you still love her?"

I rattled the ice cubes in my glass, took a sip, and contemplated my wretched heart. If I looked beyond the disillusionment and self-pity, and assessed my marriage for what it was, did love remain? I thought, on my part, it did, but was too drunk and emotional to be certain. I needed time and perspective, both of which Lorna had granted me. She had also granted me torment, of course, and loneliness. Our union had gone from being blessed – witnessed by God, no less – to a tumult of lies and heartaches. I was guilty of spectacular nothingness. Lorna was guilty of abuse, infidelity, and spite.

"She's an unthinkable cunt," I said.

Richard raised an eyebrow. "Perhaps you'll revise that opinion with a sober mind."

I smiled and shrugged, took an ice cube into my mouth and crunched it between my teeth. "And you?" A vague gesture in Richard's direction. "A special someone?"

"Very special," he replied at once, and I watched the emotion touch his face like rain. His gaze faded and skimmed away. "Constance. My wide-shining light. My shelter from the storm."

I swallowed the ice. It leaked into my chest and I imagined it, as bright as dye.

"And you didn't bring her tonight?"

His eyes snapped back to mine. Clear again. "She died eight years ago." He finished his drink with a hiss, showing his teeth.

"I'm so sorry," I offered.

"Not at all." Richard set his tumbler down and ran his finger around the rim until it sang. "I'm a stronger man for having

Constance in my life at all. And her death was a deeply spiritual moment. Quite beautiful, in fact."

I had no idea how to respond. All I could do was hold his gaze, and even that was challenging.

"Her light saved me," he said.

I nodded; all I could manage.

A rare lull in the conversation, which was lifted when a frightful redhead, her nametag illegible, invited us to dance. We declined, politely of course, and she shuffled away, leaving us to smirk in a juvenile fashion.

Richard tapped the base of his tumbler on the table. "Another drink, friend?"

I replied, "A double, I think."

And so continued our evening, with conversation, always affable, touching upon many topics, and the alcohol flowing with disconcerting ease. The deejay's choice of music ensured the dance floor was always full, and the class of 1987 kept things lively. Beneath whirling lights we saw bravado and coquettishness, ostentation and acquiescence. There was naked skin, stolen kisses, groping, fumbling, embarrassment. Richard and I opined that, of the latter, there would be even more the following morning. We watched it all from our pedestal, wearing smiles some would no doubt consider supercilious, though, again, I prefer Richard's term: detached. "These people live clockwork lives," he said, flapping a hand at the dance floor. "They do the same thing day in, day out, marking the hours like wooden figurines in a clock." Needless to say, we exchanged contact information with only each other at the end of the night. The old fashioned way: with business cards. None of this Facebook nonsense.

"I live in Marlow," Richard said as we walked to the taxi rank. "Not such a drive to Thame. I'd like to see more of you."

"Absolutely," I concurred. "I've had an enjoyable evening. Very much needed." And it *was*. I already felt lighter, somehow, as if a stone, resting against some vital place inside me, had been lifted, or at the very least nudged aside, allowing me access to the man I'd been before Lorna came into my life. By noon of the next day – before my hangover had even worn off – that stone would fall back into place, and I'd again be secured to the emotional pillory of dissolution. But at that moment, with Richard beside me and my head lightly spinning, I was unbound.

"I can see why we were such good friends at school," Richard said. "We're really quite alike."

"I'll say." I smiled at him.

"The same disposition, politics—"

"Kindred spirits."

"Quite." He laughed, swaying a little, the heels of his expensive shoes clicking off the pavement. His shadow, beneath the streetlights, appeared disproportionately longer than mine. "And here we are, into our forties, with women absent from our lives."

"Better to have loved and lost," I offered. "Or so they say."

"So they say."

We arrived at the taxi rank, where our separate cabs were waiting. Mine would take me to a better grade of hotel than the Bellston Mark. Richard's would take him to his home in Marlow, four miles away. I thought, for a moment, that he was going to invite me along, so that we could imbibe into the early hours while Shostakovich blared from Denon speakers. He didn't though; he held out his hand and I took it, shook firmly. I wasn't to know he had other plans – that Alexandra Locke, his latest victim, lay bound and gagged in his garage, and would be dismembered and disposed of before morning light.

"It's been a pleasure, Richard," I said.

"Absolutely," he agreed, and patted the pocket in which he'd placed my business card. "I'll call."

"Do."

And with that he got into his taxi. I watched as it pulled away, out of sight, wondering if I'd discovered my thread. And I *had* – only it wasn't one I controlled, one I could weave. Rather, it dangled loosely from my state of mind, and Richard had hold of the end.

He pulled. I unravelled.

***

Is there anything beyond redemption? Without hope or worth? Surely even the cruellest acts have extenuating circumstances, and the cruellest souls a vein of good? This is certainly true of Richard Chalk, my old friend. Yes, I saw his murderous side, but I also saw his kindliness. Small things, like calling his elderly mother to say that he was thinking about her - a thirty-second exchange that doubtless made her day. And much bigger things, like organising a fun-run to raise money for Huntington's disease. I wonder, did Richard balance his wickedness because he feared for his mortal soul, or did he genuinely wish to do good? I cannot pretend to understand the mind of a serial killer. Only one thing is for certain: he flashed between light and dark like a coin-flip in the moonlight.

Redemption, perhaps, for the man who murdered eleven women in eight years, but my marriage was beyond salvation. In the weeks following the reunion, I endeavoured to repair what was broken. I first took the old-fashioned approach; I sent Lorna flowers and gifts, and had Steve Wright dedicate "Nights in White Satin" to her on BBC Radio Two. These things didn't work. If anything, they further soured her opinion of me. So I embraced my spiritual side (something Lorna constantly requested I do) and sought the advice of a medical intuitive. She – her name was Echo – claimed my Prana was agitated and my chakras out of line and referred me to an energy healer. I went not because I believed it would work, but because I wanted Lorna to see how committed I was to winning her back, and how open to change. Alas, my efforts were in vain; Lorna had no investment in reconciliation. Our separation had graduated to an irreparable rift – as I was to discover over a "reality check luncheon" at Gee's in Oxford.

"How do I look?" I asked her, seated, wine in hand. Lorna had ordered tap water – would not allow herself anything as daring as Perrier, and certainly nothing alcoholic, for fear this luncheon be regarded a pleasure. I wanted her to loosen up, of course, enjoy herself, but she sipped water, ate salad, and sat board-stiff throughout.

"The same," she replied. "Gaunt." She had on a flesh-tone lipstick that made her mouth appear a thin, uncompromising line. "Why? Is there a reason you should look different?"

"I've had my chakras aligned," I said.

"Your chakras?"

"I'm energetically balanced." I inhaled vigorously and took another sip of wine. "Feels splendid. Apparently, my sacral chakra was in a perilous state."

She sighed and looked away from me, her expression one of disdain. Such an ugly reaction. It twisted her face like a rag. Hard to imagine it the same face that would pulse pleasurably while we made love, and glow afterwards, sometimes for hours. I wondered if any part of the old Lorna – the one who'd whispered "I do" seven years ago – remained. I reached across the table, perhaps to grasp it, if it were there, but she pulled away, folded her hands, placed them in her lap.

I touched the tablecloth where her hand had been only seconds before. I imagined a cat chasing reflected light.

"This luncheon—" I started.

"Lunch," Lorna interjected. "It's 2012, Martin. Nobody calls it luncheon anymore."

I bit my lip and wished Richard were sitting beside me. We'd have ordered from the luncheon menu with glee. "This lunch," I said. "I'd assumed its purpose was to discuss reconciliation."

She looked at me again and her eyes were chips of granite. "All I wanted was to meet with you. Briefly. Lunch was *your* idea. And no . . . we won't be discussing reconciliation. It's time for a reality check, Martin."

"You want a divorce?"

"Yes." A quick, unwavering reply.

The waiter came over and Lorna found a smile for him, ordering her sterile salad (she even turned down the vinaigrette) while I – unsmiling – ordered the veal. I could feel my carotid artery thumping as I enquired into the tenderness of the meat. The waiter assured me it was gourmet, and I assured him that nothing less than absolute atrophy of the muscle would suffice.

Lorna raised her eyebrow but said nothing. Her hand – no ring on her finger, I noted – was back on the table. I imagined driving my fork through it.

"Divorce," I said. "What would your mother say?" Lorna's mother was a devout Christian who kept the scripture closer than her undergarments. No doubt she would decry the putting asunder of that which God joined together. "She'll be beside herself."

"This is not about my mother's contentment, it's about mine." Lorna flicked tawny hair from her brow and sipped her tap water. "Besides, she gave me the number of an excellent solicitor."

"She did?"

A dry smile in reply.

I groaned – more of a growl, actually – and glugged my wine, spilling it down my chin, managing to draw the attention of the table to our left. I stared at them, eyebrows knitted, chin stained, until they went back to their meals. Then I reached across the table and grabbed Lorna's hand before she could pull away.

"Lorna, darling, I—"

"Let *go* of my hand." She kept her voice low, but I could see the stringy muscle in her forearm tensing as she tried to pull free.

"Let's just—"

"Do you want me to scream?"

I let go and her hand snapped back so forcefully that the table wobbled, and her glass almost toppled over. Again, we drew the attention of other diners. I saw their scowls and heard them mumble disapprovals. It took a few moments for the general hum of conversation to resume.

"If you insist on making a scene," Lorna said, rubbing the back of her hand, "I'll leave."

"You already left," I said.

"Show some dignity, Martin."

"Perhaps if you were to show some compassion . . ."

"Oh really!" Now it was her turn to scowl. "It was compassion that brought me here. I could – *should* – have had my solicitor send you a letter."

I closed my eyes and recalled a breathing exercise my energy healer – Leaf, his name was Leaf – taught me: four-seven-eight breath. Slowly inhale through the nose for a four-count. Hold for seven. Exhale for eight. I repeated until I reached a plain of calm as broad as a motorway. No, a runway . . . a runway of calm that I could take off from and soar, jets trembling.

"Your nostrils are flaring, Martin."

Four-seven-eight.

"Martin?"

"I don't want a divorce," I said, and looked at her squarely. "I believe our marriage worth rescuing. I can change, Lorna. I *have* changed. Let me prove it to you."

I saw something in her eyes. A smoothing of the granite. As close as she would come to lenity. It made me ache for the woman who had promised herself to me, and who could make me breathe, as if for the first time, with a well-chosen word, or the gentlest touch.

"It's over," she said.

And this ache . . . I buried it, like I would have to bury all hope of reconciliation.

"Over?"

"Yes, Martin."

I'd had more enjoyable luncheons, if truth be told. We sat in near silence, merely picking at our food (the veal was indeed gourmet, but my appetite, sadly, absent). I looked mostly out the window, but occasionally at Lorna, hoping to see a trace of the woman I had lost. But she was a stone, dull grey and bluntly edged. She avoided eye contact, and the closest she came to conversation was to remark on Alexandra Locke, the Hemel Hempstead woman who'd been missing for four weeks. A chap at a nearby table was reading the *Telegraph*, the pages folded so that her black and white image stared woefully at us.

"That poor woman," Lorna said. "I wonder if they'll ever find her."

She excused herself a short time later to use the facilities, and I did something I'm not proud of; I fished her mobile phone from her coat pocket and read several text messages (the phone was password protected, but you don't share almost one quarter of your life with someone without learning a little something about them, and I accessed the device on only the third try). I sought evidence of another man, if I'm being honest, reasoning that my solicitor should have all information pertinent to the separation. I found nothing incriminating, however, only a number of messages to her harridan friends that were unnecessarily spiteful towards me. *He's a pithless cretin and I can't wait to get him out of my life,* one of them read. And another: *I'm doing the right thing, Molly; I couldn't live another second with that pompous arse.* Reading them made me remember the vindictiveness and anger directed at me in the final year of our marriage, how she brimmed with scorn, and pulled away when I tried to get close.

Lorna returned from the ladies' room and grabbed her coat from the back of her chair. The phone was safely back in her pocket by this time, but I still seethed. *Pithless cretin,* I thought. *Pompous arse.* I could barely look at her.

"I should leave," she said.

"Yes," I said. "You should."

Granite eyes and an uncompromising line. "My solicitor will be in touch."

"Don't expect me to make this easy for you." Spoken through clenched teeth, this sounded anything but pithless.

She swept from the restaurant, tawny hair bouncing, and I poured another glass of wine. I considered ordering a Glenfiddich, a double, and then another . . . drinking until the world's hardness was smoothed away, but to do so would be to risk making a scene. So I chose, as ever, spectacular nothingness.

The next few weeks were difficult, a whirlwind of angry phone calls, legal advice, and threats. I sought comfort from my family, who gave as much as they could, but have never really been attuned to matters of the heart. "An incorrigible woman," my father offered. "If she were a dog, I'd have her put down." My mother's approach was less cutthroat, but equally unhelpful. "A lot of the time it comes down to a woman's sexual needs," she said. "Perhaps you'll be happier with someone less . . . particular."

Little surprise, then, that Richard Chalk became my primary source of support, as good a friend – at least to begin with – as one could hope for. I let him into my life and offered my trust. I served it to him, as vulnerable and atrophied, and in as many pieces, as the veal at Gee's. When I needed to spill my soul, he was there, always with the right amount of empathy, and always telling me what I needed to hear.

I invited him into my home.

I showed him photographs of Lorna. So help me God.

"Her eyes," he said. I'm sure there were other comments, but I can only remember those two words: her eyes.

How strange that I should open myself to him so quickly, so readily, given the twenty-five-year gulf in our relationship. A person will experience much in the years between secondary school and middle age, and their character – their state of mind – will adjust, sometimes for the better, sometimes for the worse. Even so, I thought I knew Richard. I thought he was my friend.

"We're really quite alike," he said to me, as he so often would. Perhaps he believed, if he said it enough, he could make it true. I admit, even I started to believe it.

"Quite," I said with a smile.

"What a shame we didn't stay in touch when we finished school," he said. "All those wasted years."

"We can make up for it now," I assured him.

We were sitting outside The Angel in Henley-on-Thames, a beautiful September evening, if a little cool, with the late sun dancing on the river in burnt oranges and pinks, and traffic chasing across the stone bridge that arced to our left. I sighed with rare contentment and sipped my ale: Brakspear Oxford Gold, of good body. Richard had ordered the same. And so we sat with our identical drinks, beneath the wing of evening light, cut from the same cloth, you'd think.

"Are you feeling any better?" Richard asked.

"Actually, I am." I looked at him and nodded. "Thank you."

"Good ale," he held up his glass, "and good company. Works every time."

But it was more than that, lovely as these things were. And it was more than the pink light on the river and the somnolent buzz of traffic on the bridge. I felt I'd turned a corner in the last couple of days. Perhaps *many* corners. I was resolute, where before I had been wavering. Strong, where I had been . . . *pithless*. Also, I had grown to loathe Lorna, where once I'd known only love. We'd had furious exchanges on the telephone, mainly because I'd refused to sign the petition for divorce (some small power, and I revelled in it). Her cruelty shocked me. She insisted, over and over, that she regretted ever having laid eyes on me, and how thankful she was that we'd never had children. She wished a car accident on me. A "crippling" one. And cancer – *cancer!* It was as if she were digging into a depthless sack of abuses, and hurling them at me one after the other. I gauged from this just how deeply she was hurting, and how cruel of me not to give her what she sought. Thus, that very afternoon, I acceded – put pen to paper, sealed the petition in one of my personalised toile-lined envelopes, and dropped it in the pillar box.

Were there tears? Yes . . . many, in fact. But they were not all tears of woe. They fell, and I found strength. They splashed on my shirt, and I found relief. So yes, I wept, and for a long time, but even a cocoon has to crack.

Richard called at precisely the moment I thought some company would be nice. He asked if I wanted to join him for drinks by the river – his judgement, as ever, exact.

The Thames's rippling surface deepened with bronze colour. A boat called Mystery sliced through, creating a V-shaped wake that rolled and broke musically against the banks.

"Such fortuity," I said, "meeting you, renewing our friendship at a time I needed it most. This has been arguably the most challenging period of my life, and I'm grateful to have had you beside me."

"Destiny," Richard said, although for a moment I thought, because of his lisp, he'd said, 'death to me.' He raised his glass and I touched it with mine.

Another boat chopped through, too small to have a name, its engine blatting disagreeably. Both Richard and I cast it reproachful glances.

"And you'll be there for me," he said, once the boat was out of earshot, "when I need you?"

"*Should* you need me," I said. "You're perfectly grounded, Richard. I'm sure there's not a problem you can't handle yourself. But yes . . . I'll be there."

"Thank you." He smiled and sipped his beer.

"That's what friends are for."

"Indeed."

I looked at him carefully, his fist curled around the pint glass, the setting sun casting the same bronze shades into his eyes. The right side of his mouth twitched. His sunken cheeks caught the evening shadows. I saw it then, I think, for the first time. A scarring, but beneath the surface, pulsing lightly against his skin from the inside. The man had issues, and they ran deep. Being his friend, I should have asked about them, but I had too much going on in my own life. I wasn't ready for Richard's problems. Not even close.

And you'll be there for me when I need you?

I turned back to the river. Almost red now. It rippled like a flag and chattered endlessly against the banks, and the traffic on the bridge buzzed and threw javelins of light that were like warnings.

***

He called at the beginning of October. A stormy, miserable night. I hadn't heard from him in some weeks – he hadn't returned my calls or e-mails – so hearing his voice came as some surprise. The timbre of that voice was more surprising still. I was so used to a firm, assured tone, which both reflected his character and compensated for his lisp. What I heard that night was altogether different: a trail of meek sound punctuated by sobs and cracked breathing.

"I need you, Martin," he said.

The drive from Thame to Marlow should not take longer than thirty minutes, depending on traffic and your chosen route. I took the M40, and being after nine PM – closer to ten – on a Thursday night, the traffic was light. Even so, it took me fifty minutes to reach Richard's house. The weather was dreadful, with heavy rain lashing my car and ugly gusts blowing me into the next lane. HGVs rumbled by, creating maelstroms that I believed would whip me from the road and carry me away. Dirty water sprayed from beneath their rear tyres, covering my windscreen. I gripped the steering wheel so hard my knuckles throbbed. I wonder now if the elements conspired to keep me away. Given everything that happened that night, I wish they'd succeeded.

Richard's house was small, detached, and surrounded by trees that griped in the wind. There was a single-car garage butted onto its east face – an addition, judging by a vague discrepancy in the brickwork. His Volvo was parked in the driveway, but I didn't think this unusual; perhaps the garage was used for storage. I parked on the road and hurried through the rain to his front door.

It took him a while to answer. I thought the doorbell broken, and was about to knock when I saw his image through the frosted glass. The lock rattled and he opened the door, using his weight to keep it from slamming wide in the wind.

"Martin . . ." He appeared, as ever, kempt, dressed in a clean white shirt and corduroys. Following his telephone call, I'd expected to find him in disarray, but the only evidence that something was wrong was his puffy eyes and, as I noted a little later, a single spot of blood on the toe of his left shoe. He stepped back and the door pushed wider. "Do come in."

I was not so together, rattled by the drive, my clothes damp and leaves in my hair. I kicked off my shoes and followed Richard through to the living room, an elegant place, where Beethoven fluttered from stereo speakers and a tot of Glenfiddich had already been poured for me. I sat, and Richard placed a towel over my shoulders as I took several quick and warming sips from the glass.

"Thank you for coming." He sat opposite me in a high back Chesterfield, crystal tumbler resting in his palm, his legs crossed. That was when I noticed the drop of blood on his toe.

"Not at all." I looked at him, searching his swollen eyes. "I came as quickly as I could, but the weather—"

"And I, cut off from the world, remain / Alone with the terrible hurricane."

I frowned, then my eye flicked, again, to that glaring drop of blood.

"William Cullen Bryant," He smiled and sipped his whisky. "*The Hurricane.* It describes aloneness and fear in the face of doom." He followed my gaze, noticed the blood on his shoe, then wet the tip of his thumb and smeared it away. "Doom," he said again.

I finished my whisky, surprised at how quickly it had gone down, and surprised more at seeing my hand tremble as I set the empty glass upon the table. "I'm not familiar with it," I said.

"It's how I feel sometimes . . . isolated, scared, surrounded by darkness." On cue the windows shook, thunder exploding in the wet night. "I just want it to end."

I recalled sitting with Richard outside The Angel, and seeing something beyond his well-dressed, well-spoken exterior, perhaps the hurricane he was referring to. Maybe he had terminal cancer, only months to live, or some deep-rooted psychological concern that could only be suppressed through medication. Again I reflected how little I knew him, yet here I was in his house, in his life. The first threads of anxiety touched me as more thunder cracked outside. I wanted to leave, risk the storm again, but I had promised to help with his problem, just as he had helped with mine.

"I'm here for you, Richard," I said. "Whatever you need."

He took a framed photograph from a side table close to his chair and handed it to me. "Constance," he said, then grabbed my empty glass and stepped to the drinks' cabinet to pour another shot.

"Not for me, Richard," I said. "I have to drive home."

"Nonsense," he said. "You'll wait out the storm."

More anxiety, but I nodded and thanked him, then studied the photograph while the windows trembled and Beethoven's "Symphony No.5" floated into its fourth movement. She was plain, Constance, to say the least. Not the beauty I'd envisioned, given she'd been described as a wide-shining light. Her marigold hair and clear eyes were offset by a palsied smile and a web of acne scars on her right cheek. Also, her hands were clasped in such a way as to indicate a disconnect in her motor functions. Richard returned with my drink, which I exchanged with the photograph. I wanted to say something supportive, but all could manage was, "Let's hope there's not a power cut."

"I have candles," Richard said. He sat down, crossed his legs, stroked the photograph. "I never told you how she died."

"No."

He gazed at Constance's imperfect face and sighed, and at once I knew the reason for his call: he was still in mourning. Deeply spiritual though her death may have been, there were times when it consumed him.

"1994 was a terrible year," he said. "The worst of my life, by far, though with a silver lining that blinded me. My sister, with whom I was incredibly close, was killed in a skiing accident. A week later my grief-stricken father threw himself from the top of a multi-storey car park in Wycombe. You can imagine the effect this had on me and my mother. We spiralled into depression, side-by-side, yet so alone. She lost her job. I lost mine. My home, too. One moment everything was intact, and the next it was in pieces. *Everything*. I went from corporate conventions and health spas to psychiatrists and Prozac."

I nodded. Not that I could gauge the level of his despair. All I had lost was a wife who didn't love me, and I felt resentful at the world for that.

Richard snapped his fingers. "That's how quickly the hurricane hits, and your life is flipped upside down."

"Yes." I took a sip of whisky and the thunder boomed again.

"And then I met Constance. The silver lining." His fingers on the photograph, stroking, as if she could feel. "Long story short: things got better. She was the house I lived in. She gave me security, warmth, and comfort. And when the storms came, she gave me shelter. We got married in '96. A fairytale wedding in the Bahamas. Everything was perfect for another year, eighteen months, and then one morning – we were in the conservatory having breakfast – I noticed her hand trembling while she drank her grapefruit juice. Very subtle, but no mistaking it."

He demonstrated, but I knew what a trembling hand looked like; I had two of my own.

"You don't assume . . ." Richard's words faded and he shook his head. A single tear leaked from his eye and he smeared it away with his thumb, reminding me of the blood on his shoe. "You don't assume the worst from something like that. Not immediately. You just get on with your life, and in most cases forget it ever happened. But Constance started to exhibit more symptoms, some subtle, others not so. Flashes of irritability and a feverish temper. Distractedness, clumsiness, lots of weeping. I thought it was premature menopause. She told me not to be ridiculous. Anyway, we went to the doctor and ran some tests."

He put the photograph back in its place and drank his whisky. His eyes were distant, still wet. I plucked a leaf from my hair, but didn't quite know what to do with it. I twirled the stem between thumb and forefinger. The leaf flickered, gold and red. I sipped my drink and felt the weight of it – the weight of the night – pull at me from inside.

"Do you know anything about Huntington's disease, Martin?"

"Huntington's . . ." I twirled the leaf. I could see the tiny veins beneath its red skin and thought it looked too healthy a thing to detach and die. "It's like Parkinson's disease, isn't it?"

"There are similarities," Richard said, "Both are neurological maladies. Both are degenerative. Parkinson's affects the central nervous system, while Huntington's – I'm simplifying – deteriorates the areas of the brain responsible for movement, cognition, and personality. It usually begins around middle age and progresses until there is little or no quality of life."

"How dreadful," I said.

"Indeed." Richard nodded. "Constance was diagnosed in 1998. A tall, strong, intelligent woman – the house I lived in, remember? Hard to believe anything could bring her down. But within five years she was a jerky, slurring shadow of her former self. She fell apart, brick by brick, and once again I felt the storm gathering."

I could hear the trees outside, twisting in the wind. I gathered the towel closer to me. "Miserable." Another sip of whisky. "Miserable way to die."

Richard looked at me. His eyes were clear but they appeared to shake in his skull like the windows in their frames. "Yes, but that's not what killed her." He grinned and I counted his teeth. All six hundred of them. "Not exactly."

"Richard, I . . ." The leaf, still between my fingers, caught my eye, softly glowing. "I'm afraid the Glenfiddich is going straight . . . straight to my head."

"We were living in this house. Not ideal, but it was the home we bought together after we were married, and we loved it. I had the dining room and a portion of the kitchen converted into a bedroom and bathroom so that Constance had no reason to go upstairs. I rarely left her untended, if I could help it. Sometimes I'd nip to the shops or mow the lawn, never longer than half an hour, and she was always fine – would sit where you are now and listen to an audiobook, or watch one of her Doris Day musicals. But there was one afternoon when I had to go into the attic to replace some damp insulation. It took a little longer than expected – maybe an hour – and when I came down I found her standing at the top of the stairs, not holding on to the banister or wall, just . . . standing there, jerking and swaying, looking down the flight at the hallway below. Maybe she had come up to ask me a question, and forgotten what it was, or maybe she had climbed the stairs to prove she still could. So many maybes,

Martin, but what I think – what I truly *feel* – is that she was waiting for me to do exactly what I did."

The room swayed as I waited for him to continue. I thought it peculiar that I should feel squiffy on only a measure and a half of single malt, but put it down to a combination of the alcohol, the harrowing drive, and so many recent stresses. I rolled my hand, gesturing for Richard to continue. The room dipped and the walls seemed too far away.

"She looked at me," he said. "Her face was full of anguish, pain, sadness . . . can you even imagine?"

I could, in fact; I imagined her face like a detached leaf softly glowing, curled at the edges, tiny veins beneath the skin.

"I placed my hand between her shoulder blades." Richard blinked and several tears spilled onto his cheeks. "She nodded, or jerked her head. I'll never know. But I pushed, and down she went. Her head hit the newel post, the bottom wall, and then the floor. I'll never forget the sound – like three gunshots. Then I took a deep breath, walked downstairs, and watched her die."

"Good God, man," I said. Actually, I didn't; I *slurred* it. A crash of thunder echoed my unease. Richard was lowering his mask, showing me the shadowy thing beneath – a thing I had only glimpsed until now. It was all so disturbing. I tried to stand but my limbs felt loaded with Novocain and I dropped back into my seat with a little gasp.

"Her eyes," he said. "I saw the life leave her body through her eyes, and it was sublime. They shone fiercely for three or four seconds. Exquisite, tiny novas. I almost felt that I could scoop one into each palm and carry them into every dark place. It was awe-inspiring. Invigorating. Then they faded, and I held her hand and stroked her hair. I wept, too." He wiped his eyes and showed me the tears on his fingers, fat as pearls. "Haven't stopped weeping, in fact."

"Please," I said. "I don't want to hear anymore."

"It *had* to be done, Martin. You understand that, don't you?"

"No, Richard, I don't."

"Her house was in ruins," he said, a touch impatiently. "It couldn't shelter me anymore, so I razed it to the ground. I released her."

Again, I tried to stand. Again, I slumped, boneless, back into my seat.

"Then I stood alone," he continued. "Yes, I had regular sessions with a psychiatrist. Yes, I was prescribed seemingly countless meds. But they didn't help. When the hurricanes came – as they did, and often – I recalled the light in Constance's eyes. It gave me the strength I needed, and the darkness went away." His mouth twisted into a strange shape, too wide, too greedy. "At least for a while."

I reached for my whisky and knocked it over, quite deliberately. No more of that.

"What did you give me?" I asked.

"Rohypnol," he said. "Just enough."

"Why did . . .?"

"It will all become clear, Martin."

"Thought you were . . ." I twirled the leaf between thumb and forefinger. Red and gold. Such a pretty leaf. "I thought you were my friend."

Richard smiled and righted the glass. He used three Kleenex to mop up the spilled whisky. "Moonlight Sonata" started to play, a piece I have always loathed, due mainly to it being the one composition that even philistines are familiar with. Now I have cause to loathe it more.

"That light was so alluring, so powerful." Richard disposed of the sodden tissues and strolled over to a handsome mahogany cabinet. From its bottom drawer he took a box, and from the box he took a stack of newspapers. Thunder crashed. The windows trembled. Similarly, I shuddered as Richard stepped towards me and dropped one of the newspapers face-up on the table. It was an edition of the *Bucks Free Press* from November 2005. A young woman's face stared at me from the front page. She had short blonde hair and a smile that could lift your feet from the ground. A memory-feather tickled the back of my mind, but I was too numb to grasp it. The headline – unimaginative but succinct – read: VICKY STILL MISSING.

"Victoria Channing," Richard said, and with her full name the memory clicked into place. She was a local woman who was believed to have been murdered by her boyfriend. He had passionately maintained his innocence, and no charges were brought against him, but Vicky was never found, dead or alive. Now her eyes regarded me brightly and with faint accusation, the way they had for several weeks, until they disappeared from the newspapers altogether.

"From Great Missenden," I said, voicing details as they resurfaced in my mind. "Twenty-three years old. Worked at the Roald Dahl Museum."

"Yes." Richard nodded and grinned and every one of his six hundred teeth glistened. "I stabbed her three times and she died in my arms. I thought the light in her eyes would last forever."

I jerked in my seat the way I sometimes do on the verge of sleep. That myclonic spasm. That flash of terror. Only this time the terror sustained. I looked at Richard with eyes like pools of cracked ice. "No," I slurred, my drumming heart adding syllables to the word. I shook my head and slurred it again: "Nuh-oh-oh-oh."

"I was wrong," Richard continued. "Nothing lasts forever." He dropped the *Reading Evening Post* onto the table. It landed with a slap. Another young woman stared at me from the front page. "Rosemary Hill. I cut her throat with a Stanley knife in February of 2007. The light in her eyes was brief, but had a russet tinge that warmed me for months afterwards."

"Richard, I—"

Another newspaper. Slap.

"Elaine Emmington. Seventeen years old. My youngest victim. In my defence, she looked so much older."

I screamed. It was more of a warble, really, while "Moonlight Sonata" played and the thunder boomed.

"Her eyes," he said. "Goodness, her *light* . . ."

I wanted to run, of course, but there was no way. My body felt loaded with iron ball bearings, that would slip and roll heavily with even the slightest movement. So I closed my eyes and willed myself to float away . . . out of the seat, through the ceiling, through an upstairs room where Richard may once have made love to the wife he killed, through the roof and into the night. I could be as light as the leaf in my hand, carried for miles, until the storm exhausted itself and I landed in the greenest of meadows. Richard crippled this fantasy by dropping newspapers onto the table and giving summaries of the women he had killed. His voice was an anchor attached to my delicate stem. I twirled the leaf and concentrated on it, and suddenly I remembered my energy healer – Leaf, his name was Leaf – and the breathing exercise he taught me. Four-seven-eight. I applied it, but was only midway through my second set when Richard dropped the final newspaper onto the table. "Alexandra Locke," he said, and all the air rushed from my lungs. The fact that she was still in the news, and instantly recognisable, made it all the more real. I looked at her image, my heart thumping against my ribs like a fat fist.

"The police are looking for her," I said ridiculously, as if Richard didn't know this.

"Yes. They'll find her buried in my garden. In fourteen pieces." He paused before clarifying. "Easier to bury if they're . . ." And he made a chopping motion with his hand.

My fear was absolute. I think that if a crocodile had grabbed me in its jaws and death-rolled me to some deep, dark place I would not have been more scared. I made one last attempt to leap out of my seat and actually succeeded, but managed only three or four steps before collapsing. Richard came towards me. He planted one foot on my upper arm and rolled me onto my back.

"Silly," he said.

"Gur," I said. The room swam. Richard stood above me. The light behind gave him a halo. I would have laughed if I hadn't been so drugged.

"Do you know why I called you here tonight?" he asked.

"Going . . . kill me," I blurted.

"Quite the opposite, old boy." Those teeth again. "My house is in ruins and the hurricane is more vicious than ever. I can feel it howling in my head, taking me apart. I can't go on like this." He gestured at the newspapers on the table and then used the same hand to wipe his eyes. "I want you to release me, just like I released Constance."

"Don't . . . understand."

"Suicide is so crass. So classless. And if I could do it, I would have already."

"You want me to *kill* you?"

"Yes."

"What on earth makes you think . . ." My eyelids fluttered. I drooled. ". . . could do such a thing?"

Richard smiled. "Because you're not some wooden figurine living a clockwork life."

"Gur."

"You're just like me."

"No!" I growled and shook my head. "I'm *nothing* like you. I could never . . ."

"Kindred spirits, remember?"

"*Never.*"

He crouched beside me and placed his hand on my chest. I wonder what he thought of my heartbeat – a storm unto itself, raging and banging. I faded, gripped his hand, though I didn't want to. The edges of the room closed in until only Richard's face remained, as if seen through a keyhole.

"We'll see," he said. "I think you'll be surprised what a man is capable of."

And with that I drifted away, like the leaf, swirling and gone. Beethoven accompanied me for a while. Beautiful, tormenting notes, but even they faded.

I looked for my green meadow but found only rain, only darkness.

***

I awoke to find myself in a room I soon recognised as Richard's garage, but there was no workbench, no lawnmower, no tools hanging from nails on the walls. The up and over aluminium door was the only standard garage feature. Polythene sheeting had been tacked to the walls, and the linoleum floor sloped away on both sides to narrow drainage chutes that reminded me of the gutters found on autopsy tables. A bare bulb depended from a length of dusty cord, its glow attracting two moths that repeatedly knocked their plump bodies against the glass.

Lorna sat opposite me, coarse rope binding her wrists and ankles to the chair, a rag pushed into her mouth so tightly she couldn't work her tongue to push it free. There was blood in her hair and smeared across her top lip. I remembered that single spot on Richard's shoe and wanted to scream. Her left eye was a mess of swollen tissue but her right eye was wide and filled with terror. In seven years of marriage – ten of being together – I had never known her to be terrified. It sickened me.

Richard stood behind her, knife in hand, the edge too close to her throat. "You're awake," he said. "Good. Take a moment to compose yourself."

"Richard, what—?"

"Deep breaths help."

"What are you *doing?*"

It was then that I noticed my arrangement: I, too, was bound to a wooden chair, but not completely; my right arm was free. I had a gun in my hand.

"So you don't believe you can take a man's life?" More tears leaked from Richard's eyes. I watched two of them drip into Lorna's hair. "I believe, under certain circumstances, you can."

I shook my head. "Don't do this, Richard." Tears of my own now. Too many of them. "Please."

"What did she call you? A pithless cretin?" Richard used the tip of the blade to flick hair from Lorna's face. "Now's your chance to prove her wrong, and save her life in the bargain."

I looked at the gun, fat and oily and *real*.

"Maybe the love has gone. Or maybe not." He curled his upper lip and shrugged. "One thing is for certain . . . you don't want to see her die like this."

"*Please.*"

"I'm going to cut her throat in exactly ten seconds."

"No . . . dear Jesus, *no*."

"Then I'll chop her into easy-to-manage pieces and bury her in the garden."

Lorna screamed through the rag. A raw, muffled sound. Her throat bulged as it filled with air that couldn't escape.

"But you can stop me, Martin."

"Nuh-oh-oh-oh."

"You can save us all."

I whimpered like a scolded dog and considered putting the gun to my own head.

"Ten seconds," Richard said, and pressed the edge of the knife to Lorna's throat. "This is it, old friend. It's time to see how alike we really are."

***

"Ten."

I wonder, now, if Lorna's uncompromising attitude, not to mention our bitter separation, in some way impacted my hesitance to pull the trigger. It was easy to remember the ember of derision that so often burned inside her – evident in her behaviour at Gee's, when clemency would not have cost anything, and despite my efforts at accord. Nor had I forgotten that she'd wished a "crippling" car accident on me. Cancer, too. Heat of the moment, maybe, but still hurtful. I looked at the gun in my hand as her cruelties teetered in my mind. I'm fairly certain that if our marriage was intact, and blissful, even if Lorna had shown an iota of affection, that I would have blasted Richard's brains against the polythene wall. But that wasn't the case; Lorna didn't like me – an understatement; she *hated* me – and I didn't like her much, either.

"Nine."

I could let her die or kill Richard. Neither choice appealed. It was like being faced with two doors – one leading to hell and damnation, the other to insanity and rue. The gun trembled in my hand, as foreign to me as a Neolithic relic or alien rock. I have no idea what type it was. Something beastly, with a squat barrel and a magazine locked into its grip. I didn't know if I had to load a bullet into the chamber or release the safety catch (if I could find it). I assumed Richard had made it as simple as possible – just point and shoot. Not that there was anything simple about that.

"Eight."

After all, what makes someone a killer? What rare ingredient makes them capable of taking another person's life – of determining who lives or dies? Maybe it's something we all possess, a chemical or electrical impulse locked deep in the brain, that for most of us can only be accessed via extreme circumstances . . . and maybe not even then.

"Seven."

Rain rattled against the garage door. An explosion of thunder made the roof creak and the bare bulb tremble. Would this storm never end? I had a feeling that, whichever door I chose, I would hear it for the rest of my days.

"Six."

Thix. Stupid lisp. Stupid Richard. I looked at him and screamed. Raw, cascading sound. My throat felt like a rainstick filled with broken glass.

"Five."

Lorna screamed, too – or tried to, at least. Her throat was dark with the effort, veins as thick as the ropes that bound her. And how could her eye – that single, glaring orb – be filled with such terror *and* reproach? Yes, *reproach.* For *me,* as if she didn't have more pressing things on her mind. Her body shook, wrists and ankles pushing against the ropes. She couldn't believe that I hadn't yet pulled the trigger, or that this was even difficult for me. She always said I lacked backbone. *Pithless,* the ever-famous adjective. And here I was proving her right, my spectacular nothingness on display.

"Four."

Yet more thunder boomed outside and I looked at my soon-to-be-ex-wife (maybe sooner than she'd hoped) with broken eyes. I saw things – random details – I'll remember in my nightmares for years to come: the fine hair on her forearms and a loose thread hanging from the hem of her skirt; the scar on her knee she'd gotten from falling off a see-saw when she was eight years old; the pale band of skin where her wedding ring used to be. There was blood on her blouse. One of the buttons was missing. It was easy to imagine her getting ready that morning (I knew her routine as well as my own), drying her hair and applying makeup – small things done daily, not knowing that she was doing them, perhaps, for the last time. I saw fresh blood trickling from her swollen left eye, and a damp corner of the rag dangling from her mouth.

"Please, Richard," I gasped. It was a wonder I could speak at all. "Please, I'm *begging* you—"

"Three."

So vivid, her blood, trickling too perfectly, as if it had been painted on. I saw tiny pink sequins embedded in the varnish on her fingernails. Bruises on her legs. A broken shoe strap.

"Two."

I brought the gun to chest level and extended my arm. Tears blurred my vision and I blinked them away, then curled my finger around the trigger. Richard had positioned himself so that his head floated above Lorna like a lunatic bullseye. I could barely see the curve of his left shoulder, and his right elbow was cocked to the side, but they were such small targets and too close to Lorna. I couldn't risk shooting at one in the hope of disabling, rather than killing, Richard, and couldn't move to a better position because I was tied to the chair. It was a hopeless situation. I closed one eye (possibly the wrong one) and stared down the barrel. The sights trembled somewhere between Richard and Lorna. I tried to steady my hand but couldn't.

It was over. I had failed them both.

"Sorry," I whimpered.

"One."

Everything happened in the next second: Richard's eyes flickered with disappointment, and he tightened his grip on the knife's handle. Then darkness – total and sudden – as the storm knocked out the power. Startled, I jerked, pulled the trigger. The gun snapped in my hand like something with teeth. In the muzzle flash I saw Lorna's hair lift at the top (it *bounced,* the way it had when she'd swept out of Gee's) followed by a haze of blood. I sagged. Maybe I screamed. The gunshot rang in my ears and all I could think of were the moths in the darkness, lost, looking for their light.

***

Including his wife, Richard Chalk murdered eleven women between 2004 and 2012. Alexandra Locke was his final victim. Following my statement, the police found her dismembered corpse buried in Richard's back garden, along with the remains of his other victims (except for his wife, of course, who'd been peacefully laid to rest at a cemetery in Little Marlow). For nearly three weeks Richard's house was in the news, surrounded by police tape and with one of those white tent-things in the back garden. That was how long it took to disinter and correctly match all the body parts.

The press named Richard, "The Chiltern Chopper." He's a celebrity now, like Harold Shipman and Fred West.

Me? I'm a mess. A psychological train wreck. Before all of this, I was a successful accountant working from my home in Thame. Recently separated, yes, but with my mind intact. Now I scream myself awake every night. I've lost nearly two stone.

My hair is more white than grey. I shake a lot, too, and haven't worked for over a year. The police called my actions heroic, but I don't see a hero when I look in the mirror, and I don't feel like one when I'm fumbling the cap off my sertraline prescription. My psychiatrist endeavours to dig beneath the anxiety, to whatever supports it – a trestle, perhaps, of weaknesses and woes. Writing this account was his idea. "Explore," he told me. "Uncover." Leaf works to balance my chakras. Sometimes he sweats.

Lorna hates me. Still. The difference now is that she probably has cause to. After all, she would never have been in that predicament if not for me. *I* befriended Richard. *I* showed him her photograph. *I* debated for ten long seconds whether or not to pull the trigger. She wanted to press charges against me, but was told outright that it was a fight she would never win. She went on television, on some gauche talk-show, and completely lost the plot. She threw her shoe at an audience member and had to be restrained by a beefy TV bouncer called Tim. Or maybe Jim. Her wig fell off. Everybody saw her scar. Yes, I shot her, but I saved her life, too.

It came down to millimetres, maybe even micrometres. I have a recurring nightmare in which I lower my hand a fraction before pulling the trigger, and in the muzzle flash I see the bullet rip through Lorna's skull. A similar nightmare has me holding the gun a dash higher and watching Richard's face disappear in a cloud of blood and bone. What actually happened was that my hand was at the perfect height, and the gun at the perfect angle, that when I pulled the trigger I injured both, but killed neither of them.

The shot was analysed by ballistics experts on a BBC *Newsnight* special. According to their calculations, I have a one in two-point-six million chance of doing it again. A ridiculous number, if you ask me. But we'll never know; I'm not doing it again.

The bullet scored the top of Lorna's head. It burned through her hair, separated her scalp, and cut a groove in her skull deep enough to rest a pencil in. She required several surgeries – bone and skin grafts, mainly – and now has a thick scar running down the centre of her head. The bouncy, tawny hair will never grow back there. She buys her wigs from Les Cheveux in Amersham.

I've heard they procure their product from human cadavers. I hope that's true.

Richard was not so fortunate. The bullet struck his lower jaw and removed it completely. His tongue, too. Had its trajectory not been altered, albeit subtly, by Lorna's hair and skull, it would have hit him in the throat and killed him instantly. He resides now in one of England's finest high-security hospitals, locked in a tiny room, his hands strapped to the bedrails so that he cannot disconnect the numerous tubes that keep him alive.

I visited him in the summer. My psychiatrist's idea. "For closure," he said. He wrote to the hospital on my behalf and reluctantly I went along. It was a brief visit. I stood with two of the burliest nurses I have ever seen in a room not unlike Richard's garage: bleak, windowless, a single light in the ceiling glimmering behind mesh. There was a drain in the floor and the walls were coated with something that made cleaning blood and body waste from them easier. Richard lay in his bed, his eyes (light brown with delicate orange flecks, still the same, even now) fixed upward. Below the nose, his face appeared to have been removed by some kind of human pencil eraser. Smudged away. No teeth. No *mouth*. Just a whorl of scar tissue. A trach tube jutted from a hole in his throat.

I looked at him, this man - The Chiltern Chopper – who enjoyed Beethoven and Glenfiddich, and who I once called a friend.

We're nothing alike, I thought. I had intended to say this out loud – for closure, you understand – but couldn't get the words out. I stuttered and covered my mouth.

He didn't look at me. Not once.

"That's what he does all day," one of the nurses said. "Just stares at the ceiling. I've never seen him sleep. He hardly even blinks."

I looked at Richard a moment longer and then turned to the nurses. "That's enough," I said. "I want to leave now."

I drove home with my heart clamouring, beneath a cloudless summer sky, and as I pulled into the driveway of my lonely little house in Thame, it occurred to me that the nurse was wrong.

It wasn't the ceiling Richard was staring at.

It was the light.

Biographies

Alain Davis is a bright light in this world, trying to make a difference one soul—and one swear word—at a time! She is a lifelong book nerd turned writer, has had two short stories published in anthologies. When she is not editing in her spare time, she is writing, currently working on her first full length novel. Alain has edited short stories, full length novels, and anthologies. These projects have spanned several genres, including horror, fantasy, supernatural, romance, and sci-fi. Having cut her teeth on Stephen King novels at an early age, horror and supernatural will always be her first love. She lives in the Midwest with her husband (high school sweetheart), their three kids, and a small zoo's worth of pets. You can find her on Twitter @hopelessoptimst.

Matthew R. Davis is an author and musician based in Adelaide, South Australia. His novelette "Heritage Hill" was shortlisted for a 2020 Shirley Jackson Award and the 2020 WSFA Small Press Award, he won two Australian Shadows Awards in 2019 for Best Short Story and Best Long Fiction, and he has been shortlisted for the Shadows and the Aurealis Awards many times. His first collection of horror stories, If Only Tonight We Could Sleep, was released by Things in the Well in 2020; his first novel, Midnight in the Chapel of Love, was published by JournalStone in 2021. Find out more at matthewrdavisfiction.wordpress.com.

Steve Dillon is an award winning editor who runs/ran(?) Things in The Well, and is a Shirley Jackson Award-nominated writer of over 200 shorts and poems, many set in the worlds of

Refuge and Bliss, both of which are far from it… Contact Steve at SteveDillonWriter@gmail.com and tell him he sent you :P

Hannah Elizabeth lives in Appalachia where monsters and madness are as common as the black rock that runs through the state's veins. She lives with her family and their cat Tigger who protects them from the things that hide in the shadows.

Mick Garris is an award winning filmmaker who began writing fiction at the age of twelve. By the time he was in high school, he was writing music and film journalism for various local and national publications, and during college, edited and published his own pop culture magazine. He spent seven years as lead vocalist with the acclaimed tongue-in-cheek progressive art-rock band, HORSEFEATHERS.

His first film business job was as receptionist for George Lucas's Star Wars Corporation, operated the remote-controlled R2-D2 robot at personal appearances, including that year's Academy Award ceremony. Garris hosted and produced "The Fantasy Film Festival" on Los Angeles television, and later worked in film publicity at Avco Embassy and Universal Pictures, where he created "Making of. . ." documentaries for various feature films.

Steven Spielberg hired Garris as story editor on the AMAZING STORIES TV series for NBC, where he wrote 10 of the 44 episodes. Since then, he has written or co-authored several feature films (NIGHTMARE CINEMA, RIDING THE BULLET, *BATTERIES NOT INCLUDED, THE FLY II, HOCUS POCUS, CRITTERS 2) and teleplays (AMAZING STORIES, QUICKSILVER HIGHWAY, THE OTHERS, DESPERATION, MASTER OF HORROR), as well as directing and producing in many media: cable (PSYCHO IV: THE BEGINNING, TAMES FROM THE CRYPT, MASTERS OF HORROR, PRETTY LITTLE LIARS and its spinoff, RAVENSWOOD, WITCHES OF EAST END, SHADOWHUNTERS, DEAD OF SUMMER, ONCE UPON A TIME), features (CRITTERS 2, SLEEPWALKERS, RIDING THE BULLET), television films (QUICKSILVER HIGHWAY, VIRTUAL OBSESSION, DEPSERATION), series pilots (THE OTHERS, LOST IN OZ), network miniseries (THE STAND, THE SHINING, THE JUDGE, BAG OF BONES), and series (SHE-WOLF OF LONDON, MASTERS OF HORROR, FEAR ITSELF).

Garris also executive produced the Universal feature, UNBROKEN, based on the life of Louis Zamperini and the book by Laura Hillenbrand, directed by Angelina Jolie.

Garris is also known as an interview on POST-MORTEM, where he sits down with some of the most revered filmmakers in the horror and fantasy genres for one-on-one discussions, which began as a TV series, and has become an acclaimed podcast.

Garris' books include A LIFE IN THE CINEMA, DEVELOPMENT HELL, SNOW SHADOWS and TYLER'S THIRD ACT, SALOME, UGLY, and his latest from Cinestate/Fangoria Press, THESE EVIL THINGS WE DO: THE MICK GARRIS COLLECTION.

Eric J. Guignard has twice won the Bram Stoker Award, been a finalist for the International Thriller Writers Award, and is a multi-nominee of the Pushcart Prize for his works of dark and speculative fiction. He has over 100 stories and non-fiction author credits appearing in publications around the world; has edited multiple anthologies (including the current series, The Horror Writers Association's HAUNTED LIBRARY OF HORROR CLASSICS, through SourceBooks, with co-editor Leslie S. Klinger); and has created an ongoing series of author primers championing modern masters of the dark and macabre, EXPLORING DARK SHORT FICTION through his press, Dark Moon Books. He is also publisher and acquisitions editor for the renowned +HORROR LIBRARY+ anthology series. His latest books are LAST CASE AT A BAGGAGE AUCTION; DOORWAYS TO THE DEADEYE; and short story collection THAT WHICH GROWS WILD: 16 TALES OF DARK FICTION (Cemetery Dance). Visit Eric at: www.ericjguignard.com, his blog: ericjguignard.blogspot.com, or Twitter: @ericjguignard.

Eugene Johnson is a Bram Stoker Award®-winner and an author, editor, filmmaker and columnist. He has written as well as edited in various genres, and created anthologies such as the

Biographies

Fantastic Tales Of Terror featuring an introduction by honor icon Tony Todd, Drive In Creature Feature with Charles Day, the Bram Stoker Award®-nominated non-fiction anthology Where Nightmares Come From: The Art Of Storytelling In The Horror Genre, Dark Tides with John Questore, The Tales Of The Lost Series, and many more. He is also the owner of Plaid Dragon Publishing, a small press focused on finding new voices in storytelling and making a difference in the community. He has a master's from Marshall University in Mental Health Counseling and lives in Appalachia with his family.

Gwendolyn Kiste is the Bram Stoker Award-winning author of The Rust Maidens, Boneset & Feathers, And Her Smile Will Untether the Universe, Pretty Marys All in a Row, and The Invention of Ghosts. Her short fiction and nonfiction have appeared in Nightmare Magazine, Vastarien, Tor's Nightfire, Black Static, Daily Science Fiction, and LampLight, among others. Originally from Ohio, she now resides on an abandoned horse farm outside of Pittsburgh with her husband, two cats, and not nearly enough ghosts. Find her online at gwendolynkiste.com

Chris Mason is an award-winning author who lives on Peramangk land in the Adelaide Hills of South Australia. Her stories have appeared in numerous publications, including the Things in the Well anthologies, and the Australian Horror Writers Association's magazine Midnight Echo. Chris has won Aurealis Awards for Best Horror Short Story and Best Horror Novella, received the Australian Shadows Paul Haines Award for long fiction, and been shortlisted for a Shirley Jackson Award. You can visit Chris at: facebook.com/chrismasonhorrorwriter or on twitter @Chris_A_Mason.

Cindy O'Quinn is a four-time Bram Stoker Award-Nominated writer. Author of "Lydia", from the Shirley Jackson Award-winning anthology: The Twisted Book of Shadows, and "The Thing I Found Along a Dirt Patch Road." She is an Appalachian writer from the mountains of West Virginia. Steeped in folklore at an early age. Cindy now lives in the woods of northern Maine. The old Tessier Homestead is the ideal backdrop for writing her dark stories and poetry. Her work has been published or forthcoming in The Bad Book, HWA Poetry Showcase Vol V, Northern Frights, Eerie Christmas Anthology, Under Her Skin, Were Tales: A Shapeshifter Anthology, Space & Time Magazine, Chiral Mad 5, and others. Follow Cindy for updates: Facebook @CindyOQuinnWriter, Twitter @COQuinnWrites, and Instagram cindy.o

Norman Prentiss is the author of ODD ADVENTURES WITH YOUR OTHER FATHER, THE APOCALYPSE-A-DAY DESK CALENDAR, and LIFE IN A HAUNTED HOUSE, and he won the 2010 Bram Stoker Award for Superior Achievement in Long Fiction for INVISIBLE FENCES, published by Cemetery Dance (www.cemeterydance.com). He also won a 2009 Stoker for his short story, "In the Porches of My Ears," published in POSTSCRIPTS 18. Other publications include THE BOOK OF BABY NAMES, THE FLESHLESS MAN, FOUR LEGS IN THE MORNING, THE HALLOWEEN CHILDREN (written with Brian James Freeman), and THE NARRATOR (written with Michael McBride), with story appearances in BLACK STATIC, DARK SCREAMS, BLOOD LITE 3, BEST HORROR OF THE YEAR, THE YEAR'S BEST DARK FANTASY AND HORROR, and in five editions of the SHIVERS anthology series. His poetry has appeared in WRITER ONLINE, SOUTHERN POETRY REVIEW, Baltimore's CITY PAPER, and A SEA OF ALONE: POEMS FOR ALFRED HITCHCOCK. Visit him online at www.normanprentiss.com.

Christopher Sartin hails from the hollows of Southern West Virginia where monsters and madness are as common as the black rock that runs through the state's veins. He shares his humble abode with his beautiful wife, three daughters, and his dog, Milo, the only other male in the maelstrom of maidens.

Christina Sng is the Bram Stoker Award-winning author of A Collection of Nightmares (Raw Dog Screaming Press, 2017). Her poetry has appeared in numerous venues worldwide, and received multiple nominations in the Rhysling Awards, the

Dwarf Stars, the Elgin Awards, as well as honorable mentions in the Year's Best Fantasy and Horror and the Best Horror of the Year. Visit her at http://www.christinasng.com and connect @christinasng.

Lucy A. Snyder is a writer and developmental editor who has authored 14 books and over 100 published short stories. Her work has been nominated for the Shirley Jackson Award twice and has won the Bram Stoker Award five times. Her most recent books are the collection Halloween Season and the forthcoming novel The Girl With the Star-Stained Soul. Her writing has appeared in publications such as Asimov's Science Fiction, Apex Magazine, Nightmare Magazine, Pseudopod, Strange Horizons, and Best Horror of the Year. Lucy lives in Ohio with a jungle of houseplants, a clowder of cats, and an insomnia of housemates. You can learn more about her at www.lucysnyder.com and you can follow her on Twitter at @LucyASnyder.

Jason Stokes is an author and artist living in the mountains of western North Carolina. He's also the owner of Gestalt Media and the first of its kind digital subscription service Read this Next. When he's not at work in the studio he's raising a pair of indomitable Cornish Rex cats and travelling the world with his wife and best friend, Anna.

Peter Straub is the author of seventeen novels, which have been translated into more than twenty languages. They include Ghost Story, Koko, Mr. X, In the Night Room, and two collaborations with Stephen King, The Talisman and Black House. He has written two volumes of poetry and two collections of short fiction, and he edited the Library of America's edition of H. P. Lovecraft's Tales, and the forthcoming Library of America's 2-volume anthology, American Fantastic Tales. He has won the British Fantasy Award, eight Bram Stoker Awards, two International Horror Guild Awards, and three World Fantasy Awards. In 1998, he was named Grand Master at the World Horror Convention. In 2006, he was given the HWA's Life Achievement Award. In 2008, he was given the Barnes & Noble Writers for Writers

Award by Poets & Writers. At the World Fantasy Convention in 2010, he was given the WFC's Life Achievement Award.

Paul Tremblay is the author of the Bram Stoker Award and Locus Award winning THE CABIN AT THE END OF THE WORLD, winner of the British Fantasy Award DISAPPEARANCE AT DEVIL'S ROCK, and Bram Stoker Award/Massachusetts Book Award winning A HEAD FULL OF GHOSTS. A HEAD FULL OF GHOSTS is in development with Focus Features. He's also the author of the novels The Little Sleep, No Sleep till Wonderland, Swallowing a Donkey's Eye, and Floating Boy and the Girl Who Couldn't Fly (co-written with Stephen Graham Jones).

His newest book is the short story collection GROWING THINGS AND OTHER STORIES.

His essays and short fiction have appeared in the Los Angeles Times and numerous "year's best" anthologies. He is the co-editor of four anthologies including Creatures: Thirty Years of Monster Stories (with John Langan). Paul is on the board of directors for the Shirley Jackson Awards. He lives outside of Boston, Massachusetts, has a master's degree in Mathematics, and has no uvula. You can find him online at www.paultremblay.net. twitter: @paulgtremblay. He is represented by Stephen Barbara, InkWell

Tim Waggoner Bestselling author Tim Waggoner has published close to fifty novels and seven collections of short stories. He writes dark fantasy and horror, as well as media tie-ins. He's won the Bram Stoker Award, the HWA's Mentor of the Year Award, and he's been a finalist for the Shirley Jackson Award, the Scribe Award, and the Splatterpunk Award. He's also a full-time tenured professor who teaches creative writing and composition at Sinclair College in Dayton, Ohio.

Website: www.timwaggoner.com
Blog: http://writinginthedarktw.blogspot.com/
Facebook: http://www.facebook.com/#!/tim.waggoner.9
Twitter: @timwaggoner

Biographies

David Wellington is the author of over twenty novels, which have appeared around the world in eight languages. His horror series include Monster Island, 13 Bullets, Frostbite, and Positive. He has written fantasy and thrillers, and has also worked in video games and comic books. His most recent novel is The Last Astronaut, a work of science fiction and horror. He lives and works in New York City.

Rio Youers is the British Fantasy and Sunburst Award–nominated author of Westlake Soul and Halcyon. His 2017 thriller, The Forgotten Girl, was a finalist for the Arthur Ellis Award for Best Crime Novel. He is the writer of Sleeping Beauties, a comic book series based on the bestselling novel by Stephen King and Owen King. Rio's new novel, Lola on Fire, will be published by William Morrow in February 2021.

Acknowledgements

Special thanks to *You're Not Alone in the Dark Media*:
Alain Davis
Stephanie Ellis
Chris Sartin
Jason Stokes
Anna Ray Stokes
Row Wilson
Pace Whitfield May
Lee Murray
Chris Mason
Elizabeth Massie

All stories are original to this anthology except where noted, and have been used with permission:
The Stacks © 2022 by Chris Mason
The Girl Who Bled in a Tree © 2022 by Tim Waggoner
Shh © 2022 by David Wellington
There's No Light Between Floors © 2007 by Paul Tremblay, first published in *Clarkesworld*, #8, May 2007
A World of Ghosts © 2022 by Christina Sng
Vigil at Singer's Cross © 2022 by Matthew R. Davis
The Library of Half-Read Books © 2022 by Norman Prentiss
It Only Hurts When I Dream © 2022 by Lucy A. Snyder
Donald, Duck © 2008 by Peter Straub, first published in *5 Stories*, 2015
Disremembering Me © 2022 by Christopher Sartin
Drink, Drink from the Fountain of Death © 2022 by Eric J. Guignard
Lost © 2022 by Jason Stokes
Lost in the Forest of My Mind © 2022 by Hannah Elizabeth
Step Right Up to Marcy Lynne's Amazing Wunderkammer! © 2022 by Gwendolyn Kiste
Wide-Shining Light © 2022 by Rio Youers
Ocular © 2007 by Mick Garris

Please seek immediate help if you or someone you know is feeling that life isn't worth living or if you are having thoughts of harming yourself or others.

You can contact the National Suicide Prevention Lifeline at 1-800-273-TALK (8255) or online at SuicidePreventionLifeline.org

It's free and confidential.

Printed in the USA
CPSIA information can be obtained
at www.ICGtesting.com
LVHW021920101024
793525LV00009B/158